And Other Stories

AND OTHER STORIES

edited by
George Bowering

Talonbooks
2001

Talonbooks
P.O. Box 2076, Vancouver, British Columbia, Canada V6B 3S3
www.talonbooks.com

Typeset in New Baskerville and printed and bound in Canada by AGMV Marquis.

First Printing: August 2001

The publisher gratefully acknowledges the financial support of the Canada Council for the Arts; the Government of Canada through the Book Publishing Industry Development Program; and the Province of British Columbia through the British Columbia Arts Council for our publishing activities.

A previous edition of *And Other Stories* appeared as *Likely Stories: A Postmodern Sampler*, edited by George Bowering and Linda Hutcheon (Coach House Press, 1992).

National Library of Canada Cataloguing in Publication Data

Main entry under title:

And other stories

ISBN 0-88922-451-X

1. Short stories, Canadian (English)* 2. Canadian fiction (English)—20th century.* I. Bowering, George, 1935-
PS8329.A52 2001   C813'.0108054   C2001-910195-3
PR9197.32.A52 2001

Acknowledgements

Alexis, André, "My Anabasis," from *Despair and Other Stories of Ottawa* (Coach House Press, 1994) © 1994 by André Alexis. Reprinted by permission of the author.

Arnason, David, "A Girl's Story," from *The Circus Performers' Bar* (Talonbooks, 1984) © 1984 by David Arnason.

Atwood, Margaret, "Poppies: Three Variations," from *Good Bones* (Coach House Press, 1992) © 1992 by O.W. Toad Ltd. Reprinted by permission of McLelland and Stewart.

Blaise, Clark, "Meditations on Starch," from *Selected Stories, Vol. 2, Pittsburgh Stories* (The Porcupine's Quill, 2001). © 1992 by Clark Blaise. Reprinted by permission of the publisher.

Bowering, George, "Little Me," from *The Rain Barrel* (Talonbooks, 1994) © 1994 by George Bowering.

Burnham, Clint, "Hamlet," from the collection *Airborne Photo* (Anvil Press, 1999) © 1999 by Clint Burnham. Reprinted by permission of the publisher.

Cohen, Matt, "The Bone Fields," from *Living on Water* (Penguin Books Canada, 1989). © 1988 by Matt Cohen. Reprinted by permission of Stickland Ltd.

Dorsey, Candas Jane, "Sleeping in a Box," from *Machine Sex...and Other Stories* (Porcépic Books, 1988) © 1988 by Candas Jane Dorsey. Reprinted by permission of the author.

Elliott, George, "What do the children mean?" from *The Kissing Man* (Macmillan of Canada, 1962) © 1962 by George Elliott. Reprinted by permission of Martha Elliott.

Farrant, M.A.C., "Studies Show/Experts Say," from *Raw Material* (Arsenal Pulp Press, 1993) © 1993 by M.A.C. Farrant. Reprinted by permission of the publisher.

Fawcett, Brian, "The World Machines," from *The Secret Journal of Alexander Mackenzie* (Talonbooks, 1985) © 1985 by Brian Fawcett.

Findley, Timothy, "Kellerman's Windows," from *Dust to Dust* (Published by HarperCollins*PublishersLtd.*, 1997) © 1997 by Pebble

Contents

Doing Our Own Reading

SEVERAL YEARS AGO I was talking with a woman who had been brought up in Saskatchewan but was now involved in the writing world and living in central Canada. Here's what she said: "If I have to read one more novel that starts with a prairie farm wife, old before her time, leaning on her broom on the unpainted porch and looking out at the blighted fields, I will puke!"

I was awfully glad to hear such sentiments from a person in the book world. There was a time when I liked naturalism more than anything else in fiction. I mean when I was about twenty-one. And I do not begrudge writers and readers their love of the realist text with all its description and characterization and survival. Readers have been trained to expect description and so forth, and they want what they think is a continuity between their books and their world. Writers do, too. When a Montreal shrink told Hugh MacLennan that the characters out of his newest novel were showing up in his clinic every day, MacLennan took that as a compliment.

That is, people who will never read a Henry James novel are enjoying conventions that James promoted. "What is character but the determination of incident?" he asked. "What is incident but the illustration of character?" From this cause-and-effect system, the writer is supposed to be keeping a good distance. He is supposed to disappear from thought, and if possible, the book should seem to follow him. This kind of writer likes to say "I just started these characters off, and then they took on a life of their own and all I could do was try to write down what they did and said."

We know that such a statement is seductive, but also that it is really equine manure. Any writer can, if she wants to, have a piano fall from the sky and finish off a "character" in chapter six. And maybe even make a personal writerly remark about the musicality of the scene.

Henry James saw such a writer as a dead end. "The reality of Don Quixote or of Mr. Micawber is a very delicate shade; it is a reality so coloured by the author's vision that, vivid as it may be, one would hesitate to propose it as a model." He had even worse things to say about Anthony Trollope, who admitted that the events in his fiction did not really happen and that he could give his narrative any turn one would fancy. "Such a betrayal of a sacred office seems to me, I confess, a terrible crime," wrote Henry James.

He would not have liked Robert Kroetsch at all. We are supposed to be representing life, James would say, not a rime by Robert Service. He would not have liked Michael Ondaatje's *Coming through Slaughter* either. In that novel the author seems to be saying to the protagonist: "What ... made me push my arm forward and spill it through the front of your mirror and clutch myself? Did not want to pose in your accent but think in your brain and body ... " Keep your distance, my old *creative writhing* teachers would have admonished. The mirror is an image for realists, my old English teachers would have said—we mirror life in our writing. Or we erect a window before the world, and so on, all that glass.

In *Coming Through Slaughter*, Buddy Bolden is forever escaping through windows or mirrors. In *What the Crow*

Said, a newspaper guy can remember only the future. So much for history, James's model for serious fiction.

It has always bugged me that Robert Kroetsch and Michael Ondaatje manage to write novels and poems and non-fiction prose, but they do not write short stories. I have edited a lot of short story collections, and it bugs me that I cannot include the two writers who, maybe, best exemplify the kind of writing I am interested in.

The relationship between these two writers and the general reading public can be seen in the different directions their careers have taken over the past few years. Michael Ondaatje has been writing longer and more conventional fictions of late, and they have made him world famous and rich. He is still a wonderful writer, but now his books are not "difficult." They align themselves pretty well with history, whereas in *Coming through Slaughter*, we got the "history of ice." Kroetsch writes very peculiar poetry, and every five years or more comes out with a novel, which is very interesting in terms of the writing, but is ignored by the Canadian reading world. In Germany and Australia they think that Kroetsch is the bee's knees. In Toronto they think of him as a regional writer—like Sheila Watson.

Daphne Marlatt—why the heck can't she write short stories?

There may be many reasons why the Canadian reading and reviewing and prize-giving public like realist novels with descriptions and characters and so on, and no doubt some of these reasons would also apply in other parts of the world. But here is a thought that might be nothing but bushwa: Canada is a small, recently independent country that feels threatened by its big rich neighbours. Canada needs to get an identity and stick with it. Therefore, it needs a literature that shows us to ourselves. We read that in the prefaces to Canadian story anthologies all the time.

We need what people call a "national literature," and for many professors and reviewers that means a realist fiction with description and characters and history, however revisionist.

An example might be a central Canadian professor named T.D. MacLulich, who wrote of some "postmodern" Canadian fictions: "The games that these works play with Canadian themes may not announce the health of a national tradition, but may predict its death, crushed by the weight of excessive self-consciousness." We will leave aside for now our objections that one cannot crush a death and that self-consciousness does not weigh anything. MacLulich is interested in that central Canadian dream we have heard so much of, the Canadian national tradition. He goes on: "When there is an emphasis on technical innovation in fiction—and a concurrent denigration of the straight-forward mimetic possibilities of fiction—then our fiction may lose its capacity to mirror [see!] the particularities of culture and personality." Leaving aside our objection that a mirror prevents the "straightforward," we note that MacLulich seems to agree with the kind of sentiments that emanated from the Robin Mathewses of the seventies and eighties, that Canadians should not seek to be innovators because innovation is USAmerican—that Canadians should remain hewers of wood and drawers of water, and sweepers of porches.

There are writers on the margins of the scene, and even toward the centre, who do not have a stake in the "national tradition," who do not view fiction-writing as an instrument of national cohesion, who might even think of such ideas as a kind of imperial brutality. Who wants to be told that their writing is supposed to promote non-literary ideas such as "The People's Revolution" or "The National Tradition"?

Look out. I am going to quote a writer who did not have a stake in the Canadian tradition. Roland Barthes wrote this about criticism: "its preferred material is this culture, which is everything in us except our present." That is why the criticism of jazz, for example, is notoriously unsuccessful. That is why Michael Ondaatje's *Coming Through Slaughter*, a book not "about" a jazz musician but like jazz, tells us to forget beginning and end, and listen to the middle and all its possibilities.

You do that by paying attention to the innovative form that MacLulich fears so much. Charles Olson, the USAmerican, was right when he said "One loves only form,/ and form only comes/ into existence when/ the thing is born." Think about it. Can you love "content"? Are you enamoured of his small intestine, or recrystallized calcite, the material of Michel Angelo's statues? Nicole Brossard, the truly wonderful northamerican poet and novelist (oh, why could she not have written some short stories?) made a simple discrimination that goes much further than I would dare to: "When it comes to reality, art does everything possible to really avoid it." One senses here that she has been driven to make an exaggerated reply to someone who has been insisting on Henry James's maintaining that we should "reproduce" reality in our works. In our play.

Of course, when it comes to writing, maybe especially when it comes to the writing of fiction, there is no such thing as "content," as opposed to form or even as allied with form. What is there to contain? If a realist writer tells you that her characters "took on a life of their own," how can they be said to be contained? There is no content in a book of fiction. There may be lots of references. If Timothy Findley mentions the Duke of Windsor, he is making a reference, not to some human being once alive, but to his reader's experience of hearing about the "Duke of Windsor."

I think that the upholders of the "national tradition" believe that you ensure the survival of the country by referring to it.

I also think that people who want us to put our words to the service of their notion of a country are of the mistaken opinion that we own the words. We do not own the words we borrow to speak or write. The same is true for the rest of the world. As Guy Davenport, a USAmerican writer put it, while writing about a nowhere: "The world to an animal is food, to man a language of signs before which he is largely illiterate."

In the collection of short fictions to which this piece is appended, you will find traces of realism, maybe even lots of realism in some cases. I do not want, as a reader or collector, to extirpate description and characters altogether. I just want readers to notice the writing. Ethel Wilson said that the most important thing in a story is the sentence. She was a kind of realist but she loved form. Loved it. If you notice the writing, and the writing is good, you will love it. You might also notice in that moment of loving that the reader is the focus of the fictional act.

Sources:

Barthes, Roland, *The Pleasure of the Text*, New York, Hill & Wang, 1975.

Brossard, Nicole, *Surfaces of Sense*, Toronto, Coach House Press, 1989.

Davenport, Guy, "The Dawn in Erewhon," in *Tatlin!*, Baltimore, Johns Hopkins University Press, 1982.

James, Henry, "The Art of Fiction," in *The Future of the Novel*, New York, Vintage, 1956.

MacLulich, T.D., *Between Europe and America: The Canadian Tradition in Fiction*, Toronto, ECW Press, 1988.

Olson, Charles, "I, Maximus of Gloucester, to You," in *The Maximus Poems*, New York, Jargon/Corinth, 1960.

Ondaatje, Michael, *Coming through Slaughter*, Toronto, Anansi, 1976.

My Anabasis

André Alexis

THERE'S A RESTLESSNESS that sometimes pushes me out. I don't know where it comes from or what purpose it serves, but it's there behind most of the things I do. For instance,

1. LEAVING

I was in Ottawa and things weren't going well. I was unhappy and I knew it, and once I'm in the grip of a real depression the only thing that helps is travel.

It sounds simple, doesn't it? You pack your bags and go. But first you need a viable destination. That's what makes it complicated. If I'm in Ottawa and I go to Carleton Place, what are my chances for Happiness? Nil. Same with Toronto, Sudbury, Windsor or London. Even at my worst I need a proper destination.

Then, on January 11th, my wife received a letter meant for someone else. It read:

> Dear Andrée,
>
> I love you. I dream of you nightly. In my dreams I can smell your long, blonde hair. I caress your breasts and touch your dark nipples with my tongue.
>
> I dream of you as you were last summer. Do you remember, my love, how we lay on your bed? You were sweet as cough syrup. I dream of you like that.

Please, my love, come back to Ottawa. We can stay at the Venture. I'll give you everything. I promise.

All my love,
André

The letter was addressed to:

Andrée Alexis
160 Percy Street,
Ottawa, Ontario

And the return address, printed on the back of the envelope, was:

André Alexis
12 Newcastle Drive,
Ottawa, New York
10057

Now, Andrée and I *do* live at 160 Percy, but she is a redhead and her nipples are not unusually dark. Moreover, I had her assurance that she'd never been to Ottawa, New York. So, Mr Alexis had not tasted *my* wife.

The strange thing was that I, too, had lived at 12 Newcastle Drive, but in Ottawa, Ontario. Think how rare it is to receive a letter at your current address from someone at your previous. In the mood I was in, the coincidence was enough to set me off.

The next day, I took most of my money from our joint account, wrote a letter to my wife explaining my need to travel, packed a suitcase full of shoes and socks, and got on the train for New York.

2. SKIRMISH

The train at night is usually filled with youths travelling without parental guidance. They're up all night, drinking from wineskins filled with Lemon Gin, shouting, arguing, laughing out loud. This trip was different. There were kids all over the place, but I had a seat by a window, and I was with three adults.

Facing me was a middle-aged man in a tweed jacket and a white turtleneck. His hair was red; his eyes an odd shade of green. To his left was a woman in a tweed jacket with matching skirt. Her hair was long and brown; her nose aquiline, with flared nostrils. She had a wide face. Her eyes were round and her mouth extremely small. Facing her, to my immediate right, was a man in his thirties. His hair was dark and extremely short. His thick-rimmed glasses seemed to rest on his cheekbones, so small was his nose, and he was casually dressed.

As the train left the station, the couple in tweed began to relax. They exchanged a few words, in their American accent, and then, after awhile, the man turned to me and said:

—Quite a country you people have here.

—Yes, it's beautiful, I said.

—It's the first time we've been here, he continued, and we like it so much we're coming back, eh darling?

The woman turned to me and smiled. It didn't seem possible for her to speak with such a small mouth, but she said:

—I sure hope so …

—By the way, I'm André and this is my wife Andrée.

—Pleased to meet you, I said.

—We're from New York. We're just up on vacation, and I'm glad we picked Ottawa instead of Toronto, like we were going to … It sure is beautiful, if you don't mind the cold.

Of course, we get our share of cold in New York, but not like you people up here … Who's your friend there?

He turned to the man beside me and smiled.

—Je ne parle pas l'anglais, my neighbour said.

—Il vous demande votre nom, I said.

—Dites-lui qu'il peut me sucer le noeud, maudit américain impérialiste. J'ai pas oublié le Vietnam, moi.

—What did he say?

—He said you were a damned American imperialist, and you can suck his privates because he hasn't forgotten Vietnam.

Mr Alexis stopped talking. He tilted his head and looked to my neighbour, who smiled courteously.

—Did he really say all that? he said.

—Yes, I said. I'm afraid so.

Mr and Mrs Alexis looked at each other and began to laugh.

—Well, said Mr Alexis, you people have a strange way of talking to visitors. Does he want to fight right here or does he want to step into the aisle?

—Voulez-vous vous battre içi ou dans le couloir? I asked.

—Comment ça "me battre"? he said. Je suis pas violent, moi. J'ai dis la vérité, un point c'est tout. S'il veut se battre avec quelqu'un c'est son problème. Qu'il aille se faire enculer.

—What did he say?

—He said he doesn't want to fight. If you want to fight that's your problem, and you can go get fucked.

Mr Alexis turned and looked me in the eye.

—Are you making this up?

—I don't make things up, I said. I haven't got a creative bone in my body …

At that moment, the Frenchman smiled and said in his best English:

—I hope you enjoy your trip, hein.

—What do you mean? asked Mr Alexis.

—I love America, my neighbour answered. I love America.

Mr Alexis turned to me and said:

—You nasty son of a bitch. He didn't say any of that stuff you said.

The small-mouthed wife said:

—Leave it alone, André. It isn't worth the trouble. He's just crazy's his problem.

All three of them were looking at me. Mr Alexis' temples were throbbing. His wife was contemptuous. The Frenchman was amused.

—J't'ai bien eu, hein connard? Qui t'a dit que je voulais un traducteur? Occupe-toi de tes oignons ... okay?

He sat back in his seat, smiling graciously at the Americans.

—I love America, he repeated.

The problem with me is that I don't know how to deal with these things when they happen. I felt humiliated, but I didn't know what to do. I wanted to tear the little frog's head off, but instead I sat still and turned my head away from the three of them.

Mr Alexis said:

—You are some son of a bitch.

Then he sat back. His wife took a book from her purse and started to read. The Frenchman took off his coat, pulled a tattered *Evénement de Jeudi* from its inside pocket and sat back. From then until we crossed the American border, none of us spoke.

Just after the border crossing, my neighbour began a conversation with the Americans.

—Is it New York?

—Yeah, said Mr Alexis. We live in New York City.

—A nice city, non?

—If you like big cities. I'm from the country myself. Where you from?

—Where you from? Qu'est-ce que ça veut dire "where you from"?

They turned to me. I could see their faces reflected in the window. Naturally, I didn't say a word.

—Hé, couillon, qu'est-ce que ça veut dire "where you from"?

—You Canadian? Mr Alexis asked.

—Non, non … Français. French. Paris.

—He's from Paris, dear, said Mrs Alexis.

—You from Paris?

—Ah oui, said my neighbour. From Paris.

—That's a beautiful city, said Mrs Alexis. We were there two years ago.

The three of them began to talk about Paris and New York. They were getting along. That's what made me angry. So, when the porter came by with hot coffee, it was all I could do to ask politely for coffee and a doughnut.

The coffee was in one of those silver cylinders with a spigot near the bottom and, going up the side, a graduated glass tube that shows you how much coffee is left. When the porter pulled the black plastic regulator forward, a cloud of steam escaped and the coffee ran into my Styrofoam cup.

—There you go. That'll be two fifty.

He handed me the coffee and a square, plastic envelope in which I could see my greasy, sugared doughnut. I leaned forward, and as if by accident, I threw the hot coffee in the Frenchman's face.

The effect was immediate. The man began to wail and he tried to hold his face. Then, there was movement all around me. I said:

—Oh, I'm sorry …

Mr Alexis pushed me back.

—You careless idiot, he said.

Mrs Alexis cooed sympathetically, and the porter, not knowing what to do, came back to help the Frenchman stand up. My neighbour's face was red; the skin had already begun to blister. He let out soft, little cries of alarm. His glasses had fallen to the floor. I crushed them beneath my feet. The frames flew apart and the lenses cracked.

—Oh, I'm sorry, I said.

But no one was listening to me. Mr Alexis had gotten up to follow the Frenchman and the porter down the aisle. Mrs Alexis got up to get a better look at the action. Everyone else in the car did the same. So I pushed what was left of his glasses beneath the Frenchman's seat, and I followed the procession behind the porter, to show my concern for the victim.

At the first-aid station, which was actually the porter's enclave at the end of the car, they had managed to find a doctor. The doctor had his hand in a black box full of gauze, bandages and ointments. The Frenchman was babbling in French. No, actually, he wasn't babbling. He was saying:

—Il l'a fait exprès. Il l'a fait exprès. Où sont mes lunettes? J'vois rien sans mes lunettes. Il l'a fait exprès …

—Tes lunettes sont en mille morceaux, I said.

—You speak French? asked the doctor.

—A little, I answered.

—There's some ointment here and some bandages. I'm going to have to wrap his face. He's pretty badly burned. Ask him if he's allergic to anything.

—Es-tu allergique à quelque chose?

—Oui, he answered. Je ne peut pas prendre la pénicilline.

—I got that, the doctor said. He can't take penicillin, right?

—That's right, I said.

23

—Tell him not to worry. There's no penicillin in this ointment, but he's got to sit still so we can put it on.

—Malheureusement, I said, ils n'ont que de la pénicilline. Calme-toi ...

At this the Frenchman really began to struggle.

—Non, non, he said, ça me tuera. J'suis allergique. It kill me! It kill me!

—He says the pain is killing him.

The Frenchman struggled as if his life depended on it, and he did quite well for a man in pain. They had to call several porters to hold him down, to keep him still, to spread the ointment on his face. I left the scene as he began to kick out. I would have stayed, but the ointment reminded me of a burn I'd suffered as a child. It recalled the way my shirt had stuck to my skin, the sound of the doctors' voices and the smell of the hospital.

I was so gratified at seeing the Frenchman suffer, I didn't notice Mr Alexis had followed me back to the bay. As I sat down, he tapped me on the shoulder and said:

—You did that on purpose, didn't you?

He was taunting me, so I answered in the most litigious voice I could muster:

—I don't know what you're talking about, but I know a good lawyer, and I'll sue you if you ever say that in public again. You know what litigation is, don't you?

He stood there with his mouth open. Being American, he knew all about litigation. (It's a lovely word. It always reminded me of *ligament*, and as a child I imagined the men in court snipping the Achilles tendons of the guilty.) He snorted derisively, but he shut up.

The rest of the trip to New York was uneventful. I looked out the window at the stars and, when we passed through cloudless regions, the moonlit farms, the sharp edges of small towns.

When the Frenchman was brought back to his seat, held up by two large, unhappy porters, he was under sedation. His face was swaddled in sticky, yellow gauze and he stank of balm. Only his eyes, ears and the top of his head were left uncovered. He slumped forward in his seat.

—Bad posture, I said.

I was only trying to lighten the atmosphere, but Mr and Mrs Alexis were in no mood for talk. The small-mouthed bitch was still immersed in *The Mountain and the Valley*, and her cowardly husband was doing his best to ignore me.

3. TRAVELLING ALONE

Unfortunately, the beginning of a trip casts its shadow forward. It sets the mood.

From the moment I stepped into Grand Central Station, I began to notice people with bandages. The man at the kiosk where I bought my map of New York State had his right hand in a sling. The driver of the bus that took me to Ottawa had two of the fingers on his right hand bound to a wooden splint. And the woman who sat beside me on the bus had a Band-aid over her left eyebrow. Everywhere I turned there were echoes of the Frenchman. It didn't help my disposition.

The day after my train ride, I left New York City for Ottawa, New York. The bus backed out of the terminal and wound through the city: from Elgin to Rideau, from Rideau to Bank, and from Bank to Somerset, past the harbour and the statue of Liberty. As soon as we got out of the city, I fell asleep, and for awhile:

> I was alone on a country road. There were farmyards, and fenceposts. The fenceposts were unusual. On top of each one there was my head: my head, eyes open, every four feet or so. I got

off the bus in the middle of nowhere and discovered that all the heads were speaking at once. The countryside sounded like a terminal, and the fields went on forever. One of the heads spoke.

—*Hey you! C'mere, lemme look at you. You been walking much? Hard on the soles? Jeez, I haven't had a good conversation in ages ... Say, get closer will ya. I haven't had any human contact in so long ...*

But I walked away along the narrow road, listening to the wolf whistles, jeers and curses of every head I passed.

4. OTTAWA

I stepped down into the archetypal American city. It looked as it had looked on countless television shows, and it was much as I'd imagined it from magazines and novels. (It was a little cleaner than I'd expected, but that didn't throw me.)

The streets were manageable. Two of the main roads were four lanes wide; the rest were comfortably two-laned. The wider streets were Laurier, which ran north-south, and Somerset, which was east-west. It was easy to get around and difficult to get lost. I hate that in a city. After hours of walking about, I felt as though I'd lived in the place forever.

The Alexis' house at 12 Newcastle was as I'd expected: a red-bricked, two-storeyed, chimneyed abode whose window frames were painted white, and in one of whose windows was a white flowerbox from which dry, brown vines tumbled. In a window on the second floor, I could see a young woman with a white baboushka wrapped around her head. She stopped to wipe her brow and then went on with what looked like vacuuming, though it could have been sweeping, or mime, for all I could see.

It was cold outside, so I rang the doorbell.

—Yes?

An older woman stood on her side of the screen door, and for an awful moment I thought she was André's wife.

—Does André Alexis live here? I asked.

—Certainly, she said. You can see it on the mailbox.

—Is he home?

—No.

She stood there staring at me, waiting for the next question. It was like an intelligence test.

—Do you know when he'll be back? I said.

—No.

Then, from somewhere inside the house, a woman's voice:

—Who is it, mother?

—I don't know.

—A friend of André's, I said.

—A friend of André's, said the old lady.

Then, the young woman I'd seen in the window was with us, her hand on her mother's shoulder, smiling faintly through the screen door.

She looked corn-fed and healthy. Her eyes were big, round and green. She had freckles across the bridge of her nose. Her hair, which fell from the baboushka in strands, was red. She was wearing a shirt several sizes too big for her and I could see the plain white brassière beneath it, and the outlines of her body. She had perspired, so the shirt clung to her skin here and there.

—My name's André Alexis, I said. Has André ever mentioned me?

—Not that I can recall, she said.

—Oh, that's just like him. I'll come back when he's home. Nice to have met you …

I didn't move, but the old lady began to push the door closed.

—Just a minute. Won't you come inside a moment? I'll call my husband at work; let him know you're here.

The old woman now had to pull the door open. She stood there, panting slightly, looking at me like I was a thief. I wasn't even tempted to make conversation.

—He's right here, would you like to speak to him?

André's wife called me to the telephone and put the warm receiver in my hand.

—Hello? Who is this? André asked.

—It's André. André Alexis.

—Do I know you?

—I'm fine, fine. I was just talking to Andrée. I live with her on Percy Street. I got your last letter where you mentioned our cough syrup, so I thought I'd visit.

I was looking at his wife when I said this. She brushed the hair from her eyes.

—Who is this? André said.

—You've got a lovely wife, I said. Why didn't you tell her about me?

—What are you talking about? Are you talking about Andrée? How do you know about her?

—Hey, there'll be lots of time to talk about that when you get home. I'll pass you back to your wife.

I cut him off and gave the warm receiver back to his wife.

—Hi Ange, she said.

And rubbed first one palm and then the next on her moist shirt. She listened, then she said:

—Bye Ange.

And made a kissing sound, like balloons being rubbed, and hung up.

—He'll be home at six. Mother, you can close the door now … You can close the door. Mr Alexis will be staying.

To me, she said:

—So ... I'm Andrée, and this is my mother, Andrée. I'm pleased to meet you. Come in and sit down ... Tell us how you know André ...

5. TRUE LOVE

We sat in the living-room, Andrée facing me in the baby-blue armchair, her mother beside me on the baby-blue sofa, and I invented a long, happy friendship between myself and André. Not too long, and not too happy. I placed significant gaps here and there, lapses of time during which André and I had not spoken, to explain why he mightn't have mentioned me, to give me something to be contrite about.

The old woman sat quietly beside me, her mottled hands resting nervously in her lap, She was wearing a light-green dress, a white sweater, thick stockings and fluffy white slippers. I could tell she was in a medical predicament because, at regular intervals, she would fart, silently but obviously, so that a rank smell came from her direction every few minutes and enveloped me. (I didn't think so at the time, but I now believe this was Andrée's way of showing her distrust. Had she really trusted me, she would have put me somewhere out of the line of her mother's fire.)

When I had finished my side of the story, Andrée told me hers: they had met between Ottawa, Kentucky and Ottawa, New York, on a bus, of all places. She had recently sprained her ankle, and André insisted she put her foot on his footrest. He was reading a novel. What was it? Oh yes, *The Mountain and the Valley*. They'd struck up a conversation, and then he did something unexpectedly kind: he read to her from his book.

—"... it was night and cold and the lights of the city were haloed. I could smell the ocean as I walked the streets ..."

And she'd fallen asleep, her head against the cool window, his voice fading. The next thing she knew, they were being woken by the bus driver. It was Albany, and they could go no further because of the storm, so they decided to spend the night in the same hotel ... That night they talked and talked, they had so much in common, and André fell asleep on her floor, his mouth open on the carpet, his hair grey with dust balls ... And from that night: "We've been apart only when he goes on his business trips ... Would you like some coffee?"

You could see she was in love. She blushed at the memory of their first night, and I thought to myself: how little it takes! A man tells her to put her feet up, reads to her from a Canadian novel, then passes out on the floor of her hotel room. Is *that* what it takes to inspire love? It made me unbearably angry. And, seeing the enraptured look on her face, I felt it would be best if I destroyed everything: their home, their feelings for each other, their daily lives ...

—That's a very touching story, I said.

She said:

—I guess I better finish my housework. If you'd like to freshen up, there's a cot in the room at the end of the hall. You could lie down for awhile ...

I got up quickly.

—Thank you.

It was a relief to get away from the old lady.

The room at the end of the hall was narrow and cold. There was just space for the cot and a chest of drawers and not much else. Still, it was the kind of room I like: it was white, recently painted, with a single window. There was no confusion and little dirt. The more a room is a mausoleum, the better I sleep.

I had a lot to think about. What was I to do about André Alexis? What was fitting punishment for his loutish behaviour? Clearly, he didn't deserve his wife's love. So, the first step, after I'd convinced him to let me stay, was to alienate her affections. I would have to seduce his wife, but what was the best way to perform that service? She was obviously romantic, and she did adore her husband. (It was almost religious the way she glowed at the memory of their first night.) Did she like to talk, or was it physical affection she wanted? Should I nuzzle her ears as we squeezed by each other going in and out of doors? Did she like illicit contact? Should I touch her breasts or her arm or her bottom? How much pressure in the touch? Or was she strictly cerebral? It had been ages since I'd read *The Mountain and the Valley*, but I remembered the story: an emotionally disturbed boy becomes an unstable adult who, while running away from himself, causes the death of an innocent woman and her mother. Typical Canadian fare. Not very promising as a guide to sexual preference. Then again, maybe she enjoyed the direct approach, a declaration of erotic madness, say, or an indecent proposal made while I had an erection ... I wondered if my morning erection would serve the purpose, and then I wondered if there were some way to prolong it until afternoon ... Then there was her mother. Could I get on Andrée's good side by flattering her mother? With these questions in mind, I fell asleep.

I woke up at six o'clock to the sound of the front door closing. It sounded masculine: the paterfamilias returning, master of all he surveys, a newspaper tucked under his arm, a briefcase in one hand, leather gloves in the other, ready to touch the dog, the wife, the children. It's a sound that reminds me of having my hair tousled. I sat up and found myself in a darkened room, the light from the street-lamp outside just touching the bottom of the window. It took a few minutes, but I remembered where I was, got up and went out to meet Mr Alexis.

He wasn't what I expected. To begin with, he was thin and a trifle effeminate. I could tell by looking at him he used cologne, so I wasn't surprised when his scent reached me. His face was narrow, but he had a large jaw. I put out my hand and said:

—Hello, André. It's been a long time …

I could see he wasn't about to shake with me, so I put my arms around him and gave him the college hug.

—Good to see you, man …

He stiffened as though he'd been splashed.

—You haven't changed a bit, I said.

His wife hovered about somewhere, smiling politely. His mother-in-law was where I'd left her. She hadn't moved in hours, it seemed.

—I've got one of your letters, I said.

And pulled out the envelope so he alone could see it:

Andrée Alexis
160 Percy Street,
Ottawa, Ontario

That changed his mood. He became a little more agreeable. He said:

—Yes …

I said:

—Give us the old college kiss …

I embraced him, made the sound of a kiss and followed that with a raspberry.

There was a moment of dead silence. Then, his wife said she was going to see to the liver and onions, and she left us to renew our peculiar acquaintance. He and I stepped into the living-room, where his mother-in-law had recently farted.

—What do you want? he asked.

—Your mother-in-law …

—She's dirt poor.

—No. I mean she can hear us. I'm not sure you want that ...

—She's stone deaf and senile. What do you want?

—I want to stay for awhile. I don't want money. I want a bit of hospitality. That's all anybody wants, isn't it?

—Why here?

I held up the letter to Andrée.

—Because you owe me.

Mr Alexis looked neither desperate nor guilty. He seemed to recognize the letter. It was important, but I wasn't sure why.

—Let me see the letter, he said.

—You don't need to see the letter. In fact, you're lucky I don't kick you to death and burn your house down. I came here to see what kind of man pokes another man's wife, then writes her dirty letters. I'll hang around awhile, so you can explain it to me.

I was more aggressive than I'd meant to be, but he didn't seem to mind. He smiled. His face reddened. There was something wrong here.

—Well, I'm sorry about your wife, he said.

He frowned as his mother-in-law passed gas. He took my arm; we moved away from the old woman.

—Listen, he whispered. I didn't write that letter. Let me read it; maybe we can get to the bottom of all this ...

I didn't believe him, but I held it up so he could read it.

—Yes, I see ..., he whispered.

The evening meal was eaten in near silence, and it took hours. Mrs Alexis was as agreeable as ever, but much of her time was taken up with her mother, who sat at the head of the table. Andrée cut the breaded liver into ragged pieces and put them on her mother's spoon. Mr Alexis cut his food and deliberately smushed his portions. It looked like he was eating a liver, onion and potato paste.

—It's been a long time, I said, to keep up my end of the charade.

No one was listening. It was then I had my first inkling something was wrong.

They were clearly speaking to each other in a language I couldn't quite understand. There was something said in a configuration of peas, or a cough. An answer was given in spittle, in the angle of a fork. My case was discussed and decided, without my having understood a word.

After supper, the four of us sat in the living-room. Andrée, her mother and myself on the sofa. André in the armchair. Mr and Mrs Alexis took turns trying to draw me out, but it was clear they weren't interested. (How could you fail to be interested in a man who has pushed himself to your hearth?) At nine o'clock, they began to yawn.

First, Mr Alexis yawned. And then, Mrs Alexis yawned. They yawned together, and then Mrs Alexis yawned on her own. Andrée's mother yawned, and then the three of them yawned together. Mr Alexis yawned three times in succession. Mrs Alexis opened her mouth as if to yawn, and then the three of them rose from their places, put their hands over their mouths, and yawned.

It was the most alarming ritual I've ever witnessed.

I began to have serious doubts about my endeavour.

6. DEFEAT

That night, I sat up listening for their footsteps, acutely aware that the three of them could murder me whenever they wished. I didn't get a moment's sleep.

The following morning, the atmosphere had changed again. Andrée wasn't quite so friendly, and André was even less receptive. There was not a word exchanged at the breakfast table. Frankly, I felt insecure. I wondered what he'd told her, if he'd told her anything at all, and what she'd said. ("We can poison his eggs, Darling.")

—André, I said, I think I'll come with you. I'd like to root around the city, see where you work. That okay?

He didn't answer, but it seemed to be okay. He drank his lukewarm coffee, then we went out together.

As soon as we were outside, he began:

—There isn't anything for you here. I don't know who wrote that letter, but you've got to be gone by six o'clock. You can't stay here.

I said:

—Listen, suppose you were homeless and friendless somewhere and the only person you knew was ploughing your wife. Even if you hated him, you'd be pretty desperate for company, wouldn't you?

—I'm not ploughing your wife.

—Listen, sure I'll go. Eventually. But what I don't understand is this business with Andrée. How could you fool around on your wife and your mother-in-law? I mean, I get the feeling you're pretty unscrupulous, so how come I'm evil and you're not? All I want is a place to stay.

We had reached the bus stop, and we were face to face. He looked at me as though he knew exactly where I was stretching the truth.

—You should be gone by six o'clock or no one will ever hear from you again.

And with that, as though our encounter had been scripted, he stepped on to the bus.

7. FURTHER DEFEAT

It wasn't possible to intimidate him, so my options were reduced. I would have to seduce Mrs Alexis, eat a light meal, then leave by six o'clock. Unless, of course, Mrs

Alexis took my side against Mr Alexis. That was always possible.

I walked around the city thinking about three things: Andrée, the time, and one of André's sentences:

— … no one will ever hear from you again.

The city itself was just what I needed: America, the flag everywhere, Hoagies for breakfast, Beavertails for lunch.

I went into a bookstore and bought *The Mountain and the Valley*, just in case Andrée was erotically fixated on this particular book. It was exactly as I remembered, almost completely without interest:

> As the train left the station, the couple in tweed began to relax. They exchanged a few words, in their American accent, and then, after awhile, the man turned to me and …

Charmless prose, an unexciting story, predictable characters. Just the thing for young lovers. I resolved to use the direct approach.

When I returned to Newcastle Drive, Andrée answered the door, her face flushed, a white towel wrapped around her head, a terrycloth robe held tight at her neck.

—Just in time, she said.

And again, her attitude had changed.

—Close the door. It's winter.

I closed the door and followed her into the living-room where she unwound the towel from her head and gave it to me.

—Dry my hair. If you don't mind …

Her mother was on the sofa, staring straight ahead. I took off my coat, draped it on the armchair and took up the towel.

Andrée's hair was long. It fell to the middle of her back. Even wet, it was soft and smelled of lemon shampoo. I began to pat it dry, happy to perform this intimate service.

—Do the front, she said.

And turned to face me.

She stood inches from me, her robe slightly parted, her eyes looking directly into mine; my hands on her head, rubbing the towel this way and that. I had no idea what was going on, and to tell the truth, I was nervous.

—My mother tells me you're not André's friend at all. Never knew him in college; just met him the other day. That true?

(It was then I realized what bothered me about the old woman, aside from the gas I mean. When I'd first knocked at their door, she'd answered; she'd spoken to her daughter. If she was senile, it was a curiously selective dementia.)

—You came here to pay him back. How're you going to do that, Mr Alexis? Are you going to hurt me?

I tried to move away, but she held me tight, holding her hips on mine, looking straight into my eyes.

—He did it with your wife, didn't he?

Her mother was staring at me, cheeks pink, hands in her lap. I didn't know where to look. The whole business was suddenly frightening. I pushed her away and made up my mind to leave.

Andrée followed me to my room.

—Not in here, she said. It's too clean …

I picked up my suitcase and fled.

8. FLIGHT

I travelled East, hitchhiking.

From a car window, the towns I passed left meaningless impressions: here, a water tower was bright red; there, a farmhouse was black as cinder against the blue sky.

I was in shock.

9. THE SEA! THE SEA!

I was let off somewhere in Connecticut. It was night and cold, and the lights of the city were haloed. I could smell the ocean.

The stores had closed, and the centre of town was abandoned. On Queen Street there was an all-night diner called The Horse's Asp. For six hours I sat there drinking coffee and eating orange crullers, and staring at my hands as though my fate were written on them. The people around me grew less and less genteel as the night went on until, at three o'clock, the place was filled with men who looked desolate under the fluorescent lights.

I was profoundly confused. Why had Andrée tried to seduce me? If André hadn't written the letter, who had? Who was in control, and what had my purpose been?

At three-thirty in the morning, I left The Horse's Asp, thinking about my murderer. (I was convinced I was about to die violently, and at that time, in that place, it seemed a good way to go.) I walked towards the sound of the ocean, following the soft, yellow moon.

Despite the cold, I stood by the beach to admire the ocean's resolve, the way it beat its head against the shore. Then, no more than 100 feet away, a tall man, his back towards me, walked by with a narrow white bag on his shoulder. He didn't see me. He stopped, let go of the bag and began to dig.

It was a winter night at the beach, so it was unusual that we were there together, immersed in our worlds, seeking the same solitude, as though we shared a misery. He was engaged in his private and obscure activity, unaware of me. But for his white bag, the only clearly visible part of him, I might well have walked on, believing myself alone. I felt then how peculiar God was, how strained his sense of humour. I began to walk towards the tall man, to offer my assistance.

At that moment, he turned and saw me approach. I was 50 feet away, but I could feel his panic. It was as though I'd frightened a rat. His face was obscure, but his whole body said fear. He ran from the beach. I ran a little way after him, to let him know how close I felt to his suffering, how much I wanted to help, but he ran that much faster, and he was in better shape than I. By the time I reached the place he had been, he was long gone, and he had left his white bag on the ground.

I had destroyed the brittle moment between us. I didn't know what to do with the bag, how to return it. I picked it up and dropped it and picked it up again. It was only when I decided to keep it as a memento that I realized there was something in it. The thing was cool and soft, a little wet, hard as cuttlefish in spots, yielding in others. For some reason, I thought it was a stuffed animal, but it was a human foot.

For awhile I was confused. I thought: Why would you bury your own foot? It didn't occur to me that the foot was not his, that he'd run remarkably well without it. And how had he cut it off? Axe? Band saw? Circular saw? What kind of man carries a rotting foot around in a white bag and buries it on a beach where it's sure to be uncovered by the tide? Perhaps he'd hoped to bury it deep enough to preserve it until summer when, a stink amidst the poorly dressed, it would cause havoc. Perhaps, perhaps …

No. I had no idea why he'd left the foot in the bag. It was beyond me. It was so completely beyond me that my faith in the existence of God was renewed, and my belief in the unsounded depths of human cruelty was revived.

Leaving the foot where it had fallen, I went away dazed. I kept to the walls or walked down the centre of narrow streets so no one could surprise me. Only once was I startled: an animal ran out of Fred Martin's Sea Emporium and into an alley on the other side of the street.

10. RESTLESS

Naturally, some campaigns are more successful than others. I've discovered more ordered worlds on other excursions. (That and my depressions are what keep me going out.) This trip stays with me, though. First, because it began so forcefully before careening into defeat. Second, because I still wonder whose foot it was I'd held up. And, finally, because I still do not know who wrote the letter to Andrée that set me off.

If it wasn't André, it may have been Andrée. Lately, though, I'm convinced it was Andrée.

A Girl's Story

David Arnason

YOU'VE WONDERED what it would be like to be a character in a story, to sort of slip out of your ordinary self and into some other character. Well, I'm offering you the opportunity. I've been trying to think of a heroine for this story, and frankly, it hasn't been going too well. A writer's life isn't easy, especially if, like me, he's got a tendency sometimes to drink a little bit too much. Yesterday, I went for a beer with Dennis and Ken (they're real-life friends of mine) and we stayed a little longer than we should have. Then I came home and quickly mixed a drink and starting drinking it so my wife would think the liquor on my breath came from the drink I was drinking and not from the drinks I had had earlier. I wasn't going to tell her about those drinks. Anyway, Wayne dropped over in the evening and I had some more drinks, and this morning my head isn't working very well.

To be absolutely frank about it, I always have trouble getting characters, even when I'm stone cold sober. I can think of plots; plots are really easy. If you can't think of one, you just pick up a book, and sure enough, there's a plot. You just move a few things around and nobody knows you stole the idea. Characters are the problem. It doesn't matter how good the plot is if your characters are dull. You can steal characters too, and put them into different plots. I've done that. I stole Eustacia Vye from Hardy and gave her another name. The problem was that she turned out a lot sulkier than I remembered and the plot I put her in was a light comedy. Now nobody wants to publish the story. I'm still sending it out, though. If you send a story to enough publishers, no matter how bad it is, somebody will - ultimately publish it.

For this story I need a beautiful girl. You probably don't think you're beautiful enough, but I can fix that. I can do all kinds of retouching once I've got the basic material, and if I miss anything, Karl (he's my editor) will find it. So I'm going to make you fairly tall, about five-foot eight and a quarter in your stocking feet. I'm going to give you long blonde hair because long blonde hair is sexy and virtuous. Black hair can be sexy too, but it doesn't go with virtue. I've got to deal with a whole literary tradition where black-haired women are basically evil. If I were feeling better I might be able to do it in an ironic way, then black hair would be okay, but I don't think I'm up to it this morning. If you're going to use irony, then you've got to be really careful about tone. I could make you a redhead, but red-heads have a way of turning out pixie-ish, and that would wreck my plot.

So you've got long blonde hair and you're this tall slender girl with amazingly blue eyes. Your face is narrow and your nose is straight and thin. I could have turned up the nose a little, but that would have made you cute, and I really need a beautiful girl. I'm going to put a tiny black mole on your cheek. It's traditional. If you want your character to be really beautiful there has to be some minor defect.

Now, I'm going to sit you on the bank of a river. I'm not much for setting. I've read so many things where you get great long descriptions of the setting, and mostly it's just boring. When my last book came out, one of the reviewers suggested that the reason I don't do settings is that I'm not very good at them. That's just silly. I'm writing a different kind of story, not that old realist stuff. If you think I can't do setting, just watch.

There's a curl in the river just below the old dam where the water seems to make a broad sweep. That flatness is deceptive, though. Under the innocent sheen of the mirroring surface, the current is treacherous. The water swirls, stabs, takes sharp angles and dangerous vectors. The trees that lean from the bank shimmer with the multi-hued greenness of elm, oak, maple and aspen. The leaves turn in the gentle breeze, showing their paler green undersides. The undergrowth, too, is thick and green, hiding the poison ivy, the poison sumac and the thorns. On a patch of grass that slopes gently to the water, the only clear part of the bank on that side of the river, a girl sits, a girl with long blonde hair. She has slipped a ring from her finger and seems to be holding it toward the light.

You see? I could do a lot more of that, but you wouldn't like it. I slipped a lot of details in there and provided all those hints about strange and dangerous things under the surface. That's called foreshadowing. I put in the ring at the end there so that you'd wonder what was going to happen. That's to create suspense. You're supposed to ask yourself what the ring means. Obviously it has something to do with love, rings always do, and since she's taken it off, obviously something has gone wrong in the love relationship. Now I just have to hold off answering that question for as long as I can, and I've got my story. I've got a friend who's also a writer who says never tell the buggers anything until they absolutely have to know.

I'm going to have trouble with the feminists about this story. I can see that already. I've got that river that's calm on the surface and boiling underneath, and I've got those trees that are gentle and beautiful with poisonous and dangerous undergrowth. Obviously, the girl is going to be like that, calm on the surface but passionate underneath. The feminists are going to say that I'm perpetuating stereotypes, that by giving the impression the girl is full of hidden passion I'm encouraging rapists. That's crazy. I'm just using a literary convention. Most of the world's great books are about the conflict between reason and passion. If you take that away, what's left to write about?

So I've got you sitting on the riverbank, twirling your ring. I forgot the birds. The trees are full of singing birds. There are meadowlarks and vireos and even Blackburnian warblers. I know a lot about birds but I'm not going to put in too many. You've got to be careful not to overdo things. In a minute I'm going to enter your mind and reveal what you're thinking. I'm going to do this in the third person. Using the first person is sometimes more effective, but I'm always afraid to do a female character in the first person. It seems wrong to me, like putting on a woman's dress.

Your name is Linda. I had to be careful not to give you a biblical name like Judith or Rachel. I don't want any symbolism in this story. Symbolism makes me sick, especially biblical symbolism. You always end up with some crazy moral argument that you don't believe and none of the readers believe. Then you lose control of your characters, because they've got to be like the biblical characters. You've got this terrific episode you'd like to use, but you can't because Rachel or Judith or whoever wouldn't do it. I think of stories with a lot of symbolism in them as sticky.

Here goes.

Linda held the ring up toward the light. The diamond flashed rainbow colours. It was a small diamond, and Linda reflected that it was probably a perfect symbol of her relationship with Gregg. Everything Gregg did was on a small scale. He was careful with his money and just as careful with his emotions. In one week they would have a small wedding and then move into a small apartment. She supposed that she ought to be happy. Gregg was very handsome, and she did love him. Why did it seem that she was walking into a trap?

That sounds kind of distant, but it's supposed to be distant. I'm using indirect quotation because the reader has just met Linda, and we don't want to get too intimate right away. Besides, I've got to get a lot of explaining done quickly, and if you can do it with the character's thoughts, then that's best.

Linda twirled the ring again, then with a suddenness that surprised her, she stood up and threw it into the river. She was immediately struck by a feeling of panic. For a moment she almost decided to dive into the river to try to recover it. Then, suddenly, she felt free. It was now impossible to marry Gregg. He would not forgive her for throwing the ring away. Gregg would say he'd had enough of her theatrics for one lifetime. He always accused her of being a romantic. She'd never had the courage to admit that he was correct, and that she intended to continue being a romantic. She was sitting alone by the river in a long blue dress because it was a romantic pose. Anyway, she thought a little wryly, you're only likely to find romance if you look for it in romantic places and dress for the occasion.

Suddenly, she heard a rustling in the bush, the sound of someone coming down the narrow path from the road above.

I had to do that, you see. I'd used up all the potential in the relationship with Gregg, and the plot would have started to flag if I hadn't introduced a new character. The man who is coming down the path is tall and athletic with wavy brown hair. He has dark brown eyes that crinkle when he smiles, and he looks kind. His skin is tanned, as if he spends a lot of time outdoors, and he moves gracefully. He is smoking a pipe. I don't want to give too many details. I'm not absolutely sure what features women find attractive in men these days, but what I've described seems safe enough. I got all of it from stories written by women, and I assume they must know. I could give him a chiselled jaw, but that's about as far as I'll go.

The man stepped into the clearing. He carried an old-fashioned wicker fishing creel and a telescoped fishing rod. Linda remained sitting on the grass, her blue dress spread out around her. The man noticed her and apologized.

"I'm sorry, I always come here to fish on Saturday after-noons and I've never encountered anyone here before." His voice was low with something of an amused tone in it.

"Don't worry," Linda replied. "I'll only be here for a little while. Go ahead and fish. I won't make any noise." In some way she couldn't understand, the man looked familiar to her. She felt she knew him. She thought she might have seen him on television or in a movie, but of course she knew that movie and television stars do not spend every Saturday afternoon fishing on the banks of small, muddy rivers.

"You can make all the noise you want," he told her. "The fish in this river are almost entirely deaf. Besides, I don't care if I catch any. I only like the act of fishing. If I catch them, then I have to take them home and clean them. Then I've got to cook them and eat them. I don't even like fish that much, and the fish you catch here all taste of mud."

"Why do you bother fishing then?" Linda asked him. "Why don't you just come and sit on the riverbank?"

"It's not that easy," he told her. "A beautiful girl in a blue dress may go and sit on a riverbank any time she wants. But a man can only sit on a riverbank if he has a very good reason. Because I fish, I am a man with a hobby. After a hard week of work, I deserve some relaxation. But if I just came and sat on the riverbank, I would be a romantic fool. People would make fun of me. They would think I was irresponsible, and before long I would be a failure." As he spoke, he attached a lure to his line, untelescoped his fishing pole and cast his line into the water.

You may object that this would not have happened in real life, that the conversation would have been awkward, that Linda would have been a bit frightened by the man. Well, why don't you just run out to the grocery store and buy a bottle of milk and a loaf of bread? The grocer will give you your change without even looking at you. That's what happens in real life, and if that's what you're after, why are you reading a book?

I'm sorry. I shouldn't have got upset. But it's not easy you know. Dialogue is about the hardest stuff to write. You've got all those "he saids" and "she saids" and "he replieds." And you've got to remember the quotation marks and whether the comma is inside or outside the quotation marks. Sometimes you can leave out the "he saids" and the "she saids" but then the reader gets confused and can't figure out who's talking. Hemingway is bad for that. Sometimes you can read an entire chapter without figuring out who is on what side.

Anyway, something must have been in the air that afternoon. Linda felt free and open.

Did I mention that it was warm and the sun was shining?

She chattered away, telling the stranger all about her life, what she had done when she was a little girl, the time her dad had taken the whole family to Hawaii and she got such a bad sunburn that she was peeling in February, how she was a better water skier than Gregg and how mad he got when she beat him at tennis. The man, whose name was Michael (you can use biblical names for men as long as you avoid Joshua or Isaac), told her he was a doctor, but had always wanted to be a cowboy. He told her about the time he skinned his knee when he fell off his bicycle and had to spend two weeks in the hospital because of infection. In short, they did what people who are falling in love always do. They unfolded their brightest and happiest memories and gave them to each other as gifts.

Then Michael took a bottle of wine and a Klik sandwich out of his wicker creel and invited Linda to join him in a picnic. He had forgotten his corkscrew and he had to push the cork down into the bottle with his filleting knife. They drank wine and laughed and spat out little pieces of cork. Michael reeled in his line, and to his amazement discovered a diamond ring on his hook. Linda didn't dare tell him where the ring had come from. Then Michael took Linda's hand, and slipped the ring onto her finger. In a comic-solemn voice, he asked her to marry him. With the same kind of comic solemnity, she agreed. Then they kissed, a first gentle kiss with their lips barely brushing and without touching each other.

Now I've got to bring this to some kind of ending. You think writers know how stories end before they write them, but that's not true. We're wracked with confusion and guilt about how things are going to end. And just as you're playing the role of Linda in this story, Michael is my alter ego. He even looks a little like me and he smokes the same kind of pipe. We all want this to end happily. If I were going to be realistic about this, I suppose I'd have to let them make love. Then, shaken with guilt and horror, Linda would go back and marry Gregg, and the doctor would go back to his practice. But I'm not going to do that. In the story from which I stole the plot, Michael turned out not to be a doctor at all, but a returned soldier who had always been in love with Linda. She recognized him as they kissed, because they had kissed as children, and even though they had grown up and changed, she recognized the flavour of wintergreen on his breath. That's no good. It brings in too many unexplained facts at the last minute.

I'm going to end it right here at the moment of the kiss. You can do what you want with the rest of it, except you can't make him a returned soldier, and you can't have them make love then separate forever. I've eliminated those options. In fact, I think I'll eliminate all options. This is where the story ends, at the moment of the kiss. It goes on and on forever while cities burn, nations rise and fall, galaxies are born and die, and the universe snuffs out the stars one by one. It goes on, the story, the brush of a kiss.

Poppies:
Three Variations

Margaret Atwood

In Flanders fields the poppies blow
Between the crosses, row on row.
* That mark our place, and in the sky*
* The larks, still bravely singing, fly*
Scarce heard amid the guns below.

— John McCrae

1.

I HAD AN UNCLE once who served *in Flanders.* Flanders, or was it France? I'm old enough to have had the uncle but not old enough to remember. Wherever, those *fields* are green again, and ploughed and harvested, though they keep throwing up rusty shells, broken skulls. *The* uncle wore a beret and marched in parades, though slowly. We always bought those felt *poppies,* which aren't even felt any more, but plastic: small red explosions pinned to your chest, like a *blow* to the heart. *Between the* other thoughts, that one *crosses* my mind. And the tiny lead soldiers in the shop windows, *row on row* of them, not lead any more, too poisonous, but every detail perfect, and from every part of the world: India, Africa, China, America. *That* goes to show, about war—in retrospect it becomes glamour, or else a game we think we could have played better. From time to time the stores *mark* them down, you can get bargains. There are some for us, too, with *our* new leafy flag, not the red rusted-blood one the men fought under. That uncle had *place*-mats with the old flag, and cups *and* saucers. The planes *in the sky* were tiny then, almost comical, like kites with wind-up motors; I've seen them in movies. The uncle said he never saw *the larks*. Too much smoke, or fog. Too much roaring, though on some mornings it was very *still*. Those were the most dangerous. You hoped you would act *bravely* when the moment came, you kept up your courage by *singing*. There was a kind of *fly* that bred in the corpses, there were thousands of them he said; and during the bombardments you could *scarce* hear yourself think. Though sometimes you *heard* things anyway: the man beside him whispered, 'Look,' and when he looked there was no more torso: just a red hole, *a* wet splotch in *mid*-air. That uncle's gone now too, the number of vets in the parade is smaller each year, they limp more. But in the windows *the* soldiers multiply, so clean and colourfully painted, with their little intricate *guns*, their shining boots, their faces, brown or pink or yellow, neither smiling nor frowning. It's strange to think how many soldiers like that have been owned over the years, loved over the years, lost over the years, in backyards or through gaps in porch floors. They're lying down there, under our feet in the garden and *below* the floorboards, armless or legless, faces worn half away, listening to everything we say, waiting to be dug up.

2.

Cup of coffee, the usual morning drug. He's off jogging, told her she shouldn't be so sluggish, but she can't get organized, it involves too many things: the right shoes, the right outfit, and then worrying about how your bum looks, wobbling along the street. She couldn't do it alone anyway, she might get mugged. So instead she's sitting remembering how much she can no longer remember, of who she used to be, who she thought she would turn into when she grew up. We are the dead: that's about the only line left from *In Flanders Fields*, which she had to write out twenty times on *the* blackboard, for talking. When she was ten and thin, and now see. He says she should go vegetarian, like him, healthy as lettuce. She'd rather eat *poppies*, get the opiates straight from the source. Eat daffodils, the poisonous bulb like an onion. Or better, slice it into his soup. He'll *blow* his nose on her once too often, and then. *Between the* rock and the hard cheese, that's where she sits, inert as a prisoner, making little *crosses* on the wall, like knitting, counting the stitches *row on row, that* old trick to *mark* off the days. *Our place*, he calls this dump. He should speak for himself, she's just the mattress around here, she's just the cleaning lady, *and* when he ever lifts a finger there'll be sweet pie *in the sky*. She should burn *the* whole thing down, just for *larks; still*, however *bravely* she may talk, to herself, where would she go after that, what would she do? She thinks of the bunch of young men they saw, downtown at night, where they'd gone to dinner, his birthday. High on something, *singing* out of tune, one guy's *fly* half-open. Freedom. Catch a woman doing that, panty alert, she'd be jumped by every creep within a mile. Too late to make yourself *scarce*, once they get the skirt up. She's *heard* of a case like that, in a poolhall or somewhere. That's what keeps her in here, in this house, that's what keeps her tethered. It's not *a mid*-life crisis, which is what he says. It's fear, pure and simple. Hard to rise above it. Rise above, like a balloon or *the* cream on milk, as if all it takes is hot air or fat. Or will-power. But the reason for that fear exists, it can't be wished away. What she'd need in real life is a few *guns*. That and the technique, how to use them. And the guts, of course. She pours herself another cup of coffee. That's her big fault: she might have the gun but she wouldn't pull the trigger. She'd never be able to hit a man *below* the belt.

3.

In school, when I first heard the word *Flanders* I thought it was what nightgowns were made of. And pyjamas. But then I found it was a war, more important to us than others perhaps because our grandfathers were in it, maybe, or at least some sort of ancestor. The trenches, the *fields* of mud, the barbed wire, became our memories as well. But only for a time. Photographs fade, the rain eats away at statues, *the* neurons in our brains blink out one by one, and goodbye to vocabulary. We have other things to think about, we have lives to get on with. Today I planted five *poppies* in the front yard, orangey-pink, a new hybrid. They'll go well with the marguerites. Terrorists *blow* up airports, lovers slide blindly in *between the* sheets, in the soft green drizzle my cat *crosses* the street; in the spring regatta the young men *row on, row* on, as if nothing has happened since 1913, and the crowds wave and enjoy their tall drinks with cucumber and gin. What's wrong with *that?* We can scrape by, more or less, getting from year to year with hardly a *mark* on us, as long as we know *our place,* don't mouth off too much or cause uproars. A little sex, a little gardening, flush toilets and similar discreet pleasures; *and in the sky* the satellites go over, keeping a bright eye on us. The ospreys, *the* horned *larks,* the shrikes and the woodland warblers are having a thinner time of it, though *still bravely* trying to nest in the lacunae left by pesticides, the sharp blades of the reapers. If it's *singing* you want, there's lots of that, you can tune in any time; coming out of your airplane seat-mate's earphones it sounds like a *fly* buzzing, it can drive you crazy. So can the news. Disaster sells beer, and this month hurricanes are the fashion, and famines: *scarce* this, scarce that, too little water, too much sun. With every meal you take huge bites of guilt. The excitement in the disembodied voices says: you *heard* it here first. Such *a* commotion in the *mid*-brain! Try meditation instead, be thankful for the annuals, for the smaller mercies. You listen, you listen to the moonlight, to the earthworms revelling in the lawn, you celebrate your own quick heartbeat. But below all that there's another sound, a ground swell, a drone, you can't get rid of it. It's the guns, which have never stopped, just moved around. It's the guns, still firing monotonously, bored with themselves but deadly, deadlier, deadliest, it's *the guns*, an undertone beneath each ordinary tender conversation. Say pass the sugar and you hear the guns. Say I love you. Put your ear against skin: below thought, below memory, *below* everything, the guns.

Meditations on Starch

Clark Blaise

POTATOES: Mr Spud opened at the local mall, and hired my high school boy for his first job. He was saving for a trip to Europe, where he has relatives.

He's been taught to do amazing things with potatoes. They're just a shell of their former selves. No longer prized for snowy yields, for understated contribution to stews, now they're just parka-like pockets waiting to be stuffed. It's the fate of blandness in the mall-managed world, I tell him, to be upscaled into glamour like pita bread and bagels, chicken and veal. Stuffed with yoghurt, sour cream and cottage cheese, spread with peppers, cheese and broccoli, topped with Thousand Islands dressing and bacon bits.

What wizard thought this up?

Mother!

I still like mashed potatoes. Even the name is honest and reassuring, after the *gepashket* concoctions with alfalfa sprouts and garbanzo beans. Butter-topped, cream-coloured bins of heroic self-indulgence, inviting a finger-dip the way a full can of white enamel compels a brush.

Is there a taste explosion in the world finer than the first lick of the Dairy Queen cone, the roughened vanilla from a freshly opened tub, the drowning in concentrated carbohydrate where fats and starches come together in snowy concupiscence?

CORN: My son never knew his grandmother, whose presence comes back to me as I stand at the Mr Spud toppings bar. She only exists in these sharpened moments, triggered by significant images that otherwise baffle me. "Mother" I murmur, "what do you make of this?" Questions to my mother are questions to history, answers from her are brief parables of the twentieth century.

Don't you know? she tells me. The yearning for a clean, quick, anonymous bite is universal.

My mother found herself in Prague in 1933. Her art school in Germany had just been closed down. One of her professors offered escape with him to Rio. Many went to Paris and Brussels. These weren't the Big-Time Bauhausers; New York and L.A. weren't in the cards. These were commercial designers ("but not designing enough," my mother would joke). Shanghai, Istanbul, Alexandria, Stockholm, with the leaders taking off for Caracas and Rio. One got to Vera Cruz. Maybe eventually some of them made their way to America. My mother got to Montréal.

I was a stamp collector. I knew the tales behind those thick letters with the high-denomination stamps, the elegant handwriting in black ink turning to olive. Cancelled stamps are less valuable than mint, but I treasured them for the urgency of cancellation. My mother had known a time when the germ of genius was clustered in the back streets of Dresden and Weimar and Dessau, before the Big Bang flung it to tin shacks on the shores of Maracaibo.

The poles of her existence can move me to tears, the B. Traven world of artists from the heartland of order and austerity rotting in the rat-infested tropics. She showed me photos of an art college, hand-painted signs on a tin-roofed shack, Herr Professor in jodhpurs and bush shirt, teaching from a canvas deckchair.

"Poor old Dieter," she'd say.

She'd wanted a career in fashion design. Her surviving portfolios from art school feature ice-skaters and ballerinas. She was the Degas of Dresden. But the faces of the skaters and dancers seem grafted on, dark and heavy, like hers.

The eyes are shadowed, in the movie-fashion of the day. They stop just short of grotesquerie, for those girls will never soar, never leap. She could get the bodies, but not the faces. I can't tell if it's Expressionism, autobiography, or mild incompetence. I don't know if these were the drawings she kept out of fondness, or the ones that didn't sell. Others found their way into magazines. The idea of my mother influencing the Prague Spring Collection of 1934 fills me with wonder.

Or do I read too much into those drawings, too much into everything about her? Had she somehow, secretly, read Kafka? The idea of her Europe, of pre-war Central Europe, tugs at me, the continent I missed by the barest of margins.

There was no concept of Eastern or Western Europe in those days—Warsaw and Prague were as western as Paris. Russia and Spain, of course, didn't count; they were Asian, or African. Budapest and Bucharest had reputations for pervasive dishonesty, deriving perhaps from the perversity of their languages. So the stories I grew up with and passed on to my son were of an *idea* of Europe that hasn't existed in eighty years, a Holy Roman Empire in which a single language and a single passport dominated all others and the rest of the world suffered paroxysms of exclusion for not being European, and specifically, German.

When he was twelve, I asked my boy what he wanted to be when he grew up. "A European," he answered.

In Prague she got a job painting commercial signboards to hang over doorways, like British pub placards. One of the first signs she painted was for something called 'Indian Corn'. A corn café! Nothing but stubby ears of corn, cut in half, standing in pools of butter. In Prague, in 1933.

She had never eaten corn. Her parents considered it servants' food, part of a cuisine beneath serious cultivation. Nothing that required labour in the eating—and corn on the cob looked like work—was part of their diet. My grandparents, whom I of course never met, favoured pre-nouvelle cuisine French cooking, which meant soft, smothered, simmering things, the mashed potatoes of their day, short on fibre, low on spices, long on labour and quickly digested. Much favoured were compotes and warm puddings, since they detested anything cold as well as anything hot. Worst of all were the still-churning, molten messes that had become chic in Germany with the rise of Mussolini. Upscaling the lowly pasta. My grandfather's response to history is summarized in a single gastronomic grumble. "Why couldn't *il Duce* have been a Frenchman! At least we would have eaten properly." My grandmother, no less patrician, responded, "Be grateful. He could have been Hungarian."

Of all the stories I want to know, of all the things my mother told me of the secret lives of complicated people, I remember only these ridiculous little lines. So she painted her cob—half a cob, and the cobs weren't big in those days—standing up like a stubby candle in its pool of butter. Each kernel was treated like a window in an apartment tower, radiating a buttery light. It wasn't easy, before acrylics, before the conventions of Magic Realism, being a German artist, to devote herself to a humble corncob.

"I didn't know anything at first. Or maybe I discovered it as I worked. It was love for America," is how she put it. "A craving for Indian corn saved my life."

Franz Kafka had been living a few blocks away just a decade earlier. He'd written *Amerika* under the same mysterious craving, though it didn't save his life. Maybe America-worship was in the air, at least among those who professed no longing for Germany. For my mother, Prague was just another provincial German city with an interesting Slavic component to be respected, but faintly pitied. She couldn't imagine civilized discourse in any language but German, with the possible exception of French in well-defined circumstances. French and German divided the dignified world between them, the spheres of pleasure and labour, though her French years were still in the future.

Her boss had a son, named Jürgen Jaeger—a good movie name, and he had dabbled in films like many German-speakers in the '20s. He still thought of himself as a set-designer, a property man ("but not a man of property," he joked, and the joke has survived them all because my mother jotted it down). He also identified strongly with Hitler's Sudeten policy, feeling himself mightily abused by the majority Czechs with their dirty, mongrel ways. I am making him sound unappealing—a Hitler of sorts, another expansionist signpainter with acting ambitions, born on the rim of Germany—but my mother never did. His attitudes were too common to be evil. I'm sure most Prague-born German-speakers yearned for enosis with the Fatherland, all other implications of Hitler-rule to be put aside, temporarily.

This, then, was my mother's situation in 1933. She was thirty and unmarried, talented, attractive, and stateless. She had an admirer whose rechannelled ambition was to join the political and, if necessary, military services of the greater German state. I have seen his picture, the suggestive swagger, as I interpret it, of one leg up on the running board, elbow on the windshield, body tight against the touring-car's flank. No monocle, no duelling scars, but a leather coat, a self-regarding little blond moustache, and a short, elegant cigarette that can only be carried in a theatrical gold case. He strikes the pose of a big-game hunter, even on a Carpathian picnic in the summer of 1934. This is the man who must be eliminated before I can be born.

Pictures of my mother show her always smoking, though I never saw her smoke, nor empty an ashtray without a show of disgust.

I came into her papers five years ago. That's when I unwrapped the first of many portfolios she'd been keeping under her bed. I had never seen them, and she had shared everything with me, I'd thought, the only child, the late-born son, the artistic and sensitive man in the family. Some of these I had seen—my grandparents sometime in the late twenties at a resort in the mountains. Taking the Cure. All those faces, relaxing, carefree, getting away from business and the city and the nameless sickness that seemed to stalk them.

I look like my grandfather—her genes won out. The gene for baldness, carried through the mother. The gene for Alzheimer's disease—who carries that? My mother maintained a saving fiction all the years that she was able, that her parents could have left Germany in time, just as she had, there was an uncle in Montréal who would sponsor them all, but her father lost first the will, then the sense of all urgency. It was, in his case, a medical, not political problem.

"Who is this man?" I asked her, and she pretended to look, and to smile. "He's very handsome, mama. Like a movie star." Still no response. The photo is sepia, faded, and extremely small. If only it could be blown up, Jaeger and the touring-car, the mountains and forest in the background, I might understand just a little more. There are other pictures, equally small, taken from upper windows, overlooking city squares. Brno? Bratislava? Carlsbad? Prague, perhaps, or the view from Carpathian resort hotel. Maybe Jürgen is standing at her side, whispering, "*Sehr schön*".

"Jürgen Jaeger, mama, does it mean anything?"

She held her hand out to appease me, her fingers now blue-edged tines, but she didn't look.

I can read German, speak it enough. Her old-style hand-writing is difficult. *I tell him he must do what he must do. His father has interests in Germany. They have relatives in Leipzig.*

I read it out loud, looking at its author's face, which gives back nothing. She probably jotted down these notes in ten seconds, sixty years ago. Now, the simplest resurrected fact of her life embraces the world. If I don't take these boxes now, they will be lost. She is going away and won't be coming back, and we have decided we must leave Canada.

He says, "Der Führer may be a little crude for your tastes, but he's no fool! He knows who makes money for him. And with this Rosenfeld getting elected in America, well ... "

There is another tiny, sepia street scene. It is the most precious picture in the box. For an artist, my mother took terrible pictures. A tram snakes off the top of the frame. Half of a bundled Frau crosses the street. Uniformed men—police, army, Czech, German?—fill the space at the corner, outside a coffee shop. There seems to be an *Apothek* next door. Cold-looking children play a sidewalk game using chalk just outside its door. You would miss it if you weren't looking for it, the sign for *Korn* struggling for attention against much larger and fancier boards.

This is the picture to be enlarged, at any cost. I palm it and slip it away, knowing I am taking her soul, and fearing that something will slice through all the blown cells in her brain and reach out for it, and then destroy it.

Fly! Fly! Go west and don't stop. I tell you this as a friend, as someone who knows.

This on a worn sheet of airmail paper, initialled with what appears to be a double 'J' inside a crest, with a swastika hanging below it. So strange to see, as it were, a sincere swastika and not some gangland graffiti.

J.J., Visa Clerk, Leipzig.

RICE: In my wife's culture, Usha is called a 'cousin-sister' which means any female relative approximate in age. Actually she is Anu's first cousin, daughter of my father-in-law's oldest brother. In the ancestral long-ago, they had lived in the same Calcutta house, the *jethoo-bari*, part of a joint family numbering forty.

She is married to Pramod, and both are physicists. But instead of staying in the university world and settling down on some Big Ten campus, Pramod had taken a position in Holland, setting up a lab, and the Dutch government had recommended him for similar work in Indonesia and Surinam and before too many years, he had found himself side-tracked into sophisticated, high-level nuclear management, the protocols of which led, inevitably, to international agencies. He is now with the UN's nuclear-monitoring agency in Vienna, and Usha works as a researcher in physics for the University. They have been in Vienna for fifteen years, their children are European, they own an apartment in the city and a garden house in Wiener-Neustadt. It's a comfortable life in a country where immigration and assimilation as we know them are impossible.

We are all together this night in Vienna, enjoying a huge Bengali banquet, cooked from locally gathered fish and rice and vegetables, simmered in spices brought back from frequent trips to London and Bombay. My son and I have our Eurail passes, Anu will be with us only three days before going on to India to visit her mother and sister.

It's this life we lead, I silently explain to myself, and to the ghost of my mother. Vienna was another of her cities, briefly. The world has opened for us, no fears of the unknown. My mother shrank from the very idea of India, but tried to disguise it with images of Gandhi and respect for ancient wisdom.

How under-defined I feel, at fifty, compared to Pramod; a father who has written some books, who teaches when he must, who dabbles in cultures that have their hooks in him.

We are talking of Canada. "They've become like the British," Anu says, spooning out rice to our son. "Hateful little people."

The Sens had visited Niagara Falls last summer, and been turned away at the border for an afternoon's visit. For pleasure trips they use their Indian, not UN passports. "He said things to us I wouldn't say to a servant," says Usha Sen. "'How do I know you will leave when you say? How do I know you own a house as you say?' They are very suspicious about Indians, I must say."

"I told him to go to hell," says Jyoti, the Harvard boy. "Who needs the hassle? The Austrians are bad enough, but I always thought Canadians were better."

I remember when it wasn't so, in our cosmopolitan refuge of Montréal, when my mother and I lived like Alexandrians in a large apartment in Outremont after my father's death. We had original paintings on our walls, French-Canadian artists only. My father was an old man even in my earliest memories, a lawyer nearing retirement, then dead two months after achieving it. I remember the visits of his grown-up children from an earlier marriage, of being the same age as his grandchildren, and of wondering what, exactly, to call our relationship. My son and Jyoti are, precisely, second cousins. Usha is his first-cousin-once-removed. He calls her *mashi*, aunt.

"Have more rice, please. There is plenty."

"Mother, this isn't Calcutta," says Tapati, the MIT daughter. Everything this evening is exquisite. There is no cuisine in the world that excites me like Indian, no painting that thrills me like Moghul miniatures, no city for better or worse, like Calcutta. After India, Europe is a bore. I'm staying back for my son's sake, his ancient dream of being European.

Anu is explaining our move to the States. "To be Indian in Canada was to be a second-class citizen no matter how good you were, no matter how Canadian you tried to be. At least if we're second-class in the States we know it's because we're just second-rate." I wish I could sink into the rice, the dimple-topped pyramids of snowy rice scooped out for fish and vegetables. I want to grab handfuls of rice and smear them over my head and rub them in my face. I want to do something vulgar and extravagant in this apartment of excellence, among these diligent and exquisite people, out of my own shame, the accumulated guilt and incomprehensions of my life.

Tapati is asking our son, "Is there anything special you want to see in Vienna? I can take you there."

They are amazed that for who he is and what he represents to them—America, after all, the place and people they most admire—he speaks only English. Usha's children have been raised in Europe, but with Indian ways. Each of them speaks eight languages, but they have no country. Jyoti writes rock lyrics in German, plays in an Austrian band, studies economics at Harvard. Tapati has a Ph.D. and an MBA and now interns at the World Bank. Both are in America, but not of it—too exquisite for the mall-culture America I know.

"Anything," he says. "It doesn't matter."

"No, there must be something."

He looks to me for help. He wants Europe, he wants saturation, a way of entering. He's been studying German in high school, but it's the last thing in the world he'll admit here to his second cousins. He doesn't trust himself to understand a single word. He's heard Bengali all his life, but never thought it part of himself. He spent half his life in a French-speaking city and did his French exercises perfectly, like history. It's the legacy of the New World. Jyoti has already told him, he'd trade it all—the languages, the sophistication that dazzles his Harvard friends—for a simple work permit, for the chance to stay and work the summer at Mr Spud.

"And what about you, Uncle?"

"Berggasse 19," I say.

"The Freud house?" Usha asks. "Why that—there's nothing there, believe me."

"Wasn't he a coke-head?" my son asks in all seriousness, and the question sails over the heads of all but Jyoti, who smiles and nods. A conspiratorial friendship is starting to grow.

"Berggasse is very near my lab," says Usha. "We can take the tram there tomorrow. But it's not what you think—it's just a couple of rooms with photos on the walls."

"Bor-ring," Jyoti hums, as my boy suppresses a grin.

We're there at eleven o'clock the next morning, my son and I, and Jyoti who's brought his guitar along. He'll do Freud with us, and we'll do the music shops with him. He's promised us a tour of the lowlife dives of Vienna, the coffee shops where the Punkers hang out, the places where he spent his high school years avoiding expectations to be good and dutiful.

The first cousins have gone out for a proper Viennese lunch, *Kaffeeschlag mit Sachertorte*. Nothing that has to do with the man who once compared the ego—rational and altruistic—to Europe, and the libido—rapacious and murderous—to Asia, inspires my wife to sympathy. A foolish little man, racist and chauvinist, with bad science to justify it.

It is a sunny, summer day, cool but bright, sweater weather. Children are playing on the sidewalk of Berggasse, outside the corner *Apothek*. Jyoti says to us, "Watch this—

you think the Austrians know anything?" He asks the oldest boy, "Do you know the Freud house?"

"Did they just move in?" he asks.

"Get that?" he laughs, turning to us. My son translates it.

"You could ask anyone on this street. Old, young, it doesn't matter. One group wants to forget, and the other one never knew." We cross over the narrow street, looking for brass plates outside the formal doors. Number 19 is just a flat, as it always was, squeezed between other flats and offices.

Usha was right, it's only an old doctor's office cluttered with photos. The second-cousins browse respectfully, faintly embarrassed by all the fuss. It's all Jyoti can do not to unzip his guitar case and start banging out something scandalous for the Freud Museum. I don't know what I expected to find.

This is the room where all of them came, I want to say. Princess Marie sat there. And the young Viennese Circle— see their pictures!—met here, in this room. In this room, someone challenged the incomprehensible with bad science and bad politics, in the name nevertheless of reason. The smallest facts had the deepest gravity, chance events were all connected, public events were the ritualized form of private projection.

Son! Are you listening?

Someone dared to say our dreams had a pattern, our dysfunctions a cause, our beliefs a pathology. On the walls, the Holy Roman Empire surrenders, and Freud stands on the dais, Vienna's most honoured, most famous citizen, as the Austrian Republic is declared. Here, Freud is welcoming the President of the Republic and his cabinet on the quarter-century anniversary of *The Interpretation of Dreams*. His birth-cottage is decked with bunting.

And it chokes me, suddenly, the realization that science and music and literature can be so advanced, and do nothing to influence a political culture in its infancy. Austrian democracy was younger than Ghana's when the Nazis crushed it. I want to turn to my son and remind him of the great despairing poems I've read to him, of Yeats, of Auden, and the vast literature of the Holocaust that radiates from this room and a thousand others in this city, and echoes off these grey, sunny streets. The tradition, however faintly, I belong to. Poems about the imbalance of what we are capable of feeling and thinking, and what we have inflicted.

They've gone.

"They heard music outside," the ticket-seller tells me. "They said for you to follow the music."

At first I hear nothing. I watch the children across the street, and the old women slogging their way from shop to shop, carrying groceries in string bags.

Berggasse slopes downward, and I follow it a block, half-imagining a rhythm, a few high notes and a beat in the air. Turn right, twist left. People are in the streets now, following something.

Up ahead in a small square at the rim of a fountain I can see them, clowns juggling, and a small crowd clustered. The performers wear top hats and putty noses, their checks are reddened, and one of the boys is darker than all the others, in a borrowed top hat, crouched on one knee like Chuck Berry, cutting in front of the clowns and drummers, leading everyone in lyrics I can't understand. And at the edge of the fountain is my boy in a borrowed vest and putty nose, punching a tambourine and doing a snake-dance on the fountain's edge.

Little Me

George Bowering

June 17, 1988:

THREE TIMES a week I have my early afternoon meal at Daphne's Lunch, an ordinary place frequented by the less affluent workers of the neighbourhood and by the widows who live in the highrise apartments nearby. They know me there, and call me by my first name. In return I generally have the daily special. Today it was chicken soup and a patty melt. At Daphne's Lunch they make good soup and pretty bad patty melts.

I always take something with me to read, sometimes a magazine like *Saturday Night*, but usually a book. They know me as the guy who is always reading, I suppose, and not the garbagy drugstore paperbacks some of the shop girls open in front of their salads. Today I was about halfway through *Running in the Family* by Michael Ondaatje.

Always reading. Nevertheless I notice the fellow diners around me. It is a place for regulars. There is the fat old lady with the enormous bun of hair atop her head, and the cigarette holder clenched between her teeth. She looks like Roosevelt when she lifts her chin. There is the couple that always sits in the dead centre booth. I have never heard him utter a sound and I have never seen him meet anyone's eyes. He just sits there and eats his plain burger and drinks two cups of tea. His wife, or such I presume her to be, never stops talking. Not talking, exactly; rather she issues a constant stream of whispered curses between her nearly-meeting teeth. She has yellowish-white hair which she never washes but just pins back in sticky rectangles.

There are lots and lots of regulars. I never say hello to any of them. I am the sort of person who has to be introduced, and who soon forgets names if he is introduced. I do talk with the waitresses, and even get to know some of their names. If I get to know a name, I use it in a little bit of friendly fooling before I order the special. Once I ordered a toasted chicken salad sandwich instead of the daily special, and Delores had a hard time believing me.

Today I saw some people I had never seen before. Two of them I dont remember well at all. They were two young women enjoying Daphne's famous old-fashioned milkshakes in the can. The third person was an infant, I suppose you would call him, in a stroller. They had him parked at the open end of their booth, which was right across from mine.

I always look at children. If they are young enough I start an interchange with them. I offer winks and smiles and stuck-out tongues, and receive in return grins and stares, and once in a while a comic grimace.

So I looked at this child.

He was staring at me. Completely still, hardly blinking, with large serious eyes quietly open, he stared at me. And I was staring, I am sure, at him. Anyone watching us would think we were having a staring contest, a little child and a fifty-year-old man.

I usually dont stare. Over all the years I have managed to develop a technique of seeing enough without staring. But on this occasion I was probably staring. I was certainly not doing the usual thing—looking away and then after a while back, and then away again. I was looking at this preternaturally quiet kid.

Or maybe I wasnt. Maybe I was looking at something more familiar. I say this seemingly pointless thing for this reason: the kid had my face.

I am not saying that an eighteen-month-old child had a wrinkled old guy's face. But he did not have an eighteen-month-old's face either. He had the large head and open face of a boy about six years old. He had the face I wore when I was six years old. I have seen that face hundreds of times in photographs, and since this afternoon I think I can remember seeing it in my grandmother's living room mirror.

I had a high forehead, large brown eyes, straight brown hair that lay diagonally across my brow, large front teeth with a gap between the two top ones in front. A large face with solemn innocence in it. I was looking at it for the first time in four and a half decades.

I left half of my patty melt and went home, forgetting to go to the supermarket. That is all right, though. It is far past dinner time, and everyone around here seems to have fended for themselves. I seem to have forgotten to eat altogether.

June 18, 1988:

I dont generally go to Daphne's Lunch two days in a row, but I was there today. Despite my resolve I had a cheese-burger and fries, with HP Sauce on the fries. I picked up that trick years ago, hoping the HP Sauce would keep my friend Artie away from my fries. it didnt work, and I found out that I liked it anyway.

But what am I doing, going on about HP Sauce? I rather suspect that I went to Daphne's Lunch to see whether that child with my face might show up again. I thought that I might have a look from another angle, with different weather and sky outside, in the middle of another kind of mood. I was thinking that I might fail to see the resemblance today.

I was rather hoping that, you might imagine. But I was also curious to have another look at my young face. If he still did look exactly like me at six or seven, I wanted to see more. I dont know what I was planning to do about it. It would not do to approach the child's mother and ask her where she got him.

But one feels that one might do something. I felt peculiar every time I remembered that face last night. I felt, I think, a little afraid. Nervous, at least. I do not often consult books about my feelings. I refuse to consider anything to do with astrology, C.G. Jung or blood sugar. But I thought I would see what I could find about one's double— as long as I did not have to go outside of the house to find such references. As long as it was literary references I was looking at.

Well, I found out we have a library full of double stories. They all wrote them, not just Joseph Conrad and Dostoyevsky and Robert Louis Stevenson. They all did. Literature seems, once you start looking, to be filled more than anything else with twins, shadows, mirrors, schizophrenia, robots, puppets, voodoo dolls, and so on and on. Every society has double stories, and every age group has them. They mean a lot of different things, depending on whether the stories are about sex or religion or madness.

How lucky I am! I can have an unsettling experience in a greasy spoon, and simply look into my book room at home to reassure myself about it. One writer tells us this: that the double is not only strange, but also very familiar, because he was once within us. Another warns that we mess around with doubles at our peril because of the risk of being dominated by them. Still another cautions about a crisis of identity.

I learned after about fifteen minutes to skip through most of the stuff I was encountering. I kept seeing, as if they were staring up through the pages, the wide calm eyes of that infant with the child's face so familiar to my parents.

Oh, it was just one of those things, a fluke of lighting. Taking advantage of my distraction or tiredness. I have been having a hard time getting used to my new glasses. I wouldnt mind seeing the kid again, but it was just a lot of kaka.

Still, I wish that the usual idea about the appearance of the *Doppelgänger* was something different. If you see it you are supposed to get ready to die.

But really, a *Doppelgänger* is a twin, a creature or apparition the same size and age as oneself. There arent any little kid *Doppelgängers* for grown-ups.

June 20, 1988:

They were there again today, the kid and his mother. She had the same friend with her as before. They were both wearing plastic jackets. Hers was shiny purple. Her companion's jacket was shiny pink. Her son, well I had to presume, presume? Presume he was. He was wearing little child clothes of some sort. You didnt really look at his clothes. His head is so big you dont remember what he was wearing.

When I was in grade three I was in a hospital room in Lawrence, with a boy younger than me. But the boy had a head that was half the size of the rest of him. He had to lay it on a pillow. That did not seem like a nice place to leave me. But I thought it was interesting anyway.

But this kid didnt have a head that big. It was just like a ten-year-old's head on a baby's body, let's say. Maybe not even that bad.

I didnt know whether I would ever see him again. Them again. I got as brave as I could and spoke to his mother when her friend went to the ladies' room. This is what we said, more or less.

"I hope you dont think I'm some sort of weirdo, staring at your kid."

"I didnt notice you were."

"It's just that he looks exactly like me."

"Oh, really?"

"I mean exactly like I looked, what I looked like when I was his age, or I mean when he was ten or eight. When I was."

"He's a year-and-a-half."

"Sure."

"Thursday."

"Anyway, he is a spitting image of me when I was eight in West Summerland."

"I dont see the resemblance at all."

"I wish I had a picture to show you."

Her friend was back from the ladies' room.

"Do you think Mikey looks like this guy?"

Her friend just giggled. She was a giggler, you could tell.

"I wish I had a picture to show you."

"Well, I never saw you a year and a half ago, so I dont think he looks that much like you. You're the second person this week to say my kid looks like them. Is this a new line for picking up young mothers?"

"Someone else? Did he look like me?"

"Not a bit. He had a long thin face, kind of pointed at both ends."

Her friend giggled.

The kid was staring at me with big calm eyes.

"How come he looks like that when he is only a year-and-half old?"

"Like what?"

I looked at her to see whether she was fooling me.

"He looks so old and wise. He looks like eight years old. He looks like an eight-year-old serious thinker boy."

"I sort of see what you mean."

Her son stared and stared at me. He could have been fifteen.

June 22, 1988:

No little me kid in Daphne's today. Just this talk that made me tired. Talk with the guy who walks in exaggerating how bad his back is aching. He sits down on the red banquette right next to me. I mean he has his little table and I have my little table, but we are sitting side by side on the long banquette. It is a banquette. That is what they call it. People fall off banquettes and later require steel pins in their ankles. I have heard that.

No little kids at all. But this geezer asks me whether I can see him.

"Nothing wrong with the light in here," I said.

"My wife cant see me," he said.

"I never get involved in other people's marital problems," I said.

"Not it," he said.

"I got my own problems," I said.

People talked this way to each other in Daphne's Lunch more than you might think.

"Oh sure, thanks," he said. "For nothing."

He always was a grousy old guy.

"I got this problem with a kid that's more than he ought to be," I volunteered.

Volunteered. How did I think of that word? I might as well admit that I have been having trouble thinking of words lately. Just now I remembered a word I wanted to use a while ago.

"Well, we all got our problems," the geezer said.

I just had to forget he was sitting beside me, and go ahead and eat my grilled cheese sandwich when it came.

June 23, 1988:

The little me was there today.

We sat there looking at each other for a long time. A long time. I dont know, maybe an hour. Maybe less than that.

He wasnt wearing glasses but other than that we sure looked a lot alike. Like twins maybe.

I dont know what he was staring at me for. Maybe he stares at everybody. Maybe he was seeing what he will look like in fifty years. Or thirty years or whatever it is.

He looks to be about twenty years old I would say. Smart-looking kid. Gets smarter-looking all the time. Time.

In my dream last night a smart young Jewish professor says "I do not use time to keep back space." I looked at his dark eye and tried to look like I knew what he was saying.

I dont even know what I was just writing. I do remember an amazing number of words, though, everything considered.

I figure I am still smarter than most people in Daphne's Lunch. Includes that little me fellow.

You want a battle of wits, kid?

Still, he's a nice-looking boy. I do have to say that, dont I? Given that I'm talking about myself.

No, I'm not. This is a person in a greasy spoon. Somebody's kid. Some kid. I cant remember what I had to eat at Daphne's today. The usual, I would say. Daphne is never there any more.

I am. Both of me.

June 24, 1988:

cereal
hamburger meat
toilet paper
2% milk
vegs—brocc. or cauli.
60 w. light bulb
tea bags
toilet paper

June 25, 1988:

Twenty-fifth. Holiday of some sort, but not June.

Light was coming through the window like Mom used to be. Very bright light. Coming in like an angel.

Like a god. Coins spilling off him. Skirt made of golden daggers.

In the lunch place. I saw a kid in a stroller or sitting at a table, same thing. I mean you get something. Good to eat.

They were angry at me. Someone.

Wanted me out of there.

Later I noticed a dog staring at me. This was just around the corner. He wasnt trying to scare me. Just looking at me. I thought okay.

I didnt think okay. It was just okay.

Dog didnt look like anyone.

I never had that kind. Havent got any dog now.

June 27, 1988:

dapne

he   xtwo

eyen   like

mi yen

                                            hee

. i i

    gett msf   2 get

June 29, 1988:

Hamlet

Clint Burnham

I DECIDED: I want to get back into my mother's womb. I phoned her up to communicate something to that effect. I called after 11, so it'd be cheaper.

She was doing the dishes my Dad said, they're like that, you understand. Dad & I chatted for a while about nothing in particular. I've never been able to talk to him about much, not about politics certainly since he's voted Liberal since the days of Diefenbaker. It was now about ten after 11, & I had the TV on with the sound off, Arsenio Hall was wrapping his legs around each other and making his thumb fit behind his first knuckle. Then my Dad said here she is & he put my mom on the line.

I asked Mom how she was. Fine & her voice sounded puzzled because I usually only call on her birthday, Mother's Day. Special occasions. So I gave her the scoop. Told her I wanted to get back in her womb. The whole story was I was being evicted from my apartment as of the end of the month, the landlady's cousin was moving in and I didn't have anywhere to go, anywhere appropriate. Mom was a bit nonplussed. This was coming at a bad time. She was going on two days computer training next month, Lotus 1-2-3 & she didn't see how she could fit me in.

This was not going the way I intended it, right? It's not like I want to move back in with my folks, I want to move into Mom. She says let's be practical. My Dad pipes up on the phone, saying now let's look at this from your mother's perspective. Think of what she'd be going through. I don't see how it's such a big deal. I can't afford to live on my own, not in this city, so why not. I've had some set-backs. Between opportunities. These, these recessionary times.

Mom relents like I always knew she would. I say great. We made our plans. I was to get a hold of her in a day or two. I gave her to understand that this was just a temporary hold-over, till I got back on my feet again. Next day, I made some calls and tracked down a friend who had some space in his basement where I could store half my stuff. I took it over in two taxi rides, no real furniture, a dinette chair and a mattress that flopped out the back of the cab's trunk. I decided to keep my little portable TV I got for $90 at the Safeway years ago. Mom's probably cable-ready.

I showed up on her doorstep with my adidas bag in hand & my TV under my arm. Dad opened the door, I gave him the brush-off. Mom was upstairs in the bedroom, ready to receive me. I came in & she opened her legs. Right away she nixed the TV. I figured I could live without it, do finger puppets or something. Inside, it was darker than I thought. I pushed my bag ahead of me, & left my runners outside after I got my feet in. It was real comfortable. There was a soft glow, pinkish, coming in through her stomach. Or I guess it's her abdominal wall, Grade Nine Health class came flashing back. Then I was startled by a booming-soft noise, it was Mom talking. She was talking to me, asking how I was getting along. I told her I was just fine. I pressed my mouth up against the wall and made that blubbering sound parents do on their baby's stomach. Mom giggled, a medium-pitched rumble, and sighed and patted on the other side of where my lips and nose were.

I curled up to get in a comfy position, like I was on my couch watching TV. Then I had this sickening thought— had I dragged that old couch out of the apartment building & down to the curb? I fell asleep in the cabride over to Mom's place, and maybe I dreamt it. I'd tried to clean up the apartment as best I could, because I wanted to get back as much of my deposit as I could. There was a minute or two of tension, then I relaxed. When you're back in the womb it's hard to really get uptight about anything.

I feel so good in here! You know? There's really nothing like being home at last. It's been three, four weeks now, I'm losing track of time, like some guy in a Solzhenitsyn novel, only this is a prison I like.

Back to my first day.

Mom was really considerate too—as Moms always are, of course. She went downstairs to get a snack. Probably knew I hadn't eaten for days. I heard a door open and close softly, and the crisp rattle of a stiff plastic bag. She was taking some slices of whole-wheat bread out of the freezer. She keeps it there because she doesn't eat it fast enough. In a few minutes Mom was eating tea and toast. I felt my strength come back almost right away. I was grateful.

Now was sack time. Mom was back upstairs on her bed, watching TV. She had her hands crossed on her belly so the light was very dim. In a few minutes, the beat of her heart lulled me to sleep, like a cheap clock will a new puppy. I had pleasant dreams, imagining I could hear the blood around me in her abdomen, being gently rocked when she stood up to get something. Getting little hard-ons, but no wet dream.

After that soothing start, the next day was a bit harsh. It was a Sunday, so in the afternoon Mom sat around out back on a reclining lawn chair while Dad fired up the barbecue and made some steaks. His famous twenty minutes a side well-done specials. But it was really sunny out, so really bright and hot inside where I was. After a while, I don't know how long, I must have started to get sunstroke, because I got real paranoid. First thing, I thought I could hear Mom's skin frying from the sun. It's crazy of course, but you're a bit cut off from the world when you're in the womb, to say the least. I felt like a piece of meat left in a bag of groceries in a hot car. Then, whenever Mom turned over on the lawnchair to lie on her side or front, I could swear I could feel the criss-cross of the straps pressing into me through her stomach. More than once I took a damp face-cloth out of my gym bag and wiped my face.

Later that night was a bit better. After the meal, which I didn't really appreciate, being so hot and sticky, the night cooled down, and Mom just sat there drinking Long Island Iced Tea. I felt nice, cool and cheap. Then she got up and said she was going in to get a sweater. When we got inside she went up to the bedroom, closed the door, and took out a book to read. After maybe ten minutes, she fell asleep.

I was beginning to wonder if I was coming between my parents, which was not my intention at all, really. I lay in there for a while, thinking of this, but fell asleep before I could see if Dad would come upstairs.

When I was in high school there was this drama teacher, Mr. Fortescue, and he said that one of the purposes of drama was to work out problems in society, and he said that even doing a puppet play about something that's bothering you could help. This after a while I thought would help me here. I thought I couldn't have been the real cause of my parents drifting apart. The next day, Mom's at work and I tried to suss it out, couldn't. So what I did was do a little puppet play, only I didn't have any socks, since I was naked in my mom's womb. So I took out a pen from my gym bag and marked little faces on my fingers, one for Mom, one for me, one for Dad.

Dad is the thumb & he's pissed off. Mom, the index finger, is treating him carefully. I'm at the end of the hand, the pinkie. The idea is I try to stop Mom and Dad from fighting, but I get hopelessly entangled. Meanwhile, this is all to no avail, at least not what I intended. My finger puppet play's tickling my Mom from inside, she's at work and laughing like crazy, her prosthetic son inside, making her laugh and rubbing her tummy like she took care of him when he was a baby.

The Bone Fields

Matt Cohen

"IN THE HARMONY of spent light, words are reborn." So Stigson begins tonight. Keeping us warm are thick chunks of maple burning in a place we call the theatre. Not a building but a small meadow backed by a curved rock wall.

Against this wall we sit.

Off the rock bounce heat and light, keeping us warm, illuminating our faces, giving us the slowly dancing shadows of giants.

"I could tell you the story of the man who became his own dream," Stigson offers.

Silence.

Stigson moves closer to the fire. He is a big man and his face is large even for one of his size. A largeness accentuated by his beard. When I became Stigson's follower his beard was a luscious corn yellow. Now it is the colour of corn leaves turned brown and streaky by frost and cold rains.

"You," Stigson suddenly calls out. Without Stigson we cannot live. "You," he calls again. He is looking at no one in particular. He is looking at everyone.

Annie stands up, stumbles forward. Has Stigson singled her out without my noticing? Has the whole scene been prearranged?

Annie stands in front of the fire, her arms folded. Stigson towers over her.

"What can you offer us tonight?" Stigson asks. His voice sounds dangerous. More than usual? I ask myself; or is it only that I am always thinking that Stigson grows ever more virulent?

Annie looks out at us. I can't see her face. She seems to be shaking. On a night like this a year ago Annie's brother was selected in the same way. By the time morning came he was dead. Did Stigson kill him? Did everything I remember really happen? It must be true. That is, when I remember how to find a certain lake, a certain cache, a certain path through the forest, the lake, the cache, the path are always waiting for me when I arrive. So too, therefore, what Stigson has done. Except that death, ecstasy, even boredom are not places that can be visited. Just the memory or, in the case of death, the body. Certainly the part about the body is true. I dug the grave myself. Myself lifted Edward up and dropped him into the earth. He was heavy, I remember thinking, the real and substantial heaviness of life was still in him. Though in fact he was stiff with death. Even when his body thumped to the bottom of the grave his muscles and bones rigidly held their position. Knees bent. It was said that Edward had spoken against Stigson: dissent, jokes. Never to me, of course, because I above all am supposed to belong to Stigson. "My Judas," Stigson once went so far, meaning what I don't know because I am no Judas, Stigson no Christ, and besides—all those who would have been Romans died long ago.

Annie reaches into the pockets of her coat and her hands emerge cupped to overflowing. Stigson grins. Our fear turns to excitement. The script was planned after all— Stigson taketh away but Stigson also giveth. One by one we come forward. Under Stigson's watchful eye we swallow our portion of the mushrooms. Kettles are hung over the fire. While waiting for the drug to take effect we drink hot tea and dream our adventures of the night ahead.

Two small frogs sitting on a log. This was a long time ago, the summer I was ten years old. The log was a recent arrival: a storm had blown it down the lake and now it was resting in the lee side of our absent neighbour's dock. Stigson was a year younger than me, but bigger. Thick straw-like blond hair that spiked out from his round skull, blue eyes that begged to be lied to, largish ears perpetually sunburned. We were wildmen that summer. Stigson had been placed under my command by his parents. We had uniforms: sun-bleached jeans, shrunken T-shirts, white canvas sneakers with holes worn in the little toes, battered men's fedoras circled by greasy black bands and adorned with birdfeathers. I had twenty-two feathers, Stigson eighteen. At the beginning of the summer I had assigned us ranks—I Captain, he Sergeant; but with each new feather a promotion was required so I was now Admiral of the Galaxy, Third Degree, whereas Stigson, owing to a stretch of bad behaviour, was stuck at Solar System Commander.

Stigson and I were in half-uniform—jeans and hats, lying bellies-flattened on the dock. The frogs were the dark green of the underside of oak leaves. They longed to jump into the water but they didn't dare. They had been sitting still so long that their pores were turning into volcanoes. They knew that Stigson and I were watching them; perhaps they had even smelled the dead feathers in our hats. Like soldiers, I thought—that summer was my military history phase—at the edge of some ancient bloodied battlefield, too frozen with fear and dread to save themselves.

Stigson looked at me. Our fishing rods were on the beach, baitless hooks hungrily dangling on the sand.

One of the frogs breathed. Its underthroat fluttered in the stillness. Silent, silent, Stigson and I wriggled forward. It had taken us forever to inch across the dock. A forever of iron discipline, of exchanged looks, of breath breathed with the changing breeze. Now we were at the dock's edge. We were curving our bodies so that our shadows would not be visible to the frogs. We were about to fall into the water—this was a trick we had practised earlier in the summer, a similar occasion; as we slid through the air, but before our bodies made a splash, we would clap our hands over the ambushed frogs.

I nodded to Stigson. Silently we rolled off the dock. Our hands came down like guillotines. As the cold water shrunk my skin I felt a wild struggling under my palm. The water, the sudden sun in my eyes, the sound of Stigson whooping in triumph, the live being insanely squiggling to escape my grasp. I squeezed tighter. The frog was dry but gummy. I slid it into the water. It relaxed, its skin expanded into its normal happy slime, it began to hope I was only playing a cruel but temporary game. I didn't want to know what the frog was thinking, but I did. I decided to order Stigson to let his frog go. But he was already on the beach, digging his barbed hook into the prisoner's lower jaw, running at top speed towards the shaded grass knoll from which we were going to offer it to the big bass we knew was waiting in the deep shaded pool below.

It was early morning. The sun had turned the sky atomic blue. Stigson and I had spent the whole summer inventing this strange planet. My hat was floating at my knees. In my hand wriggled alien life and above my head a hawk scribbled a message I had just learned to decipher.

Lying in the forest blackness. Most of my body has melted into the cold earth. Only my brain is alive. Fluorescent, glowing ghostly white, it floats through the forest. "Go," I say. Soon it is working its way up through the leaves, towards the sky, finally it is in the clear and accelerating towards the moon.

Leaves rustle. The air is heavy and cold.

I listen to the earth's heart beating.

In my empty skull, acorns take root, twin oak-trees shoot through the sockets of my eyes.

This morning I shaved. Looking into the cracked mirror of a long-dead pickup truck I scraped away my stubble. Amazing that in only a week you can forget your own face. Mine always surprises me by looking so young: cheeks, chin, lips—all smooth and unmarked. The face of an execution-er I would once have said. But now there is almost no one left to execute. All of us here—in Stigson's group and in the whole area—belong to the Vegetarian Cult. At least officially. In any case none of us (except perhaps Stigson) would ever kill a person. Even an animal. But fish are allowed because, Stigson decreed, fish do not dream. Dreams are what is sacred, Stigson went on, because dreaming is life.

Life, lifespores. It was one of the first times on mush-rooms that I had the vision of Life. Lying on my back—like this—damp ground and fallen leaves trying to melt into my skin—like now, I had been afraid that I was dying, that I had already died and forgotten my life, that my body was rotting into the forest floor. Unable to move, melting into the cold soil, I closed my eyes. In the midst of the darkness an explosion of light. Otherworldly music. A storm of dancing molecules whirling through space, combining and re-combining, changing shapes, configurations, loyalties—a storm of random possibilities colliding into each other until the magic combination was achieved and BINGO—a living being.

Stigson's father was a doctor, but he preferred to call himself a physician. "My father is a *physician*," Stigson would announce solemnly when I introduced him to the children of other cottagers. Stigson, a city boy, was deemed to need my bit of country gloss, which was why he was put under my care. Stigson's father, the *physician*, was rich. Their cottage was a split-storey wonder which had a sandy-beached bay to itself. Like other doctors, even those who did not call themselves physicians, Stigson's father could paint on iodine, sew stitches, prescribe pills and ointments. And then, the week of the "accident" at the Chalk River heavy water plant, Stigson's father was called away. To cheer up Stigson I gave him two extra feathers for being a temporary orphan.

"He does radiation sickness," Stigson offered one morning. We were on one of our fishing expeditions, an hour's hard paddling from Stigson's boathouse where the canoe was kept.

I knew what radiation was. Deranged molecule and atom parts, little overcharged matter-bullets, unbalanced micropsychopaths careening tribelessly through the universe.

From his fishing tackle-box Stigson drew a plastic vial of pills. "These protect you," he said. "My father gave them to me." He scooped a handful of water from the lake, messily swallowed two tablets. He offered me the bottle. "Go ahead."

It was August. A summer day on the lake. Glassy wrinkled water. Granite cliffs that could scorch your hand. Centuries-old pine carving the bone-blue sky.

"I have a thousand pills hidden in secret places," Stigson said. That was true, I found out years later. Only by then the thousand had become tens of thousands, buried in hiding places all over the countryside, caches that Stigson, while I was supposedly teaching him, had memorized so well that even decades later he will suddenly exclaim over a remembered configuration, push into the woods through thickets that would not even have existed at the time, move aside rocks, fallen logs, an apparently random stone in the side of a hill and come up with another of his precious plastic vials.

"You'll die if you don't," Stigson said.

He was ten years old. Spiky blond hair that tapered into arrows when he swam. A bridge of freckles over his nose. A mouth that was always a bit open showing large milky teeth. A babyish looking boy, I had thought when first introduced, looking so young and so fragile that instead of feeling I was finding a playmate I thought I was being given a babysitting job. Wrong. Because Stigson, though younger, was already stronger, smarter, quicker. But most impressively: always in perfect control. For example, after he first defeated me in a running race I took him in the canoe and made him keep paddling to my pace, wanting to force him to give up. That day, early in July and the sun shining like a knife off the water onto Stigson's pale back, I watched him match my every stroke while the skin on his back turned first pink, then a bright angry red along the bony ridge of his shoulders. Until it was I who stopped. I who suggested that we beach the canoe. I who slipped into the water to relax while Stigson, bright-eyed and curious, watched from the shore. Waited until I had floated out towards the middle of the lake and then he got into the canoe and made as if to paddle away, leaving me to swim home or walk back barefoot around the edge of the lake.

"Swallow," Stigson said. He offered me a pill, our first communion.

I swallowed. We didn't die. Nobody died except for two nuclear technicians at Chalk River and those deaths were hushed up.

Mynor Jones's face looked like a baked potato left overnight in the oven. The skin was mottled and grey. Baggy, layered, and crumpled. One ear was turned out to catch the wind. A large donkey's ear with a hanging lobe discoloured by annual frostbite. The other ear, wise and/or timid, lay close to the head. Most often it was covered by Mynor Jones's lank black hair.

When he leaned towards you—possibly over the table, possibly across a fence or stall partition—you saw the timid ear ducking for cover behind the greasy black veil while the social wind-catching ear hove forward.

"I'm the old man in the ark," Mynor Jones liked to say. He lived in the house where he had been born. Slept in the bed where he had, according to himself, squirted like a rocket from his mother's womb. "I'm still living," he repeated ten times a day. It was true. Mynor Jones lived, while all the other locals—farmers, storekeepers, even the drunks—had died from radiation poisoning. "Newcomers," Mynor Jones explained. According to him, and there was no one left to contradict him, his family had been the first to settle in this particular little valley. Sent over from Scotland with the promise of railway lands, Mynor Jones's great-great-grandfather had somehow gotten off at the wrong stop, become mixed up with a group of fur-traders, found himself eventually being pensioned off with the land grant of a farm which, it turned out, existed only in the imagination of the man to whom Mynor Jones's great etc. grandfather had paid all of his cash plus two bottles of bad whisky.

"He hacked and he hewed," Mynor Jones said.

When we were out cutting with our own axes, Mynor Jones was always boasting that the original Jones could have done whatever we were doing in half the time and half the sweat. "My ancestor could take down a tree like this in ten minutes," he would boast when after an hour we were doubled up panting while the tree remained perfectly straight, nothing to show for our efforts but a ragged V-notch halfway through its trunk.

Last year Annie and I spent two full months hiding at the farmhouse of Mynor Jones. Full moon to full moon to full moon. We stayed in what had once been called a summer kitchen, was now a junkshed with a rusting wood stove and a mattress. Stigson was too proud to come looking for us. For Jones we cut wood, cleaned house, baked ourselves at his makeshift forge trying to turn the remains of his various tractor implements into hand tools. One week I made three shovels. Not bad. And carved a dozen hickory handles while sitting by the fire, my knife digging into the wood and Annie's hot vegetable soup boiling in my guts.

"Now this is the life," Mynor Jones said. "Why don't you two pill-takers just settle down here?"

Mynor Jones had whisky. Two years old, aged in various kegs he kept in basement and barn. The recipe for Mynor Jones's whisky: a gallon of last year's batch, a few more gallons of well water, add hand- or basketfuls of every fruit within a mile of the house until squishy, fill to the top with more water or juice and cover until ready for extinction.

Annie wouldn't touch the stuff, but sometimes I stayed up late with Mynor Jones in the kitchen, keeping him company over a gallon jar. "Might as well save the candles," he would say. If there was a moon, the white light reflected off the snow would create a ghostly glow bright enough to throw shadows, to deepen the hollows of Mynor Jones's face into trenches, to turn his mouth into a deep well. Light enough, too, so that afterwards when I buried my head in Annie's belly I could open my eyes to warm curved marble. But in that moony glow her lips and tongue were the colours of death, her eyes flat.

"Take me away, Annie," I would whisper. But Annie wasn't taking me anywhere because Annie was gone. Except sometimes, sometimes—sometimes in the middle of the night there was Annie stoked up like a furnace, Annie burning a full head of steam, Annie on fire, Annie in heat, Annie waking me up full of craziness and desire.

When we came back Stigson gave us the look we were usually spared and said, "I thought you were dead." In those two months, I thought, he had aged two decades. But with summer he filled out and gained strength again, his own theories always working best on himself, bouncing back higher the lower he sank, always the surest, the most confident, the most powerful.

Once we were tens of thousands. An amazing coincidence, I had thought, that the area where I had spent my boyhood summers was one of those best suited for survival. But then Stigson explained it was no coincidence at all, that for two years his father had studied the patterns of wind, rock and vegetation most resistant to radiation. This region of eastern Ontario was, Stigson said, geologically speaking, one of the most primitive in North America. Pre-Cambrian rock hundreds of millions of years old. Limestone made up of billions of prehistoric sea creatures. Even the lichen we used to start our fires had been growing for hundreds of thousands of years.

The more of us alive, the more there were to die. By this time Stigson had more pills, better pills. In those days different cults often collided with each other in their foraging. And in those days, too, the skies above the bone fields were sometimes black with crows coming down to feast on irradiated flesh. "Microwave meals," Stigson would sneer. In those early times Stigson would give sermons about how the past had been turned into the future, how the world had been driven to suicide by fast food and television.

That was when Stigson's father was still alive. He had his own theory—which was that all along there had been subtle evolutionary changes preparing the species to weed itself out using this catastrophe. Pills or no, he insisted, some of us had already developed body chemistries to cope with radiation. Just as the population was already being trimmed down by cancer, AIDS, epidemic starvation, he pointed out, before this latest disaster. Only one remaining problem: evolution needed a quantum jump, a mutation of the species, a blast into the future. What better blast than massive doses of radiation—eliminating some while creating new genetic peaks for mankind?

So that was his vision—a species-wide transformation kicked off by atomic disaster. And one day near the end I gathered up my courage and asked Stigson's father why it was we needed to change.

He was lying in bed, a massive bearded man gone to big-boned skeleton and hanging flesh, matted salt-and-pepper beard hiding the sores which had begun to infect his face.

"What do you mean 'why'?"

"Why did we need to change? Why not go on as we were?"

I expected an outburst on the moral cruelty of man, his evil towards himself and other species, his inability to live naturally among the birds and the flowers. Don't ask me why, but I had always thought this was the direction in which Stigson's father's mind was turned. "Other planets," he croaked. "Flying saucers, creatures from outer space. Where have you been all these years?"

"Here."

"Exactly. We should have been in space ten thousand years ago. That's why we destroyed our own planet. We were stuck on it. Glued by our lack of evolutionary change like overpopulated rats in a cage. Everyone knew that. Everyone knew we had to get off. But how? We lacked the—" He coughed, started jabbing at his head with his forefinger.

"Brains," I said.

"No, idiot, imagination. Evolutionary motor. We lacked the chromosomes. Every religion in the world believed in original sin—one way or another, believed in personal guilt, when the real problem was our chromosomes. Scientists began understanding that what we needed was not moral rearmament but a biological boost. It was another version of the old missing-link problem. So if the link was missing, it was up to us to create it. Some tried to manufacture it in a test tube, others worked on altering the chromosomes of potential parents—"

"And others," Stigson completed for me the night after his father died, "decided that the best solution was at once the most radical and the most democratic—a proliferation of apparently 'random' nuclear accidents that would allow the human race to be reborn at a higher level. Of course there was no plot, no actual conspiracy. Just the circulation of an idea informally discussed at various international conferences. At first the accidents were tiny. The public always blamed them on inept bureaucrats or patronage construction. But scientists knew the Three Mile Island disaster must have been caused by human error. Deliberate human error. To show their goodwill, the Soviet scientists created Chernobyl. Then came Chalk River. A couple of years later there was the 'accident' in India. After that things began to get out of hand. Like lemmings, you might say."

The bone fields began as the idea of another cult. Stigson's father, still alive, was in favour. No good, he said, burying the bodies in the usual way. Radiated corpses lying in the ground, exuding their half-lives for tens of millions of years. Better using the huge limestone quarry lined with thick layers of cement by those still alive at the time who knew how to do such things and had the necessary equipment.

And so it was, at the beginning, that the dead were driven to the site and dumped. Those were the early days when fuel, cars, civilization seemed destined to limp on for decades. In those days, for example, it was still possible to believe Stigson's father and his friends might have known what they were doing. Possible to believe that somewhere in some unsuspecting belly the new race for the new age was ripening, the evolutionary step humankind had awaited for millennia.

Now small mountains of crushed stone encircle the bone fields. The graders and bulldozers are parked in the midst of these mountains, permanently stationed guardians frozen forever when their gas tanks went dry for the last time.

When the task of burying and covering echoed through the countryside every day, the sky above the bone fields was often black with crows and vultures. Now occasionally a lone crow with a long memory circles above. All it finds is more memories. These days the dead are buried where they drop.

But still I am attracted to the bone fields. Sometimes, perched on a gravel hill or sitting behind the wheel of an old rusted grader, I'll see the others, from other cults, making their own visits. We are the survivors, whether because of our chromosomes, our pills or pure chance is unknown to us.

In summer the whiteness of the bones can be tinged with yellow.

The light of autumn sunsets turns them darker.

Rain drains away quickly. Even snow tries to melt on contact.

Back from moon, from sun, from stars. What have I brought with me? A memory, perhaps an image. A scene from a movie that will never be made. The engine of the universe, the universal engine. Beads of yellow-white electrons dancing, incandescent particles exploding. Clouds of isotopes drifting through nothingness.

Radiate
Radiate
Radiate the food you ate

Put it down
Throw it up
Drink out of a glowing cup.

One two
Three four
All we ask is one more war.

Stigson says ours is a generation of guardians. We have survived. We survive. We hold the earth in trust for those to come.

Foraging but not killing
Cooing but not billing

Journeying into our nighthearts to touch the centre, fuel the fire.

Some day, Stigson says, we or our children or our children's children will see the dawning of the new consciousness. For now we are in a tunnel whose end is only the light of our fragmented memories. We are, Stigson says, Plato's savages in the cave, but when we or our children or our children's children emerge, it will be forever.

I am lying on the forest floor, back from the moon (the stars, the nothingness), my skin like a sponge soaking up lifespores from the earth. Stigson will still be by the fire. Not now, but soon, he will come searching for me. Stigson is bigger than I am, faster, stronger, smarter. But tonight Stigson will not find me because I am afraid.

Guardians, Stigson calls our generation. He invents history as he needs to—past, present, future are the cords he uses to enslave our minds.

Not mine, I like to think.

I am no guardian.

I am the survivor who mistakenly survived.

After us there will be no one. We are the last. When we are gone, the planet will continue its slow circles around the sun, its pierced ozone layer will commence the multi-million-year process of healing, trees will gradually push their way through broken pavement. Finally the planet will either heal itself or not, become green again or collapse from its self-inflicted poisons.

I blame no one and nothing.

To blame is to say things might have been different, that if we humans had played our cards right we could have enjoyed the Garden of Eden forever. I stand up. I wrap my arms and legs around my favourite oak tree, sink nails and teeth into its understanding bark. Then jump down again. Time to start sliding—through the woods, away from Stigson, away from the fire.

Half an hour and I am at the edge of the lake where Stigson and I played our childish games. At the sandy shore a thin skin of ice. Waiting for me, where I hid it, is a canoe. Quietly I slide it across the frosty sand. In the bushes the paranoid rustle of a porcupine. The ice breaks under the canoe's weight. I hopscotch a few rocks, step into the canoe. How I love the tug of water against paddle, the sensuous lick of the lake on varnished canvas. In the woods the night air was thick and green, full of resin and dead leaves. Over the water the air is cooler, purer. Soon, from across the water, I will be able to smell the open earth of Mynor Jones's tilled fields. Perhaps even a dry curl of woodsmoke. Like the ionized colours of the twilight sky, so too the last smells of the dying planet.

I put my paddle across my knees. Tiny streams of water flow off the wood and make their silvery sounds as they splash back into the lake like miniature bells. I plunge the paddle in, draw it out, just to repeat the sensation.

From the south shore a sudden staccato of coyote yips. Lately it seems they've been dying, though no one ever sees their bodies. "They bury themselves," Mynor Jones insists, as though they can dig their own graves and then pull earthen roofs shut over top. But necessary details do not interest Mynor Jones. He knows what happens. How it happens is for other people—people from cities perhaps, the kind of people who commit mass suicide—to figure out. "Where there's a will, there's a way" is as far as he's willing to go. And then adds that when his turn comes, he intends to do the same.

In early October there was a sudden plunge from Indian summer. Two nights of severe frost followed by a heavy snowfall. If the deer had survived the radiation, the snow would have made them easy targets for hunters. If the hunters had survived. A strange sight, snow, when the trees are still thick with leaves—some of them turning their bright fall colours, others as green as spring. Stigson and others say the weather has changed and that the seasons have become more erratic. To me it always seems the same, even people's complaints about disastrous long-range weather trends.

In fact, it often seems to me that Stigson's father and his friends have not—as intended—wrought their mighty change upon the world. On the surface, yes: mail, telephones, fuel, cars—most of the amenities of the last hundred years gone. So too, of course, a certain number of people. Lately there has been no news of anywhere aside from the fantastic rumours and stories brought by the occasional wanderer hoping to earn a few nights of meals by bringing us such entertainments. But in the year following the Indian accident, the year in which it and the other "accidents" filled every layer of the earth's atmosphere, every windstream, with clouds of radioactive gases— during that year and especially near the end, you could still watch the nightly television news and see helicopters passing over ruined or deserted cities all over the globe.

Mynor Jones was waiting for me. Or so it seemed as I came out of the woods and found him sitting on the front steps of his house, drinking his terrible whisky and smoking a wild tobacco cigar. The moon was a bright sharp crescent, glistening in the November sky. The sky itself cold and perfectly clear. Like crystal, I thought, and we the butterflies preparing to be frozen.

From the darkness behind him, Mynor Jones pulled a glass. We drank. In the sharp silvery night light his face looked like a rock sledge-hammered into shape.

After a while he led me down to the garden. Half of it was a rubble already eaten or stored, the rest was covered with ragged remnants of canvas, old sheets, even some precious transparent plastic. From beneath one of the plastic covers Mynor Jones pulled two tomatoes. Mine was half-ripe; one side sweeter than summer, the other bitter and hard, tasting of cold sour earth.

"When I was a boy," Mynor Jones said, "my mother squoze the frost out of the ground. Every morning in November she mashed the ground in her fists. You could hear the icicles breaking. And in the spring, just as soon as the snow started to melt, she was out here stomping, kicking, pounding, squeezing the ice into water. She hated snow. At least once every winter she tried to pour kerosene on top and throw a match to the whole thing. Never worked. Too easy. Only way to get rid of the stuff was to smash it to bits. Or wait until summer."

I had met Mynor Jones's mother often enough. A big fat woman, during the tourist season she was to be found perched on a stool at the checkout of the local 5-and-10. From Victoria Day until Labour Day she wore the same blue print dress to work. By mid-July you could smell it as soon as you came into the store. When August was hot, the whole town reeked of it. She used to love to break open rolls of coins. So why not snow? At least on this particular evening I was willing to believe it.

"Your friend doesn't like me," Mynor Jones said.

"Annie?" I asked, knowing better.

Mynor Jones laughed, making the sound of a small rock-slide. We were still standing in the garden. The drug was at work again, melting my feet into the ground. I sank to my knees, grabbed handfuls of earth and mashed them into my face. Tiny stones scraped my newly shaven cheeks. Ice too; the temperature was dropping fast, I suddenly realized; under cover of darkness the heat was being sucked from ground and sky to be whisked away to another part of the planet. I imagined myself howling in protest, howling like those dying coyotes. I began to laugh. Mynor Jones jumped on top of me and started trying to bury my head. While we wrestled, I kept laughing and barking. The plastic roofing of Mynor Jones's makeshift hothouse was collapsing on top of us. Jones had his hands around my throat when I finally found a yellow elephant squash and brought it down on his head. A soft plonking sound that made me start laughing all over again. Mynor Jones backed off and I slithered away under the canvas, snaking through prickly squash vines until I got into the higher terrain of staked peas and green beans. When I finally came out into the open air on the other side Mynor Jones was waiting for me, bottle in hand. I drank and then spat out the terrible whisky along with a few stray bits of ground that had come to visit the inside of my mouth. My tongue was swollen. One molar felt loose.

"Not bad for an old man," Mynor Jones said, puffing out chest and belly.

"Not bad," I agreed. Then drove my fist as hard as I could into Mynor Jones's overblown gut. It was like punching a sandbag. My fist crumpled into itself and jolts of pain exploded out my elbow. Mynor Jones laughed.

We crossed the field to a road. Walked along it to a turning. Climbed the hill to where Mynor Jones's grandfather had built a smokehouse for venison and ham. We opened the door. Mynor Jones started making a fire. A row of pheasants were hanging upside-down from an oak beam along the back. No one from the cult knew how to trap birds or game. Even when Mynor Jones put a handful of meat into one of her stews, Annie pretended the chunks were just chewy potatoes. Jones trimmed some fat off one of the birds, threw it in a frying pan with an onion and some wild herbs.

"Big belly needs to be fed," Mynor Jones said. The fat in the pan spluttered. Grease fell into the fire, sending up blue flares and puffs of smoke. Soon Mynor Jones was leaning over the pan, using both hands to shovel food into his bearded face. The smell was too much to resist: I joined in, we ate until dawn when, bellies full of charred flesh, we staggered out of the smokehouse and down the hill to a stream where we could lie face first to drink, then to rest our heads in the icy water to let it thunder through our hair.

I lie beside Annie. This is the third day of snow. Stigson says that to go inside is a sign of weakness, a cause of weakness. Staying inside, seeking shelter, needing to protect the body: these are, Stigson says, the beginnings of the inevitable decline, the pushing of oneself down the slow hill that can lead only to an eternity in the bone fields.

Two weeks ago—or was it a month?—Stigson and I tried to patch it up. Whatever it is that needs to be patched, which isn't easy to define because we have never openly quarrelled about anything, just slowly drifted apart while the others in our group become listless and confused.

To make it like old times we spent the whole night walking, the way we used to, first over the paths forged by our cult, then onto the dirt roads we used to walk when we were summer visitors. Along the road we stopped at burnt-out farmhouses and reminisced about the families that had lived there, the cars they had driven only a dozen years ago, the relative beauty of their daughters and the stupidity of their sons. All dead. From time to time as though such tricks could pull me back into his circle, Stigson would loop his arm around my shoulder to pat me on the back.

At one point Stigson said, "I think this winter the final test. We're really turning the corner now. In the spring I'm certain we'll blossom again." Listening to him I felt irritated. A year ago he had allowed himself to be baptised by a visiting missionary from a Christian cult that had a farming collective to the north. Since then, like the missionary, he had been talking about "blossoming again"— the new code word for having babies—as though the Chinese revolution were coming.

"No one can stay pregnant, let alone have babies," I replied.

"In the spring," Stigson said. "When we have passed the test."

All of Stigson's recent sermons had centred around the idea that God was testing us, that he had winnowed out the weak, that all of us who remained were strong, ready for the future.

"You and Annie could have a child," Stigson said. We were in a shallow valley, yet even the slight hollow had been enough for me to feel the extra coolness in the air, and before Stigson had spoken I had been poking my feet into the grass at the side of the road to see if the dew was starting to freeze.

Now Annie is sleeping and I am lying beside her. It is not late, I am not tired. But I am in bed with Annie because she wanted to sleep and I wanted to be sure she would be warm. Last winter, too, she went through strange spells of exhaustion, unwillingness to eat, always followed by a revival. So I am trying to convince myself that this is just another episode from which she will recover.

From outside I hear footsteps in the snow. I get out of bed. I am already dressed, but coming out from the covers into the crisp air of the room I need another coat. By the time Stigson comes in I am sitting in a chair, waiting for him in the dark, boots tightly laced and an axe in my hand.

"I was worried about you," Stigson says.

"Annie was sick."

"Bringing her inside only makes it worse. Not right away but the next time."

"If I didn't bring her in, there might not be a next time."

"Fear is never a wise counsellor," Stigson quotes from himself. But his heart isn't in it.

We're talking. We're arguing. It's dark but for the reflected ghostly light of snow. Mynor Jones comes into the room. Stigson and I can't stop shouting. Suddenly I am holding the axe in the moonlight. Annie is screaming. The blade is shining dull reflected silver. I am, the way Stigson taught me, outside of myself. I see Stigson approaching me. I feel my muscles—a flock of birds knowing what to do, where to go, migrate through the darkness. I see Stigson falling, one hand outstretched, falling the way I once taught him, silent as death towards the unsuspecting prey.

Digging the grave takes two days. Finally we have to make brush fires to thaw our way through the frozen crust of ground. By the third day, when I go back to the "theatre" where the cult used to gather to sleep or to listen to Stigson's sermons, everyone has already moved on, drifted away. To the Christian collective in the north, I suspect, but they don't need to worry—no one will chase them down. The fires are out, garbage and unwanted utensils are neatly stacked in one place. I throw these remains into the smallest of the caves, then spend the day blocking its mouth with fieldstones. One day, I think, perhaps Stigson will be a great legendary martyr. And I, as he predicted, his Judas. As I walk back to Mynor Jones's house, I am thinking about Stigson, admiring him. Night falls. I am skirting the lake because the ice is not yet thick enough to bear me. If there are other sounds in the forest I cannot hear them for my own, and with each step I grow larger because I am the one who survived.

Sleeping in a Box

Candas Jane Dorsey

"Everything that is worthy is secret."
—Iris Murdoch

A SCHOOL PROJECT to measure the size of the moon. What equipment will be necessary? The principal in his office has Rex Begonias in bloom; he rotates them from his greenhouse at home, bringing them through the cold corridors muffled in a quilt. He listens to the project idea expansively, but instead of granting permission begins to tell me about the cooking demonstration he gave earlier in the day. I haven't eaten yet today and his description is tangible in my mouth.

I have brought my blind dog in order to illustrate how I will explain graphically to the children the impossibility of measuring something without the right tools. A fine scientific principle. It is a long time since she last left the apartment and she is excited by the smell of children. She gyrates on the end of the leash almost as she did when she was young, dancing to the changing wafting odours she detects as currents in a stream. I could demonstrate with her a different measurement, one I cannot make; children's passage through this space is obvious to her, even though there are none here now and she couldn't see them anyway.

My apartment is down the hall from the large theatre in which the visitor from Earth performed. She sang well, but she wouldn't talk with us, and she gave us no encore though we applauded ferociously.

After the performance a few of us stayed in our seats, chatting among ourselves, and by an accident of acoustics Danno and I could hear the voices from backstage. Her manager was berating her for not talking between songs, for not responding to the applause.

She replied but what she said was not quite decipherable, spoken as it was in that charming accent.

Afterward I was in the corridor, fumbling for the key to unlock my apartment, when she came out of the theatre, alone and looking rather forlorn.

"Would you like to come for tea?" I asked.

She wanted to know how far it was; she had to be back at the hotel before a certain time.

"I live here," I said, ducking under a painter's scaffold and opening the door. We were only a few metres from the theatre access door; she was amazed.

Inside, the apartment is charming: soft, easy furniture and big windows. The dog snuffled over to the singer, nosed her silk-clad knee. Her nose left a damp mark on the silk but the singer didn't notice, absorbed as she was in the view. I pretended to be blasé about the windows, though they had cost me a lot, and put on the kettle. Chara and Danno came over, we drank tea, the singer from Earth quiet, watching us, smiling formally whenever we looked at her. Her name was Meia.

On Earth it is not so difficult to know how big the moon is. My old lover once told me he could hold up his hand, thumb upwards, and at arm's length his thumb tip covered the moon. That's how big it is, where we all live, a disc no bigger than the thumb-nail of the average Terran. Under that nail we live jammed like so many grains of annoying sand, to be cleaned out now and again with a brush or the blade of a knife.

The singer from Earth stayed after the others left. I finally had to tell her I was going to make supper. Was she going to eat at the hotel? I asked.

"I have no plans," she replied. "May I eat with you?"

"I do not have enough," I said.

"We can share," she said. "I don't eat much, really I eat like a bird."

While I got out the plates and brought the food out of the cooler, she leaned against the counter. "Can I help with anything?" she asked.

"No, it's fine," I said. She reached a hand absently to pick up a piece I had just sliced. I put my hand over hers. "Wait," I said.

"Can I get out the rest?" she asked, her hand on the cooler door, opening it even as I said, "That's all."

The cupboard, of course, like the old rhyme, was bare. She wasn't stupid, she figured it out.

"That's all you have?"

"Until tomorrow. Yes. It's the end of the tenday. We have rations, we have to make them last."

"But at the hotel, I get—"

"Yes. But you are from Earth. You have priority."

"I will not eat after all. You will eat with me, at the hotel, as my guest."

I wanted to go very much, but I know the Moon better than she ever will. "They will not let you bring me in," I said.

"I beg your pardon?"

"I will not be allowed. I will eat too much."

"I will insist. I am their guest, after all."

"You should reread your contract."

She prepared to go. "Wait," I said. She stood looking at me, silk clothes so bright, in front of my very expensive windows. "Never mind," I said; "goodbye."

I said nothing more. Nevertheless, she seemed to think she should.

"I will come back," she said after a silence. Then she went.

I didn't expect to see her again.

I don't know if her visit had anything to do with it, but it was the morning after when I got the idea for the school project. I was down in the library, doing a little research, and I met the man who had been my first lover. I hadn't seen him in years. He had brought a delivery up from Earth. He was so pleased to see me that he stayed for some time with me, kissing and hugging me and talking about his children, who are teenagers now. "Leaving you and deciding to have children were the best decisions I ever made," he said effusively, between kisses. Then he went away to arrange for the return trip.

The library has an ice-cold water fountain. I drank a cup and refilled it. On Earth you can drink as much water as you like, leaving the tap running between cupfuls. It's one of the reasons I like the library.

Explaining my idea to the principal, I talk with my hands a lot, illustrating the relationships within the concept. The dog is restless and wants to get at the children. I don't mean to make it sound ominous. She just wants to play.

How big is the moon? How big are any of us? When I am as hungry as I am now I feel thin but not very small. Though I am as narrow as a thread, my hunger makes me enormous.

*   *   *

The windows look so real. Cars, aeroplanes, pedestrians walking in and out of frame, out there on Earth, as if they were outside my walls. The singer from Earth is fascinated.

Really, *from* Earth: she has now left Earth for this place, strange though I find that. She walks around my apartment, touching things. I don't like her to touch too much; she'll see what's fake. The blind dog is tracking her by sound, orienting herself by bumping the furniture. The dog is allowed to touch.

Meia is her name; I suppose I should try to remember that. She will want me to call her by her name. All the Earth people do. She will want me to ask her how she is settling in, and profess interest in her reactions to the move. She will want me to ask her what she finds most different, most similar, most challenging and welcoming. Well, if these conversations give me back enough, maybe I will take her to the library. She will like the water fountain, but only after she has been here long enough to appreciate it.

The library is not for newcomers. It is for people who have been sleeping in this particular box for a long time.

*   *   *

Night, according to the windows. Meia is here again. Talking at length for the first time, saying—do I want to know?

"I don't care so much about the size," she says. "It's the colour of it." Is she talking about the food, her room, or her lover? I forget. She notices me forgetting.

"Why do you do that?" she suddenly says.

"What?"

"That ... removal. That deafness. All you people here do it. You ask me questions and then you don't hear the answers and half the time you ask me the same questions again the next day. Why ask me the questions if you don't want to know? Heaven knows it's hard enough to figure out what you want me to answer. I'd be just as happy not to say a thing."

129

"But then you'd touch things."

I didn't mean to say that, it just came out.

"Touch things?"

I turn away but I can't get away from the conversation to which I committed myself. "You touch our things. They're ours. Some of them came from Earth. They were expensive. They belong to us, not you. If you want something, get it yourself. Don't use up ours."

"You mean, there's a rule about it? Nobody told me."

"We don't tell people from Earth. They'd get uncomfortable and we can't stand that. But if you move here, someone finally tells you things. I'm sorry it had to be me."

"Why? You are my friend. I'd rather you tell me than some stranger."

"No, I'm not your friend. I told you, we don't touch other people's."

"Other people's what?"

"Everything. Other people's everything."

"Welcome to the moon," she says.

"It's called the box," I say. "The moon isn't this place, and this place isn't the moon. Look," and I gesture out my windows.

"It's not Earth either," she says. "Those windows are transmitted from down home just like everything else."

"Oh, yes," I say, "but they cease to be Earth soon enough. Do you know how to measure the size of the moon?"

"No," she says.

"Start by touching it," I say. "That's the answer. And we never will. So the moon's as big as we imagine it to be."

"Which is how big?

"Well, today, it doesn't exist at all," I tell her. "She can tell you," and I indicated the blind dog, who all this time had been fawning at either Meia's knee or mine.

"She's allowed to touch things," Meia says, sharper than I gave her credit for being.

"Yes, but she can't see," I say with sorrow.

"Is that my option too? To touch and be blind, or to see and be alone? Or to get myself a deaf cat, or a lame bird, or another dog like this? Or some of these phony windows?"

"No," I say. "It's not like that. The dog is old; I'm used to her now. I have friends, lovers, we have our lives. We know what's what, so we don't have to dissemble with each other. We know where the windows come from, but we know where they go, too. That's the difference."

"And I can't be one of you and know too?"

"You will be, whether you like it or not. Unless your singing is so fine that they ask for you back."

"I didn't exactly have a choice about leaving—only a choice of exiles. When I played here, it seemed fine. Now I see where the punishment lies."

"We are all bitter. Maybe not about the same things."

I go up to her and put my fingers through her hair to her warm scalp. I can feel her firm skull holding my hands apart.

"I like my head held," I say. "Do you? I think I live there, inside my head. If you ever want to touch me, really reach me, touch me like this." And I stroke her ears, her brow, through her hair, and her strong neck. She looks at me with a surprised, then a troubled, finally a rebellious face.

"Why are you doing this?" she whispers.

"To make you understand," I say. "Besides, I have always liked your singing."

She pulls her head away roughly, pushes the dog's head away from her lap, gets up and half-rushes, half-stumbles to the door.

I want to keep a proper silence, to teach her, but suddenly: "Do you see why I didn't want it to be me?" I had to ask her.

131

"No," she says, "but I am sure I will sometime under-stand. When I have been well and thoroughly boxed-in to this place." And she goes out, as I intended her to do.

For the first time, I miss her a little, later.

*   *   *

In the library, there are workers around the ice water fountain. They are putting in a wall. I walk to the fountain. One of the workers is Danno.

"This is the last day," he says. "As of next tenday, it's to be restricted. Card holders only."

"That's not right," I say. "This is the library!"

But there is nothing to be done. I go home to my apart-ment, where the blind dog waits.

Project to measure the size of the moon. How long is a piece of string? The schoolchildren will learn more than triangulation, but I don't tell the principal about that. I have my own ideas about how big the Moon has become. I have spent a lot of time walking through these halls, and living in that apartment with its clever windows. This morning when I woke up, it was because I had tried to stretch in my sleep, rolled over in bed, and struck my shoulder and arm right down to the knuckles against the wall that bounds the bed. The pain abolished sleep. I have been here a long time but my body will not always forget.

What do the children mean?

George Elliott

H E GRUMBLED out loud as he walked. He had to walk to town, scuffing his boots through the rough gravel, breathing dust when a rig passed, stopping every forty rods or so to wipe the damp off his face. Kith offered to drive him but he laughed that gentle, looking-down laugh of his and said he'd walk.

(Kith was his daughter-in-law. She married young Tom that year barley went up to a dollar a bushel. She was a Sparling.)

So he materialized, out of the base-line road where he lived, on the eighth concession. (You don't see much traffic on that base-line road nowadays. Drive down the eighth some day and when you get to the base-line corner look over to your right towards the far greenery. That's the deep-cut creek valley, Old Johnson Mender used to live in there. That's all. It's an abandoned side road now.)

Old and alive he was as he walked. Up his road, under his sky. His sky that started up from the fingery little poplars, misty and blue two concessions away, and curved up over the eighth and down to the gently rising land where the township ends. His sky holding his world.

Grey hair perched out from under his straw hat in tufts. There was the leather look to his face, but his cheeks were pink warm. In under the shaggy brows, his eyes moved easily. They were old eyes but they weren't washed out yet.

The last time he had been to town was many years ago. Now it looked strange, bare and freshly painted. He kept his eyes straight ahead as he went by the blacksmith's shop, closed up now, and the harness shop that had been turned into an implement agency since he saw it last.

He remembered that the place where he was going was catty-corner with the bank and directly across from the Queen's Hotel. They'd changed the front quite a bit in sixteen years: slat blinds in the windows facing the street, so you couldn't see in any more. The glass door had new gold lettering that told the office hours.

He made the door shiver when he stepped in from the street. Inside it was too quiet, that was what was wrong. He wanted to get used to it, so he looked all around slowly. When he got to the wicket, it was easy for the clerk to tell he was hot and blustery, probably mad.

"Look here, young man," Mr. Mender started, the words rattling on each other as he spoke against the quiet, "I want three beautiful children. I want to take them with me. They must be young, full of spirit, and ready to do what I tell them."

The clerk settled himself on the high stool, leaning forward on his elbows on the counter. He tilted his head a little to one side before he spoke. One of those cantankerous old know-alls. Thinks we'll jump when he barks, does he? The clerk used his voice to cut and mock Mr. Mender.

"You're rather old to be asking for three children, aren't you, sir?"

"Rather old!" exclaimed the old man. "Listen you, I'm Johnson Mender, I'm the only man in this township with the right to ask for any children. You young whelp! Get out your order book and take my name and address and no back talk. That's the way this place was run not so many years ago."

The clerk's face went pink and he was angry with himself. He couldn't catch a hold on the words to hurt and still this old man. He backed out of the cage and called for the manager.

The manager came and looked. His eyes went wide, then he smiled. He took Mr. Mender's arm and, together, they walked through the gate that kept customers separated from the business side of the office. In the manager's private room, Mr. Mender sat uneasily. The clay-splotched overalls and patched smock he had on were what you usually saw across the desk from the manager sixteen years ago, but they didn't seem right that day.

"It's been a long time since you were here, Mister Mender, About sixteen years, I should judge." The manager, Mr. Mender decided then, had a grocer-man's face, round, red and smooth; the kind of face that sticks to the job and hides whatever's inside. The old man remembered back, too, and smiled.

"Yes, yes, sixteen years ago this summer. But about my order to that clerk. I have to hurry home and get started."

"Hold on, Mister Mender. I'd certainly like to accommodate you this time, but, after all, there's your record. It's all on the books, you know. We can't ignore that."

"You mean Froody? And Honey Salkald? Why, they're both . . ."

The manager interrupted. "Yes, I know, Mister Mender, I know. You took those two children and the collateral seemed all right at the time, but Froody's mother never came around. Neither did her daddy. Neither did Honey's dad. You promised, remember? But we've had to give you extensions every year since."

"And I think there's still time. Look at Honey's grand-dad. Look how well he shaped up before he died."

"Grandparents don't count, Mister Mender. I'm sorry. No, you've defaulted twice so we can't fill any new requests."

"But you can't refuse me like this. You know I would never come here like this if I weren't serious. How else is there? If you refuse like this you cut me off. Don't you understand? I've been working on these new ones ever since Froody and Honey ... "

"Yes, Mister Mender, I know. But what you don't seem to understand is there are new developments in this business. They haven't been tried out too carefully yet, but there are going to be changes in the collateral rate at least. We have to go easy for a while and watch our balance sheet pretty carefully, much as we'd like to help people like yourself. What's troubling me is I'm the man in charge here, always have been. You've dealt with me before, yet I can't let the children go as easily as we used to. Those are orders. But I know what I'm doing to you. You old-timers have put me in a difficult position. And in your particular case, we thought you'd pretty well given up after you lapsed on Froody and Honey."

"But I'm old. You know better than to talk to me about changes. I know what you're talking about and all that jiggery-pokery makes me sick. Make you fellows mighty weary in a while, you mark my words. Collateral, lapses. That's all stuff. I'm eighty-seven years old. There's not much time left. I only need three children and you've got to give them to me."

The manager's face was troubled and firm. He followed Mr. Mender to the door. They stepped into the sun-baked street together. Slowly, for Mr. Mender's legs had gone stiff and old, they walked down the main street to the town line where the concession road began.

"I hope you understand my position here, Mister Mender. I'm only in charge of a local branch. If I were at head office I'm sure something could be arranged. Lord knows I'd like to help, because I think you are on the right track."

Old Johnson Mender made little throat-clearing noises and kept on walking to where the sidewalk ended and the eighth concession began.

"Would you care to tell me who the cases are, Mister Mender?"

"Yes. I'll tell you who they are, mister wise man. I'll tell you. Come over here and sit down. I'll tell you."

So the manager and Mr. Mender sat down in the dry grass by the side of the road. They were just outside the town. There was a new-cut barley field beside the road. A proud old elm in the fence bottom hung its big branches over them. Poplars lined both sides of the concession that narrowed straight into the township—reaching-up poplars, up to the sky. The manager's glasses glinted coldly in the warm sun.

While he listened, the manager thought of what was happening at that very moment. My world, he thought, is that field of barley there, long cleared of stumps, ploughed and cultivated, sown to barley and clover last spring, carefully harvested, stocked and threshed, and the clover left to get a root-hold for the winter. All order, all order, the manager thought. But his world is this long grass and weeds that grow thick-stemmed and too tough to destroy along the road where people go, up and down the road, close beside that.

"The first one, mister wise man, is my son, Tom. He's a fool. He's my son and a fool. He's down there right now at his house below the hill, sitting on the porch and rocking. And all he has inside him is 'This is my little farm. That's my barn and my root house and those are my mulberry trees and those are my chickens. I haven't missed a Sunday at church in twelve years. I get along good with my neighbours because I mind my own business. I don't owe anybody any money. That makes me a fortunate man!' And that's all he has to say to himself, mister wise man. What was it that stopped him there? He's fifty-five now, so I'm sure you'd get back the child I'd send there. Look, get this through your head. He's my son. He doesn't want to know

139

who I am. He's afraid: so all I am is his father. That's good for some folks, but my son, he needs to know someone like me. Nothing bad would happen. Worse than that, he doesn't know who his wife is. Never once has he ever tried to get through to either of us.

"Kith, that's his wife, she came to me not so long ago, stern and proud, trying to hide it, not wanting to break down and wanting to, all at the same time. She did, and I tell you it's not good for an old man to be full of pity only. Not good."

The old man stopped to remember. He twisted a pig-weed out by the root. It was red, covered with clay. The leaves would wilt by the time the two men were ready to leave.

"What kind of a life is that? Him proud-bound and dying in himself—and with a lonely wife. There are other things.

"I can see one of the children you could give me sitting on his shoulder, tugging at his ear and lifting up his eyelids and kicking him where his heart is to make it go. Imagine that heart going for the first time. It'd hurt at first and be a puzzle, but he'd come around.

"Then I got to send one to young Mordy MacDonald yonder. I tell you, mister wise man, Mordy is too proud. He's arrogant. Know what that word means? Arrogance is a sin and I've got to stop it.

"What makes a no-special-account family think it's got to lord and mister it and look down the nose on other people, like the MacDonalds've been doing since they first came here?

"What Mordy doesn't get is the juice that's in him is the same as the juice that's in everybody else. He bleeds when he's cut. He has a three-holer like everybody else. He puts his thumb down on the haft of the fork to get at his peas.

"Mordy's daddy started it all. Thinking he was too good for this country. He came here with nothing, like everybody else's daddy. There's no room now for what that old man did to Mordy.

"There's Mordy in his yard, looking up from filling the cow trough. He sees Swifts' barn next farm up. He sees Alex Thompson's barn across the road. He thinks they may have just as good barns as his, they may take off just as good crops as he does, but they haven't got the name.

"See what I'm driving at? Mordy's kids want to play with the Swifts. They want to buck-buck, how many fingers up at school in recess time, but Mordy'd skin them once he found out. They're getting too old for school now. Pretty soon they'll decide Mordy's all right. I got to catch them before that happens.

"You think this is all a lot of talk, mister wise man?" The old man mopped his face with his polka-dot handkerchief. His breath was coming faster.

"Now, Mister Mender, don't say that. You know better. I understand." Somehow the manager's face didn't appear as mean or troubled out here in the township as it did in town. He was where he wanted to belong: out among the living, but swallowed up. The long twitch-grass swam around his vision.

And, somehow, old Johnson Mender's eyes got all washed out. They halted in their moves from the horizon to the barley field to the manager's face and back again, halting and slow they were. The pigweed he'd pulled was already wilting in the sun.

"Go on, Mister Mender."

"The best thing for Mordy would be for him to be lifted up away from his farm with his head turned away from his name on the mail box. A child from your place could show him his neighbours. He'd come down and get to know Alex and the Swifts. One day he might cry inside over a little thing like shaking hands."

Something of the old man's fierceness came back to him; but whenever the sun winked on the wispy metal frames of the manager's glasses, Mr. Mender felt pity for the manager too, but mostly regret because it was in the manager's hands to do something for the almost blind. And when the old man started to speak again, the resentment of the manager was gone from his voice. He stopped calling him mister wise man. It was as though the old man's thoughts were now being put into his throat, into the words, by the unexpected excitement of dreaming out loud.

"Yes, that minister is almost blind. I was going to use the third one for the minister at the river church. Poor man. His softball league. Monthly reports. Marrying and burying. His balance sheet. Social services. He can't remember what was in him when he first started preaching. Nowadays when be gets together with the church wardens, all he can think about is he isn't making much money. He's never told anybody, but he'd like a church in the city. In the city. If he only knew he was here among his people.

"The other day his wife asked him if he'd let her have some extra money because she wanted a new hat to wear at the presbytery meeting in town. He didn't even see what the hat was. He didn't hear what his wife was saying. An easy thing like that. He gave her the money and she got the hat. Does he call that social service?

"And his sermons. You'd think he never heard of mothers or fathers, living or loving. They were what was in him when he first started preaching. They're not in him now. He hasn't preached a sermon in six years. We sit in our pews every Sunday but Sundays might as well be Saturdays or Thursdays. I thought sure he'd have heard his wife when she asked for money for a new hat.

"Boy, think of it. A child from your place at a Sunday morning christening. Right in the minister's arms. Looking up at him with eyes that say what needs to be said. You know that, don't you? You know I'm right. You know it'd work and you know you'd get the child back."

Excited inside, the manager nodded. He took his glasses off and for a second his sun-beat face was broken and eager. His fingers worked at the creases in his trousers as though he would jump up and start back to town. Instead he put his glasses back on.

"Why did you default on Froody and Honey, Mister Mender? I want to let you have the children, but I can't."

Mr. Mender pushed himself over and up to his feet. He walked in the weeds beside the road out into the township. The poplars, whispering and comforting, passed him on, one to another, into the country, towards the lake.

The manager stayed sitting by the side of the road. The disorderly weeds were big, green, swimming big in the corners of his sight. A stomach feeling in him was the fear that he was what made Mr. Mender dwindle so small as he walked away. He moved his eyes from near to far to keep the old man in sight, but the poplars kept passing the old man along from one to the next and on.

And the twitch-grass, yellow green and hard to kill, the nodding Queen Anne's lace, the blue devil, up over all, the roadside life filled his sight. All that was left was the road out into the township. The road that went back into town too. He got up and turned.

Where the base-line road crosses the eighth concession, there are two rural delivery boxes, one for Mr. Mender and the other for his son, Tom. This was where Kith found her father-in-law when she came up the hill for the mail. He was slumped against the anchor post behind the mail boxes. She ran back down the hill, calling for Tom.

Tom came and carried his father down the hill, under the mulberry trees that shaded the porch, then up on the porch to the horsehair sofa. He laid him down.

"I'll phone for Doctor Fletcher," Tom said; "loosen his shirt and swab his face."

Kith was left alone with old Johnson Mender. Before he opened his eyes, he considered the warm old smell of ripe mulberries. He opened his eyes and saw Tom was not there.

"Kith," he whispered, "I was going to do something about Tom. Can't now. You'd have seen it right away. It would have made you glad. Everything would have worked out. Could've changed him, but they wouldn't let me. Too late now.

"I had a plan, Kithy. Wonderful plan. Three little children. One takes a little run and a hop, floating easily down here right under the porch roof one afternoon, just an instant. But enough. Another glides into Mordy's yard. Another, shining clean and humming, looks up at the minister at the christening next Sunday morning. Too late now. They wouldn't let me."

His voice and his eyes became washed-out whispers. Kith could feel him strain for every breath. She heard Tom's footsteps in the house. She bent over the old man quickly.

"Wait, Daddy, wait," she spoke in his ear, "don't go. What children? What do you mean? What do the children mean?"

Studies Show/
Experts Say

M.A.C. Farrant

HOW MUCH butylated hydroxalade does it take to make one mutant cell?" This is the question I pose to Isobel over dinner. "One millilitre? A quarter of a teaspoon?"

"Why don't you just shoot yourself and be done with it?" Isobel screams as she packs her bags. "I'm leaving you. Sicko. Pea brain. Bag of shit. You've got gas up the ass. And I'm taking the antibiotics with me."

"You'll be sorry," I tell her. "Studies show that being cut off from friendships and family doubles a person's chance of sickness and death. Not only that," I call from my sick bed, "but Experts say it is not enough to marry someone because they make your heart pound, two people's lifestyles must come together as well. What's a nurse without a patient?"

The main thing that worries me about living alone is this: what if I should stop breathing in my sleep? Sleep Apnoea. What if no one is there to wake me, shake my shoulder or, if necessary, administer mouth to mouth? What if I am found dead in my bed, a rotting cauliflower, one ghastly hand still clutching my *Merck's Manual of Diseases*?

For this reason I call up Georgina, single mother of two, my client-girlfriend from the Welfare Office.

I say, "About forty percent of women who separated while still in their thirties will never re-marry. Now's your chance."

The chest pains start on the first Sunday after Georgina moves in. We send the kids to McDonald's and spend the rest of the afternoon in Emergency. I tell them this is my fifteenth heart attack.

"Skinny guys don't get heart attacks," the intern says. "It's probably just gas."

Driving home I say to Georgina, "What does the medical profession know? They've yet to discover why I am dying."

"Everyone dies," says Georgina. "In fact the outer limit of the human life-span remains at about 110 years and that figure hasn't changed since the beginning of recorded history."

"But you're not supposed to die in the prime of your life," I yell. "Not when you're a 42-year-old, white-collar Welfare Worker, three-bedroom home-owner secure in the middle-income profile bracket."

"You worry too much," says Georgina. "Worry wart! Next you'll be getting Herpes." Georgina is laughing.

"Very funny," I say. "Right now I'd be more worried about this pain in my lower right quadrant. I think I have a fever."

"Show me where it hurts," she says, unzipping my pants as I'm driving.

I pull over. She does the rebound test for Peritonitis, the way I taught her on our first night together. Nothing.

"Probably just a gas bubble," she says, hiking up her skirt and getting comfy.

Georgina lasted three weeks. She accused me of having pre-menstrual syndrome. That son of hers, Ronald, definitely has psychological problems—he called me a basket case. And I'm still recovering from the blow Curtis landed as they were leaving.

"There's a strong possibility I may be bleeding internally," I call as they head towards the waiting taxi.

"Porter Jones," Georgina shrieks from the sidewalk, "you don't need a true love, you need a fleet of ambulance attendants."

Fortunately, as a Welfare Worker, I am eligible for stress leave at three-quarters of my regular pay. I hate to admit to failing emotions but it's the only way I can get off work to minister to my swollen liver. My doctor has refused to see me. The things I could say about the medical profession.

Before long a person called Wanda follows me home from the health food store.

When I finally speak to her, as a test, I say, "I have this pain."

"People with pain almost always have something wrong in the body," she says and I am ecstatic. I know I have made a match. Wanda clinches it when she says, "I can always tell a victim of 20th Century Disease. You need me."

"Okay," I say. And go to bed.

Wanda is an old hippie: long flowering skirt, hairy legs, several pounds of beads hanging off her neck. She has taken to preparing herbal remedies for me, teas, poultices. She gathers the herbs from her own garden and administers them while chanting and nodding her head towards the eastern sky, her long grey hair falling over her unhinged breasts. And furthermore, she is an excellent masseuse.

"Doctors are rip-off artists," she says.

True. True. True.

We are like-minded, Wanda and I. The things she says about the medical profession. For instance: how come, how come and how come?

How come we can land a man on the moon and we haven't yet found a cure for Agoraphobia?

149

How come doctors play so much golf while all over the world people are starving for adequate recreational facilities?

How come doctors get all the money while lay people like me are having to shop at the Nearly New and make a cult out of getting by with less?

She also says, "Doctors don't know dick. Anybody can see you're allergic to everything."

To this end Wanda has removed every piece of synthetic material from my house. This activity hasn't left me much. The TV, my dishes, the kitchen table and chairs, my Dacron wall-to-wall, even the plastic toilet roll holder. All sit in a pile on the front lawn. The shower curtain. A windfall for the Sally Ann.

She has painted the interior of my house Maalox-white, using lead-free paint. White walls, white ceilings, white floors. My house looks like the inside of a laboratory. I sleep on a white cotton futon; Wanda allows white cotton pyjamas. She vacuums dust from her naked self before visiting me from the custodial tent outside; she monitors my condition twenty-four hours a day.

She brings me cauliflower soup, the cauliflower hand-grown in the finest organic soil.

"Mineral deposits found in cauliflower are effective in treating advanced cancer of the colon," she assures me. Every day the cauliflower cure.

I spend my days wandering through the bare room in an orgy of illness. I've never felt better in my life.

Before long, Wanda sets up a roadside stand and is charging admission.

"Opportunity knocks," she says. "The doctors aren't the only ones to make hay out of gas."

She has called me the Bubble-Man. Sightseers now file through the flower beds and peer in at me through my curtainless living room window. I bask in the attention, their awe-filled eyes caressing me like benevolent heat lamps. Judging from the crowds, Wanda is making a killing.

Lately she tells me that Bubble-Man T-shirts are selling like crazy. She says she is about to become President of Bubble-Man Industries, manufacturers of disease memorabilia: stool samples, vials of blood, plastic throat swabs.

"Okay," I say, "but can you tell me why I am dying? I have this pain."

"In the neck?" Wanda asks.

"All over."

"Well, keep it," she says, "that pain has corporate significance."

"All right," I say, "but get me some ginger ale and some Vick's cough drops, cherry-flavoured. And fix my pillow and rub my back and bring me some magazines and bring me the thermometer. I need all the care I can get and don't you forget it."

"Not on your life," Wanda says.

All the sightseers are wearing white cotton pyjamas. Television networks are plaguing us for prime-time interviews: Bubble-Man has suddenly become an important news item and we are getting offers to do commercial endorsements.

Now everyone I know is gawking at me through the living room window. In envy. Covetousness. Isobel and all her relations. Cousins I never knew I had. Former co-workers. The entire staff from the Department of Welfare. Georgina, Ronald, Curtis, their neighbours from the housing project. No one is immune. All gaze in wonder, mouthing at me through the living room window: "We never knew you'd be famous, Porter Jones. We never knew you'd be a person of importance."

Fulfillment on their faces. Tears in their eyes.

My head is spinning. I allow members of fundamentalist religious organisations to touch the hem of my pyjamas. Cripples and maniacs sit reverentially outside my window. For hours.

But then suddenly the doctors descend. Swarms of them are poring over my body, taking tests, peering in my orifices. "Wanda, Wanda, this wasn't in the plan. You said doctors are the plague of the earth!"

But Wanda's nonplussed. "Things change," she says. "And studies show that businesses which use consultants wisely are more likely to flourish than those which do not. You have to be sensitive to market forces if you want to survive."

So I am charitable to the doctors, serene in my national sickness, swollen with illness-identity. I'll be a good business investment for Wanda. "A barium enema? No problem. Suck on this little metal tube? Delighted."

But when the doctors finish testing me they ponder: how come, how come and how come?

How come Porter Jones has all this attention?

How come he is lying bloated with gas on a cotton futon and is not in one of our technologically advanced medical centres?

How come a businesswoman-hippie has control of this amazing new gimmick when there are research foundations to vie for, new medical centres to be had?

The doctors buy out Wanda's interest in Bubble-Man Industries and move me to a specially sterilized Bubble-Room at their Centre.

Wanda is pleased with the settlement. "Buy low, sell high," she says as she's leaving. "Besides, I'm onto something. There's this guy, paralyzed from the waist down from eating Aspartame. He needs me."

My bubble has burst. After six weeks of further testing at the Centre, the doctors can find nothing wrong. As well, interest in me is waning; the polls show that VCRs are turning family television viewing into video campfire gatherings. This means that I am no longer being watched—I have achieved viewer saturation. My ability to command the public's attention is no longer significant.

My removal from the medical centre happened this way. I was spending my brief but halcyon days there, as usual, nursing one of my invisible, lurking turnouts or else giving interviews through the Plexiglas of my Bubble-Room when a workman burst through the door and began stripping the Saran Wrap from the walls.

"What are you doing?" I gasped. "Don't you know I'm the Bubble-Man? I have 20th Century Disease. I'm allergic to *everything*!'

"Got orders to re-do this room, Mac," was all he would tell me.

Within hours the Bubble-Room had been transformed to resemble the inside of a church: altar, font, cross, stained glass windows. Six hospital beds done over to look like pews. Three nuns, three priests, all dressed in deathly black, prepared to take up residence.

"Electromagnetic clatter from millions of man-made sources is drowning out the whispers from heaven," they explained. "We're donating ourselves to medical science. Research. Soul transplants. That sort of thing. Please make way for the cameras."

In desperation I called up Georgina. "I'm being turfed out," I wailed, "thrown back to the polluting forces, my only possessions, the white pyjamas on my back, my portable heart monitor. How come, how come and how come?"

Today I have Diverticulitis. Yesterday it was Scabies. Last week, gritty deposits on my tibia. It's incredible the way I go on living.

I have moved in with Georgina; Isobel got the house in our divorce settlement. Because of my many illnesses I am totally unable to work. Fortunately my union at the Welfare Office provides me with a lifelong disability pension at fifty percent of my regular wage. With the money Georgina makes as a Welfare recipient, we get by pretty well, especially since we sent her kids to a group home—all those preadolescent hormones were giving me migraines.

It took a while to adjust to life post-Bubble but I am now, once again, at home with plague, virus and allergic reaction. Still, I am always on the lookout for a new disease which will explain my condition. Unfortunately there is not a doctor in the country who will see me.

Lately I have been troubled with Narcolepsy. I am liable to keel over in mid-sentence. It's like dropping dead, only I fall asleep instead. Nevertheless, I was able to get Georgina pregnant. I can't remember when I did this but she assures me that I am the father and not that ambulance attendant, Arnold, who is always hanging around. "For one last auto-graph," he winks as I plunge to the ground.

But I have fond thoughts for the child. Maybe if I can hold out through the deterioration of my sight, hearing and appetite which I know is in store for me, and the incontinence and the mental disturbance, as well. Maybe if I am still alive when the child is old enough to realize that studies show/experts say that he was born to die, that living is just a series of unexplained, uncomfortable medical conditions, occurring one after the other, sometimes all at once, perhaps then I will show him my scrapbook. Pages and pages of newspaper clippings from my Bubble-Man days, boxes full of disease souvenirs: the T-shirts and white pyjamas. It may be a distinct advantage for him to go through life with a once-famous father. On the other hand, perhaps I shouldn't influence him unduly—he'll have his own diseases to discover.

The World Machines

Brian Fawcett

AROUND NOON on my nineteenth birthday, Old Man
Nelson showed up at the small shack I lived in. I heard
him coming, talking to himself as usual, and I opened the
door as he reached for the doorknob. He would have
walked in without knocking, just like most people. With
him I didn't mind—he owned the land my shack stood on,
and he'd never once asked me to pay any rent.

"Put your coat on, son," he said in his slight
Scandinavian accent. "I got something you need to know
about. It's your birthday present."

Old Man Nelson drove a huge black Oldsmobile that
looked like a gangster's car. But he didn't look like a gangster. He looked like what he was: a retired logger who'd
made a lot of money and who told stories about everything
under the sun except how he'd made his money. I don't
remember how I got to know him, but since I liked to listen
to his stories and I lived on one of the many properties he
owned, we came as close as young men and old men come
to real friendship. For a couple of years, I spent quite a lot
of time listening to him.

"You know," he began, as he turned the big Oldsmobile
out of the alley, "them buggers who run things don't do it
by themselves, eh?"

He knew this question would interest me because we
frequently talked about how things were run around the
city. I'd noticed, among other things, that even though the
Mayor and Council of our small town were stupid and
short-sighted men, they exercised a degree of authority and

control they couldn't possibly have understood and certainly didn't earn. There was a kind of gap between what they said about how things worked and the complex and overlapping processes by which even I could see the city operated. This gap, which I merely sensed without understanding its workings, was a disturbing darkness that resided at the core of the city. I could never quite forget that it was there.

I began to see it while I was a small boy, watching the city crews dig up the streets, install pipes in the holes, and then fill in the holes. The next year they would do the same thing over again. One year it was water pipes. The next year, sewer pipes. Another year, gas. Then they replaced the pipes. I believed, as most children do, that the world and every action in it had a purpose; that it was under some sort of benevolent and rational control, even though I'd already begun to realize there was very little evidence to back this up. Watching the crazy way the crews dug up the streets every year convinced me, by itself, that whatever was going on wasn't rational or benevolent on any terms I could understand, but I continued to believe at least it operated on some sort of logic. But what was that logic, and what did it serve? As I grew older, finding the answer to that question preoccupied me, and consequently, Old Man Nelson's opener snapped me to attention.

"What do you mean, they don't do it by themselves?"

Old Man Nelson had a way of telling stories that made things fuzzier before it made them clear. That was one of the reasons I liked listening to his anecdotes and stories. Listening to them was like walking into a fog and coming out with money in my pocket. All I had to do was show some curiosity, then nod my head in the right places to assure him that I was listening carefully. He'd talk, and I'd generally learn something interesting or useful.

"Well," he said slowly, "those buggers don't know much of anything. They just know where the switches are, and they like having people running this way and that more than they should."

I nodded, but kept silent. It made sense, but this wasn't the right time to question. I let the fog spread.

"Out by the lake I'll show you something you've never seen before," he said.

I'd been to the lake dozens of times, and I'd never seen anything unusual, except maybe the time my sister got a bloodsucker up her nose.

"You've never seen it because you didn't expect anything unusual to be there," he said, fielding my unasked question perfectly. "That's the way these guys do things. They put things where nobody expects them to be, and so nobody looks right at them. You can't see what anything is unless you look right at it. Even then what you're seeing can't be understood if you don't have the words to get a hold on it."

"Who's 'they'?" I asked. We shared a taxonomy but our vocabularies were slightly different. For instance, Old Man Nelson called the mayor and council 'them buggers'. I referred to them as 'those assholes'. Maybe the difference was because they really hadn't done anything to me yet, and Old Man Nelson often complained that they spent most of their energy thinking up ways to screw him.

"The bosses," he said.

"You mean those assholes down at City Hall?"

"No. Them buggers don't know nothing. I mean the big bosses." He paused. "The ones you never see. If you're really doing something you don't go strutting around like a rooster, crowing about it."

"So what do these big bosses do, anyway?"

"They run everything, and they make sure nobody gets out."

I sat in the roomy imitation leather seat beside Old Man Nelson and watched the shacks whiz by outside the car window, mulling over the idea. I wondered for a moment if he was talking about God, and decided he wasn't. He didn't believe in that crap, and neither did I, any more. The idea of God used to be comforting. This idea wasn't. I didn't know a lot, but I had figured out that anyone with that kind of power wasn't going to be interested in me. Power was for assholes, and I didn't want to be an asshole. I didn't know what I wanted to be, but I knew that there were a lot of assholes out there, that the world was full of assholes, and that the world seemed to be changing in such a way that only assholes would be able to get anywhere in it. Old Man Nelson was about the only adult I knew who wasn't an asshole, come to think of it.

"You asleep?" he asked, as much to prevent me from falling asleep as anything.

I could sleep anywhere, any time, without the slightest provocation. I think he admired that talent more than anything else about me. He often said that if he didn't talk to me constantly I'd drop off on him. Then he'd laugh and tell me to get lots of sleep now, because when I got old like him I wouldn't ever get any sleep. He didn't sleep much, he said, because he knew too much, and if he let his guard down, them buggers would walk all over him.

"I'm not sleepy today," I said. "What did you mean when you said the bosses run everything?"

Old Man Nelson paused, as if figuring out a way to make it simple enough for me to understand. Whenever he was thinking hard an odd expression came over his face, a grin that made him look part goat and part elf. "People get up in the morning and then they sleep most of the night, right?"

"Right." I didn't bother to complicate things by pointing out that he didn't sleep that way.

"Why?" he asked flatly.

"What do you mean, why?" I replied. "Because that's how things work. You can't stay awake all the time. If you tried, you'd get too tired to stay awake, and then..." I sensed that I was digging myself into a hole. "Darkness makes people sleepy," I finished lamely. "I dunno."

"If everybody got up when they wanted to, and slept when they wanted to, the bosses' system would get buggered up," he said. "Some people would sleep all the time, like you, and some would sleep all day and stay up all night, and some people wouldn't sleep at all."

"I guess."

"And things would start to change."

"Yeah?" I said, starting to see some shapes in the fog. For one thing, I was going to have to revise my theory about change. Instead of changing things, the bosses were keeping things as they were.

"Yeah. So the bosses keep it all going the way it already is."

"If everybody did what they wanted wouldn't everything just break down?"

Old Man Nelson gazed at me patiently. "At first, that's about all it would be. But after a while people would start seeing what really needs to be done, and when that happened, things would start to change."

"So how do the bosses keep things from changing?"

"That's what I'm going to show you," he said.

"So what you're saying is that the bosses don't want anything to change, and that's a bad thing, is that it?"

"Sure. They don't want real change, anyway. Things in the city can grow bigger, like trees do, and if they grow bigger people think things are changing when they're not. But if something different—really different—starts to happen then the bosses might lose."

"Might lose what?"

"I dunno. I've never figured out what it is they're so damned scared of losing. Money, maybe, but maybe something more.

"Something more?" I asked. "Like what?"

Old Man Nelson shook his head. "You wouldn't understand if I told you."

"How come you know all this?" I asked. "Is it because you don't sleep much yourself?"

Old Man Nelson thought that one through before he answered. I felt the car slow down.

"I dunno about that either," he said, finally. "I guess I got a funny ticker in me. Damn thing doesn't work like it's supposed to. I keep waking up with my heart pumping like a pack of dogs chasing a rabbit, and I start seeing things."

The car speeded up again, and I watched the shacks along the roadside get blurry until they seemed like one, long, continuous shack. They began to peter out, and for a while, all there was to look at were blurred birch and poplar thickets.

As we started up the long ridge that overlooked the lake, the countryside started to change. The trees got larger, and, I noticed for the first time, more evenly spaced. Old Man Nelson was whistling quietly. The tune was unfamiliar, but catchy. We reached the crest of the ridge, and I could see the brilliant blue water of the lake below.

"Down we go," said Old Man Nelson, and abruptly pulled the car off the main road, through a shallow thicket of willows and onto a narrow paved lane I didn't know was there. For a second I thought he'd gone crazy and was smashing up the car. We'd been going at least fifty miles per hour.

"Not many people know about this road," he said, as if that explained his peculiar method of entering it.

"I sure didn't," I whispered, beginning to breathe again as he slowed down.

I couldn't see the lake anywhere, and it should have been easily visible as soon as we pulled off the main high-way. The lane we were slipping silently along was strange. I could see it hadn't been used much, because the tarmac was still clean and black. The underbrush crowded closely along it, and in places had begun to infringe on the margins. I didn't know what to make of it, and I sat there, expecting the lake to appear any second. But it didn't, and Old Man Nelson kept driving.

Then the underbrush along the sides of the lane thinned out and disappeared, and the evergreens went with it. The evergreens were replaced by geometrically spaced poplars, their pale olive-green trunks unspotted and straight. The lane flattened out, and seemed to turn back on itself. I felt panic rising in me; I'd heard the stories about old men kidnapping people and killing them, although I couldn't really relate those stories to Old Man Nelson. As if to reassure me, he chuckled to himself and told me it was just a little farther.

The lane curved through the poplars again, and ended abruptly in a small clearing. At the head of the clearing the ground rose sharply and there was something like the front of a building cut into the hill. It was odd-looking, construct-ed as an arch with two pillars about twenty feet high on each side of the doors. The doors themselves were glass, like the kind they put in supermarkets. They even had the recessed rubber mats in front of them that make the doors open automatically.

Old Man Nelson brought the Oldsmobile to a halt at the far edge of the clearing, and I stepped out into a field of plants. They were flowering, and I recognized them as Indian paintbrushes. Like the poplars, they were native to the area, and like the poplars they had obviously been planted in a rigid geometry that made them seem as foreign as they should have been familiar. Then I remembered that it was still early summer, and that Indian paintbrushes bloomed much later in the year, in August.

"They're smart sons-of-bitches," Old Man Nelson said as I knelt down to pick one of the red flowers. "They get them to bloom right from the time they come up out of the snow until freeze-up. But they don't taste good like the real ones do."

I pulled one of the nectar tubes from the flower and sucked the transparent liquid from it. It tasted bitter and I spat it out.

"You should listen to me better," Old Man Nelson laughed. "Let's go inside and I'll show you some things."

He walked toward the glass doors and sure enough, they opened when he stepped on the rubber mat. We went inside and I followed him down a dim corridor.

"What is this place?" I asked, the questions bubbling out of me involuntarily. "Who owns it? Are you sure we're supposed to be in here?"

"You ask too many questions all at once, and none of them are the right ones," he answered, his voice echoing along the corridor.

"Who built this place?" I continued, searching for the right question without any idea of what it was or how to find it. "How long have you known about it? Does every-body know about it? How long are we going to be in here? Do you know the people who run this? Do you know how to get out of here?"

"Wrong questions, wrong questions!" answered Old Man Nelson, waving his hands but not stopping to turn around.

I gave up and followed him silently down the dim corridor. The walls moved back, and above me in the gloom I could just barely make out a network of steel pipes that stretched out and up in both directions. Here and there the network was penetrated by steel walkways and platforms, each with an array of wheel valves, switches and small coloured lights. From the low even hum I knew that whatever the installation was, it was working, operating. What it was doing, I had no clue.

Except for Old Man Nelson and me, it was deserted. I was lagging behind—for an elderly man, Old Man Nelson walked swiftly, certainly, and I found myself scrambling to stay up with him. When I got even with him, I caught at his sleeve.

"What is this place?" I asked, almost pleading. "Where are we going?"

Old Man Nelson gazed at me without slowing his pace, and without answering my questions. As I grabbed at his sleeve again, he swerved out of my grasp and into an alcove I hadn't seen. He stopped, and waited for me to enter behind him.

"Wait," he whispered. "We can't talk here."

I obeyed, and found myself following him down a long, narrow corridor with a low ceiling. Up ahead I could see that the corridor ended in a set of glass doors much like the ones we'd come in by.

Old Man Nelson stepped on the rubber mat, the doors opened, and he walked through them into a room that was instantly flooded with bright light. I followed, skipping into a run to keep the doors from closing against me.

"We can talk here," he said calmly.

The flood of my questions washed over him until he waved me back.

"I'll start from the beginning," he said. "This installation is one of their machines. I don't know for sure how large it is. Very large, obviously. It isn't the only one I've seen either. I discovered another one, smaller and not so fancy, years ago, just before I left the Old Country."

"What is it for?" I asked. "Who built it?"

"The bosses built it," said Old Man Nelson. "They built it to prevent us from changing the way things are. They keep them hidden to prevent people from finding them and understanding what they're doing. If people found out how much of their lives were controlled they might tear them down."

"But we're here," I said. "You found two of them, and now you're showing me this one."

"Hah!" he scoffed. "You're gonna see how much difference that makes. I've been trying to show this thing to people for thirty years now, and you're the first one I got to see it."

"Thirty years? I'm the first one?" I felt equally tempted by both questions.

"I took my own boys out here but they just laughed at me. They couldn't see what I was talking about."

I knew he had three sons, and that he didn't have much use for any of them. Two were already wealthy logging contractors, and the third was at some big university back east studying to be a lawyer. Old Man Nelson's criticism of them was always the same: 'too goddamn busy making money to see what the money was making them into.'

"You're saying that this thing has been here for thirty years?" I asked, not quite believing that it could have been. It looked new, and from the entrance, very modern.

"I only said I've *known* about it for thirty years," he said, smiling at me as if I should know better. "It wasn't this big when I first found it."

"How big is it?"

Old Man Nelson scratched his chin just as if he were trying to decide how far it was to the corner store.

"I walked it out this way, a few years ago," he said, pointing in the direction we'd been going. "I figure it goes almost all the way to the river, which is about nine miles. Down at the far end you can hear the river if you put your ear to the wall. The last time I checked it didn't go as far to the north, but then that was where the newest machinery was, so I don't know how much it's grown."

"What does it do?" I asked, after a moment of silence.

"I can't answer that for you," he said. "I can show you what it is, but I can't tell you what it does, exactly."

I waited for him to explain what he meant by that, but he didn't elaborate. Another silence ensued, but it wasn't, I realized, really silent. Beneath our voices was the sound of the machine, which alternated regularly between a deep rumble and a drone-like hum.

"Can we go farther in," I asked, "so I can figure it out for myself?"

"We could," he said, "but it wouldn't help you. Besides, there's a danger I might lose track of you, and I don't know if you could get out on your own."

"Can we try to go farther anyway?"

"You can always try," he said, his tone shifting, as we were suddenly discussing another matter. "But it's the same here as anywhere else. You'll reach a place where you're not capable of taking in what you're seeing, and when that point is reached you stop being able to understand. If you can't understand things, you come under their control. That's no good. You've got to take this in a little at a time."

I didn't understand what was going on and I didn't really understand much of what he was saying, and instinctively I began to look around me for something material that would enable me to. He lapsed into silence, and I turned and sidled over to examine one of the walls of the room. When I touched it, it was utterly smooth, undefined, although from a distance it had appeared to be rough concrete. I jerked my hand back, alarmed.

"It's like that," he said. "That's the frightening part. From a distance, it seems to make sense, and it can almost look familiar. But the closer you come to it the less definition it has. That's one of the ways you recognize their materials."

"Are there other entrances?"

"Lots of them. They're all over the place, but it's difficult to recognize what they are when you see them. The one we entered by is the only one I know how to reach. I guess you could say that it belongs to me."

"Are you here a lot? I mean, do you spend very much of your time in here?"

Old Man Nelson sighed. "You better start to watch your language more carefully. I don't 'spend' time—that's their way of thinking. I lose time here, but I don't spend it, because I get nothing back, and neither does anyone else. And I'm here a lot. More and more as the years go on."

I wasn't used to fluorescent lights, and my eyes were getting sore. Worse, I was having trouble breathing. The room—and the whole installation—was air-conditioned, but all that did was to flavour the air with an acrid dustiness. I wanted to get out, but I also wanted to find out as much as I could about the place.

"Where are we now?" I asked, gesturing at the walls around us. "What is this room?"

"It's sort of a museum," Old Man Nelson replied with an ironic chuckle. "I've found a few of them like this. The only difference between this and the rest of the installation is that out there, anything resembling a question and answer sequence activates the control panels. In here, as far as I can tell, nothing happens. That's why I brought you here to answer your questions."

"How'd you find out about that if you've never brought anyone else here?"

"I didn't say that. I said that no one else has been able to see what it is. You should listen more carefully." He took my arm and pushed me gently in the direction of the doors. I balked.

"One more question?"

"Okay, ask it. But no more."

"I don't understand how this can be a museum. There's nothing here except bright lights and walls I can't see properly. Museums are supposed to be full of relics, dead things. This place is more like a waiting room."

"This is a museum—at least on the bosses' terms. A museum, as far as they're concerned, is just a warehouse to store dangerous substances in, a place where things or ideas are put in order to make them inactive. Does that answer your question?"

It didn't, but I nodded anyway. "I guess so," I said.

I followed him back down the corridor and into the larger cavern with its overhead array of pipes. Old Man Nelson turned back the way we'd come. I wanted to see more, so I quietly slipped off in the opposite direction. I was hoping that by the time he noticed, I'd be so far away he'd have to let me go on by myself. There was nothing about the installation that was frightening to me now. Already it seemed familiar and dull, and it didn't feel like I was in any physical danger. After all, the place was empty except for the two of us, and the machinery far above my head, humming steadily.

I walked several hundred yards without looking behind me, and heard nothing from Old Man Nelson. When I turned around to see if he was coming after me, he'd vanished. That didn't alarm me. I knew roughly where I was, and getting out was simply a matter of following the long corridor back to the entrance where, no doubt, Old Man Nelson would be waiting.

I walked, the sound of my footsteps lost beneath the hum, for what felt like several miles. But the landscape around me, if that's what it was, stayed the same. Then, among the gun-metal grey of the pipes overhead appeared other colours: at first pastels, and then richer primary colours. The effect was of a riot of colour. I was gazing up into them when I bumped into Old Man Nelson.

"Are you impressed?" he asked.

"With what? With all this?"

"With the colour," he laughed. "Do you know where you are?"

Until that moment I thought I knew where I was. But since I had no idea how Old Man Nelson had gotten there, I was no longer so sure. Without waiting for my answer, he took me by the arm and walked me through a set of automatic glass doors. I was startled to find myself outside the entrance we'd entered by.

Old Man Nelson didn't offer any explanation. He just told me to get into the car.

"It's getting late," he said gruffly, as if he regretted the entire episode. "I've got some things I have to take care of."

Overhead, the sky had clouded over, and the poplars were shimmering in the light breeze, exposing the silvery undersides of their leaves like they always do before it rains.

*　　*　　*

But it didn't rain that afternoon. It should have, but since that afternoon, nothing else has been the way it should be, or the way it used to be. We drove back to town on the dusty gravel roads. Old Man Nelson didn't have much to say and neither did I. He dropped me off at the shack and as I got out of the big black car I thanked him for showing me the machines. He just laughed in a preoccupied sort of way.

"You don't have to thank me for that," he said. "The buggers were there all the time. Now you gotta figure out what they are, and how to remember what they are. After that, you'll have to decide what you're going to do about them."

*   *   *

I knew exactly what to do. Those machines were composed of pipes and there was a network of pipes in the ground all through the city. Obviously, they were connected. I turned my small shack upside-down trying to find where they entered. Then I realized that my place wasn't like most—I had no running water, no toilet, no gas. I checked the electrical system, but found nothing unusual except a third bare copper wire that seemed to have no purpose.

For weeks after that, I drove everyone I knew crazy as I checked their houses for pipes. I found apparently disconnected pipes and irrelevant wires everywhere I looked, but I couldn't establish a pattern to any of it, no logic. I gave up when my mother, after eyeing me carefully while I searched her house, suggested that perhaps I should see a doctor about my problem.

*   *   *

That August, Old Man Nelson died. I didn't get to see very much of him after he showed me the machines. He just didn't come around. I wanted to go out to see the machines again, but we didn't have the kind of friendship that allowed me to visit him. He'd always come by on his own time, and now he didn't seem to have much of it for me. It was as if he were in a hurry, all of a sudden. He told me himself that he was busy—"planning something important," he said when I ran into him on a downtown street one hot afternoon. He looked tired, older than before, his step slower, his breathing laboured. I didn't think too much about it because his eyes were as bright and alert as ever—maybe more so.

I had a hard time finding out the exact details of his death. His wife didn't like me, and because his sons knew the old man preferred my company to theirs, they didn't like me either. I sent a note when I heard about his death, but nobody answered it. I even phoned his wife. But since I didn't really know what I wanted to ask her, and she was aggressively not interested in talking to me about anything, our conversation was a short one. From what I was able to piece together, Old Man Nelson organized a family reunion of some sort—all his sons were in town before he died, and so were a number of relatives. The reunion—a picnic—was held at the lake less than a mile from the stretch of road where he'd pulled the car through that thicket to show me the entrance to the machine.

At the picnic, the old man had attempted to take the family for a walk in the woods. When they refused to go with him, he flew into a rage, storming off deliberately, according to his son, into one of the impenetrable alder and devil's club thickets that surround the lake.

When he didn't come back, a search was launched. They found him in a small clearing at the heart of the thicket. At first they thought he was sleeping, his head cradled comfortably on a mossy log amid the Indian paintbrushes that filled the clearing. The paintbrushes were in full bloom, but the old man was dead. His wife said that it was his heart.

I went to the funeral, even though I knew Old Man Nelson had been a vocal atheist. A preacher got up and had a few things to say about the life beyond, and how, although he didn't know 'the deceased', as he put it, he was certain that Old Man Nelson was going to his deserved reward. None of the sons delivered a eulogy, and there weren't very many people there, considering Old Man Nelson had lived in the town for close to fifty years. I didn't go to the interment, and the family didn't hold a wake. They all looked impatient during the service, like they were needed elsewhere.

I hitch-hiked out to the lake a few days later. The man who gave me the ride thought I was a bit nuts, wanting to get out on a stretch of deserted highway, particularly since it was fire season and a small fire was burning in some slash only two or three miles away.

"You never know when those fires can take off with the wind and burn off a whole goddamned hillside," he told me.

"Not this one," I replied, and slammed the car door shut, waving him on.

I found the lane easily; it was simply "there," as if it had been waiting for me. But as I walked down the gently sloping tarmac, I sensed a change: the poplars were losing their leaves, and as I reached the turn where before the trees had grown in regimented order across the flattened park-like landscape, instead of order I saw carnage: trees with broken tops, trees blown down, and here and there between them, mounds of debris: old house siding, bits of stucco, broken bottles, scraps of pastel plastic. In the clearing where the glass doors with the columns had been, there was a sizeable gravel pit, the bottom covered with about two feet of slimy water rhinestoned with gasoline and diesel. The air was rife with the stink of garbage and petroleum.

The entrance to the machine itself was different. The glass doors had been removed and in their place were heavy steel doors of the same gun-metal grey of the first pipes I'd seen inside. The rubber mats were gone, and so were the columns.

I tried the door, and it opened—not automatically, and not easily—but it did open. I hesitated, not sure if it was safe to enter, and as I did so I heard a familiar laugh. I spun around, and there, just beyond the gravel pit, I thought I caught a glimpse of Old Man Nelson disappearing into an alder thicket.

I hurtled after him, down into the pit and through the scummy water, and up the slope into the thicket. But there was nothing there but the trees. Not a thing moved but the dappled sunlight filtering through the trees. I stood still for a moment, and then my ears picked up the faintest hum. In front of me was a clearing, and as if what the old man showed me had never been, the Indian paintbrushes bloomed in honeyed disarray beneath the smoky August sun. I sat down among them and waited. The hum grew louder, and I remembered that I'd left the doors to the cavern open.

Kellerman's Windows

Timothy Findley

1

KELLERMAN STOOD in the open window, his elbows braced against the sill. He couldn't sleep. His body would not lie down. His eyes would not close.

Midnight—July—and all the rooftops of Paris were spread out before him, every one of them a stepping stone to the next. Kellerman had always thought this. *With a running start, you could leap from rooftop to rooftop all the way to the moon.* He'd said so to Shirley: *look at them out there! You want to play hopscotch? Bring your stones and bring your chalk; leave your worries on the doorstep ...*

She was asleep now, curled on the bed in the room behind him, her wine glass half emptied on the table beside. her. *I'm tired, Marty. Tired. I can't play games tonight.*

It didn't matter. She was there.

Kellerman turned again to the window, his wine glass in hand, the bottle on the sill. Looking out at the slated roofs and the sky, he felt like a child who had just unwrapped a gift and the gift was exactly what he'd hoped it would be.

A rooftop! A chimney!

He drank.

"Here is where it all began," he said. Not so loud that Shirley would hear him, only so he could hear himself. "I'm alive—the same as I was before." he said. Alive and in Paris staring out at its beloved skyline. *In my time, fifty years ago, every young man's dream began out there beyond this window, Paris. Women. Fame.*

Name one who would not be Hemingway.

Can't. It's what we all wanted, back then. So, I might not be Hemingway. But I am me, Martin Kellerman—who made his own way and became his own writer.

He set the glass down, careful not to let it tip, and lighted a cigarette. *Lethal, who cares? Smoke and Paris—the stink of Gauloise everywhere—the stink, the smell, the scent, the perfume of them.*

"Wonderful!" Aloud.

He blew a cloud and waved his hand in it. *Smoke and Paris go together like smoke and mirrors.* Haussmann's incantation. Haussmann, the city planner. Haussmann, the magician. *Paris? I'll give you Paris. Ta-dah!*

Kellerman poured more Côtes du Rhone, enjoying the heft of the bottle as he tipped its mouth to the glass. Its weight, in itself, was a pleasure:—*not yet empty*, it told him.

Yes. It was a good thing he had done—was doing. Coming back to the beginning, nearing the end. One more book to finish. One more triumph. And Shirley with him. With him still, in spite of twenty-six years of tumultuous marriage—glorious—ghastly—tender and terrible times. Three children. Fourteen books. High on the lists. Low on staying power. *You'll have to run faster, Marty*, his publisher had said. *Sure. Nothing to it!* And then, one day: *I can't run any more.* The words not coming. The mind refusing. The body not responding—turning on him, just when he needed it most. *Give me a rest*, he'd said. And this was it. Paris and rejuvenation.

"Marty? Come to bed." Shirley's voice was almost a whisper.

"Can't," he said. "Go back to sleep."

"You all right?"

"Fine. Just fine."

"You know what the doctor said."

"Sure. He said to my mother: *Mrs Kellerman, you have a healthy baby boy! Rejoice!*"

Shirley snorted and turned in the bed. "Your mother had five healthy babies, Marty. The other four are all dead."

"Go to sleep."

"Yes, sir. Yes, sir. Anything you say." She was already going, drifting back towards her dreams; her breathing deepening, her fingers uncurling, letting go—her left leg reaching for the bottom of the bed. With a sigh, she left him.

Kellerman turned again to the window and drank more wine. *To hell with what the doctor said. I'm alive. I'm living.*

2

He could not believe it. Forty-six years ago—almost half a century—Kellerman had stood in this very same room, watching the very same skyline.

Nothing changes. Everything changes. Everything the same and everything different.

All those windows out there glowing—luminescent in the dark—were the same as he had seen when he was twenty, but all the lives beyond them would be different now. Many deaths and many births—leave-takings—arrivals—changing circumstances ... *There, for instance.* One storey down, across the street, an old woman stood in the middle of her living-room, staring at a photograph.

She must have been seventy-five or eighty—her pure white hair pushed back and away from her face. She wore a pale blue wrapper and a high-necked gown. All around her, the tabletops were cluttered with mementos—other photo-graphs in frames, empty vases, porcelain figures, cut-glass goblets, one bronze horse.

The woman kissed the picture in her hand and held it then against her breast. Perhaps her dead husband.

Perhaps a child. Turning, she gazed into a distant corner. *There?* she seemed to say.

No.

She turned again and fixed her sights on a shelf containing books and Indo-Chinese dolls.

There?

Perhaps.

She crossed the room with a swaying motion, almost dancing, threading her way between the tables and chairs. At the shelf, she removed some books and put the picture in their place. Stepping away, she looked at what she had done.

No. It was wrong. One too many faces staring back at her. She snatched up the photograph and passed from sight, only to reappear in the dining-room, whose windows, unlike the others, were closed.

It took her no time at all to make her final decision.

There.

The photograph, which Kellerman of course could not decipher, had been set between two candlesticks on a gaming table whose polished lid had been raised against the wall.

Perfect. Perfection.

The past was now complete—and in its place.

The old woman made for her decanters on the sideboard. Wine was for the daytime. Midnight wanted Cognac.

3

Kellerman heard voices directly opposite. Two people—both unseen—were having an argument. Every window was opened wide in what appeared to be a very large apartment.

The wrangling moved from room to room. Accusations! Denials! Threats and counter-threats! All with such vivid articulation. Kellerman thought of waking Shirley just to hear the words. All the words for rage and hurt. All the words for infidelity and shame—and all the words like breaking plates, hurled into the night. Much about betrayal, everything about love. And then the final *never again. JAMAIS!* And slamming doors. All the usual—all too familiar—but, this time, spoken by two men.

Kellerman could hardly breathe. He felt as if he had taken part in the argument himself. He closed his eyes and, when he opened them, one of the couple across the street had come to the window. He stood there staring down. Seconds later, the other appeared below. He did not look up. Instead, he slung a jacket over his shoulder, took a few steps to the corner and was gone.

Kellerman didn't move. He knew he would not be seen. The abandoned lover in the window opposite was blind with self-absorption. In all the world there was only one other person—and he had disappeared.

Kellerman watched. The man, though balding, was young—perhaps no more than twenty-seven, twenty-eight. What hair remained was short-cropped and red and the head it revealed was turned towards the sky—*as if some passing angel would tell him what to do.*

As if some passing angel …

Robert's invention. Robert's game.

As if some passing angel would teach me how to dance.

As if some passing angel would drop a million-dollar bill.

As if some passing angel would …

Tell me what to do.

Robert was their only son and the only one of their children who was gay. *Gay*—a word that Kellerman detested, but a word that Robert had worn with pride.

What's wrong with *homosexual?*

Nothing, Dad. It's just not cool.

What's *gay* about being kicked to death?

No answer. Robert was dead—the victim of gay-bashing. Skinheads.

Well. At least it's over now.

Kellerman watched the young man turn and walk away. As he watched, something impelled him—perhaps some passing angel—to whisper: *don't get "lost in the jungle."* Another of Robert's inventions. His last and favourite game.

4

To Kellerman's right, beyond the intersection, he could see the Hotel Luxembourg. Its windows were slowly going dark, since now it was well past midnight. Travellers, dazed with jet-lag, bed down early. Still, one set of windows, two storeys shy of his own, was lit. In one of these, a young man sat transfixed, gazing out at the street. He was smoking a cigarette and drinking wine. Kellerman's *doppelgänger.*

Beyond this young man, the room was blue with the flickering light of a television set. Through the second window, Kellerman could see a bed and, on the bed, a dishevelled young woman propped up with pillows. She was sucking a strand of her own dark hair and staring vacantly at what was on the screen. Because of the heat, she had thrown back the sheet, revealing her naked legs. One bare foot beat time to music Kellerman could barely hear.

Doppelgänger poured more wine into his glass from a bottle taken from the sill beside him. Kellerman thought: *it's me, forty-six years ago, with all my dreams intact. Paris. Women. Fame. And lying in between the shirts and underwear in my suitcase was a manuscript half written that was going to take the world by storm.*

He could see all this—he could read it in the young man's shoulders pushing forward into the dark above the street—in the tilt of his head as he measured out the distances between the roofs. *The rooftops of Paris—out there waiting. Stepping stones all the way to the moon.* And the moon shining down, its aureole touching the city of light.

Bring your stones and bring your chalk, leave your worries on the doorstep ...

Now he was back—with another manuscript half written that would take the world by storm, if only his god-damned publisher would give him time.

5

Kellerman turned away from the window.

Shirley?

She was fast asleep, her breathing gentle and steady. The only sign of tension was the grip she had on the piece of Kleenex in her hand. *My clutch,* she called it. She carried them everywhere—even into the shower, where Kellerman would find them wedged like velvet stones between the liquid soap and the shampoo.

Shirley. Guide and companion—vexing—mysterious— filled with laughter and loaded for action—going to do battle with every kind of darkness, her own and his. And Robert's, in the grave. Mother of three—enraged and stricken with grief that would never end—endowed with boundless astonishment in the face of daughters whose wonders had no limit. Rachel. Miranda. And all their brood.

Kellerman paused on his way to the bathroom and looked down into Shirley's face. *I got me a lioness,* he thought. *What do you think of that, Mister Hemingway! A lioness—and I didn't fire a shot!*

Kissing his fingertips, he laid them against her lips, and like a child with its parent's hand, she kissed them back without waking.

In the bathroom, Kellerman opened a second bottle of Côtes du Rhone and, drinking from its mouth, he toasted himself in the mirror.

"Hello," he whispered. "Welcome back." And took the bottle through the bedroom's darkness to the window.

6

Down below him, the Cognac Widow was dusting and polishing her treasures.

You're mad, dear lady! It's one o'clock in the morning!

And there was music.

What?

He couldn't tell, but it was coming from her windows— her dining-room windows now standing open with the rest. Not a waltz, but a jagged tango, to which she moved with duster in one hand, glass in the other—partnered by ghosts, applauded by dolls and photographs and one bronze horse—her empty vases sprouting flowers and all the cut-glass goblets overflowing with champagne.

Lighting the last of the Gauloise, Kellerman leaned against the window frame, his hip pressed into the sill.

Two bottles of Côtes du Rhone and one whole package of cigarettes.

Well, no. He had shared the first bottle with Shirley. There was her half-empty glass to prove it. And surely these were yesterday's cigarettes—a partial package only—ten at the most. Or twelve.

Whatever. Certainly this was the last of them.

He focused on the Hotel Luxembourg.

Am I still there?

Yes.

Doppelgänger, shirtless now, had risen to his feet and was leaning far out into the night. His head turned upwards, he twisted towards the sky and took a deeply contented breath. Kellerman watched it filling the young man's chest and heard him exhale.

From the bed, the woman called to him: "for God's sake—aren't you ever coming in?"

No—not yet. Don't. Stay out here under the moon. You will never, never, have this moment again. It has to last you all your life ...

Kellerman himself leaned out.

Kellerman—forty-six years on.

And all the rooftops of Paris spread out before him.

With a running start, he could leap from one to the other all the way to the moon.

When he fell to the floor, he thought he must have tripped mid-flight. The last thing he said was: *damn.* But Shirley didn't hear him. She was sitting with her children in her dream.

7

In the morning, when she found him, he was lying on the carpet with the open window above him and his pyjamas soaked in red wine.

Shirley sat down beside him and took his hand. Closing his eyes, she kissed him and tidied his hair and did up the buttons over his heart and took his hand again.

Done. And well done.

Not a shock. No surprise. It had been half expected. Truth to tell, it was why they had come.

Taking Cover

Keath Fraser

L ADIES AND GENTLEMEN, to kick off we'd like to welcome
you officially. Children and singles too.

WHOOP WHOOP WHOOP WHOOP WHOOP...

This is the emergency distress call for anybody locked out
of their rooms during a red alert. Knowing how to whoop
may save your lives.

In a few minutes you will all be shown to rooms that are
sealed hermetically. The different corridors have coloured
handrails and you should remember the colour of yours.
For your own protection it's imperative to stay inside your
rooms as much as possible, because corridors are less well
protected from the radiation outside—and incidentally
more likely to harbour other people's germs. Visiting hours
you'll find posted on the back of every door. But as the
corridors are narrow you should make plans to visit other
rooms well ahead of time to avoid congestion. If the con-
tamination level in the corridors is high they may be closed
for extended periods. Suddenly and without warning. It
should be remembered this auditorium will be closed till
further notice and no public meetings scheduled after you
are admitted to your rooms. This space is contaminated.

The world is contaminated. It's a fate worse than death.

To pet-owners apologies are due. Noah was kinder to pets but Noah had fewer people to accommodate. Since there's a limited supply of uncontaminated air everybody here is in competition. Children shouldn't lose heart. Their pets may prove defiantly resilient outside and even survive this internecine war. Suffice to say the penalty for smuggling in an animal is the pet itself. So no dogs, cats, hamsters, crocs or cockatiels.

On the subject of breath you ought to be aware of the Tibetan Monk Chant. This consumes less oxygen than normal breathing, and has the additional advantage of exercising the lungs. It's also helpful in meditation and relaxation, and serves as a warning to others that introspection is in progress.

m m m m m m m m m m m m m m m m m m m m m m m m
m m m m m A A A A A A A A A H H H H H H H H H
H H H H H ...

This teaches you how to hold your breath for long periods at a stretch by exhaling slowly from the bottom of the spine.

As you will all be here for quite a while, learning how to pass the time is an important means of understanding how to survive. How to manage, how to cope, how to keep your heads above water. You're all in the same boat. So to weather the storm and tide you over, to keep you high and dry as well as steering clear of disaster, here are some rules:

No dumping on your neighbour, okay? No hogging hot water during the shower hour. No showers more than once a week. No loud tape decks. No flushing of toilets in the middle of the night unless absolutely necessary. No metal in the garburetor, olive pits, sanitary napkins, pencil stubs. No pissing in the shower. Otherwise we have a lot of happy-go-lucky refugees doing what they feel like with no regard for the community and the business to hand, i.e., survival through mutual co-operation.

Privacy is privilege. Social shame remains an ethical system. The ways of doing time are oriental.

No people whose word for "yesterday" is different from their word for "tomorrow" can be said to have a loose grip on time.

You are requested to make your beds wash your dishes flush your excrement mop off your tiles dust the furniture polish your mirrors vacuum the carpet recycle your water but remember:

This is no place for the morose. This is a clean well-lighted place. A place in need of your decorating ideas. The vigorous here are in one another's minds the sick in one another's arms the young in one another's dreams. Our theory of space is transformational. This is no place for the languid. No place for the worn-out and despairing, for the self-important the mean the small-talkers. This is no place for the unregenerative. This place is no place you thought would save you.

Nothing transfigures all that dread but you.

Breathe normally so as not to use up more than your share of oxygen. No jogging in the corridors, around rooms, on the spot. Light torso movements all right, likewise isometrics, toe-touching, but no pushups or arm-wrestling. And definitely no aerobics. Dancing's allowed in your own rooms during our hour of recorded dance music every evening, but don't expect heavy rock, Strauss or hoedown. Nor any mournful melodies. Count on foxtrots and the Bossa Nova. Discourage your thirst: the supply of uncontaminated water is strictly rationed.

Where you are going space is constricted and time capacious. Time makes everything happen but space is what you perceive. Being under siege will entice you to temporize. Taking cover will incite feelings of living in a glass house. Resist these temptations. Time's in the imperative. Throw stones against empty walls. You might even survive.

Expect to receive broadcast messages from the theatre of war when and if available. Expect these in nutshells. Don't expect them to harp upon the long and short of expiration. Forget about obituaries. Listen for new ways of understanding old expressions. Of grief, of eating your heart out, of passing away. Of being smashed to smithereens. Give voice from the bottoms of your hearts. Be wise after the event.

Anybody who wants to broadcast on our community station we will list in our weekly program: topics like ceramics, self-improvement, memoirs. Nothing discouraging please. Nothing negative. No goddamn whining to see the stars again. And for heaven's sake, no gardening tips.

Those of you with children will find games and correspondence courses provided. It will be up to parents to educate their children to the new constriction. Unlike some shelters this one encourages children, but it would be delinquent not to remind you that having any more at this time would require a sacrifice you might not like. Childless couples should realize their own space is limited and no new rooms are available should they suddenly give birth. We inform you of this with a heavy heart.

Singles among you should remember that no doubling-up is permitted. The single rooms are just not adequate. Those found co-habiting will be asked to give up one of their rooms to families in need of additional space. A single room needn't be lonely for anybody involved in community activities. We have a small bank of information available about other singles listing their interests and aspirations. Dial the number in the manual by your telephone. Be brief. This shelter is on a party-line and many of you may not be familiar with party-line etiquette.

This is the case with children in the habit of using phones whenever they feel like it. Children should be discouraged from using the phone unless they ask permission. Please, no goddamn pranks. In the last war no one, let alone children, had access to a phone in the underground bogs they used to call shelters. The telephone has been installed to prevent you feeling down in the mouth. Use it wisely.

What else? Golfers are reminded to give up their clubs and putters. They are going to have to replay a lot of life's links in their heads. They're going to have to mow them and hoe them and irrigate them alone. By the way, ladies, there is one hibiscus in every apartment, which likes to be watered once a week with a pinch of fertilizer once a month. If you spot thrips, murder them or they'll eat your root.

WHOOP WHOOP WHOOP—

Always whoop from the abdomen, never the thorax. The worst whoopers will not survive in the event of another bomb. Fallout in the corridors may cause a slow and painful—

Give up what you knew about the good old ways of taking cover. Lay the groundwork for a new way of feeling at home. Lick your rooms into shape. Gird up your loins for a long lean time.

During which it would be better to toy with new ideas and mince no words. Your perception is idiomatic and begs other space. War is hell. War lasts. It is the original sin. Heaven blazing in the head.

When you feel like throwing in the towel when you feel like burning your bridges when you feel like kicking the bucket

just remember: to get a new lease on your room refurbish it. You are apt to believe that grass is greener on the other side of the fence. This is a fatal mistake. Nothing here is the same old story. Not looking for greener pastures, not keeping up with the Joneses, not making a beeline for security. Nothing flies the way of the crow. Out there is definitely no man's land.

You're all in for a long haul. Feeling down in the dumps will become a residential virus. By the look of you, it already has. Expect to find yourselves up the creek without a paddle, fishing in troubled waters, going down for the last time ... But don't give up. The war in the world may disappear. Don't presume, so may the world. Acquire detachment.

In a moment you will be asked to take off your clothes. This act will be your final preparation. Your first precaution to ensure that as little fallout as possible reaches your rooms.

There's no need to be embarrassed. In the end we'll turn out the lights and you may shed your clothes by the light of the Exit sign.

Remember—what you are used to is now old hat. Like pulling up your socks or flying by the seat of your pants. You are accustomed to buttoning up, belting up, pulling yourselves up by the bootstraps. You used to be clothes-horses.

No more. Here your baggage will be stored in lockers until it's safe to return it to you. Everything you require, showers and robes, will be found inside your rooms. Inside your covenants. Inside yourselves. You're among the lucky. You're taking cover.

All your troubles are packed in old kit bags. You've decided that discretion is the better part of valour. Displaced and anxious you are willing to turn the other cheek because the alternative is a slow and painful death.

But cross that river when you come to it. Right now you're tired and anxious to retreat to your rooms where you can cherish old possibilities. Like wading out with the tide on a clear August day dreaming of your best friend's wife's buttocks. Like barbecuing fritters for the gang on your backyard Hibachi. Or playing tag with your spaniel in the park, where he did his business, scratched up the lawn and came bouncing back. Down here we encourage the exchange of snapshot albums. We delight to imagine you seated here. Spitting images.

Yet these are erstwhile pleasures because in the end you may suffer nausea, run out of oxygen, deplete your food, fall apart inside from radiation. Waste away, suffer, go up like smoke under a direct hit, perish.

For the succour of all you will discover in residence an interior decorator. He's another reason to keep your phone free. We encourage the arts and feel the cost of a decorator will meet with your approval. He comes with the shelter and although you will never meet him he'll help to brighten up the dark days and months ahead. His services are subsidized by the questions you admit.

Does anybody exist at the end of the line if he doesn't speak? How else do you know if the forest exists? Why do we need a voice at the end of the line anyway?

Anybody interested in receiving one of his calls can count themselves eligible. He wants you to know he is not a crack-pot. He merely wants to change the way you listen. So when your phone rings and he refuses to speak—give him the time of day. Sit back and take a load off your feet. Let him breathe in your ear.

He speaks in no pictures you'll recognize. He may not even be a he. Listen to him breathe. He is used to reticence, indifference, hangups. He hates darkness and isolation. The darkness he finds obscene. He breathes and even pants.

Your world may light up. It may not. You may call him an impostor. He may be one. Greatness lies not in being strong, but in the right use of strength. Our decorator's strength is in his fingers. He dials, he calls you up with new sets of old numbers, old combinations with new prefixes. He'll try to turn you into voyeurs. The effect could be narcotic. You may feel like rearranging your rooms. You may begin to see the forest for the trees, that you're still in the swim, that unlike Heraclitus you are able to dip your foot in the same river twice.

Pay attention when our decorator in residence rings and fails to reveal himself fails to tip his hand fails to live up to his promise fails to meet you half-way fails to darken your door ...

For in here your received notions of human nature will undergo change. Nature will not survive man's assault on himself. The luxury of ideologies leads only to the grave.

Your blood cannot survive invading anaemia. Your senses cannot survive radiation that blisters your skin cooks your eyes gnaws your eardrums ulcerates your tongue oxidizes your nose.

The sensible thing is to check for leakage every day. Check your gauges. Report changes in levels of radioactivity.

You are all contaminated. All victims of what is everywhere in the air. Take stock of changes in yourselves, any dessication, any deterioration, any convulsions of your tongues. The way you speak measures your degree of resistance to residential virus. To severe dislocation. The penalty down here for talking shop is fallout. It hangs in the air like dust.

m m m m m m m m m m m m m m m m m m m m m m m m
m m m m m A A A A A A A A A H H H H H H H H H
H H H H H ...

Make up your minds to empty them. The dialect here is new. Old-fashioned war permitted a return to normal life every morning. This is no longer possible. Your nightmares last all day every day. There is no way of distinguishing day from night. What you forget no longer exists, what you don't remember no longer infects you:

no more clover in July no more asters in September no more plane trees or lotus or dragonflies in autumn no more milliners no more pianos no more concert halls no more stadiums no more theatres no more chicken coops no more Toyotas not to mention legislatures congresses courts no more brass bands no more lexicography no more Chinese food no more trust company officers no more archery no more bicycles no more comstockery no more Visa and Mastercard no more libraries no more junk mail no more Constantinople no more capuccino ice cream no more gerrymandering no more Sunday newspapers no more hindsight no more friends in cafés no more parachuting no more Hovis bread no more popery no more waterbeds no more stockbrokers no more sciroccos no more adjudications no more blueberry-picking no more lapis lazuli no more ferry schedules no more hugger-muggers no more topping lifts no more donut diners no more cosmography no more eggs no more area codes no more Malvern Hills no more simony no more butter lettuce no more butter no more mystagogues no more jujubes no more store detectives no more Latinists no more cryptography no more kid gloves no more tabernacle choirs no more mergansers no more oysters no more pointillism no more natural light.

No more fresh air. Those who insist on poking your heads outside will return with radiation sickness. You will keep throwing up. You'll lose control of your bowels. You'll bleed from your noses and your ears. Your hair will fall out. You will probably die.

Here while it lasts is a less noxious world. Breathe in, breathe out. You will discover you have noses. You will smell what is denied your common sense, You will smell apple skin in the air, cologne on dogs, chocolate in daffodils. Grass bleeding, a lake stirring, the sea rotting. You will smell the engine-rooms of freighters on the night wind. Train stations, golf balls. Hair in the sun, motel swimming-pools, metronomes. Chicken feed, $10 bills, printer's glue in the spines of books. Shingles in heat, cat gut in racquets, missals in church. Baseballs, teabags, tarpaper. Bark on trees, violins at concerts, cement in mixers, turkey in the straw. Salt marshes and roller-skates. Fingernail filings, African violets, decaying teeth, watchstraps. You will smell turpentine in sagebrush, ammonia in brie, popcorn in lobsters. Sprinklers, pitch, tires on asphalt, suitcase handles, blow holes, Bombay, holy water in fonts, goose shit. You will smell furniture polish at parties, sewing-machine oil in rifle barrels, lights at a play. Spider monkeys, newsprint, lobelia.

Do not believe the source of life is extinguished. Do not believe it isn't. Do not be generous without being kind. Don't believe the quiet person has less to say. Don't be sanguine about the place you're going to. Don't, on the other hand, repine. This is no place for the senseless. Not even if the place makes no sense at all. Your sentence now is life. The idiom can be translated but never commuted. Love starts here in the vernacular.

You may not be Chinese. But you're becoming oriental. You have glittering eyes. Your eyes amid many wrinkles are wise.

The world is on fire. This place is covered. Take off your coats. The light is going out. Stand up and shed all your clothes. Do not be ashamed. Use the light of the Exit sign. Stand up.

Keath Fraser

Tell yourselves not to be afraid. Tell yourselves the fear is in your minds. Address yourselves to the cave inside. Take off all your clothes. The light is going out. Tell yourselves you are taking cover. Tell yourselves to shed the jejune remains of style, your flirtations with persistence, your resolutions to lead less solemn lives. Tell yourselves this place is ideal. Tell yourselves the world is on fire. Tell yourselves the light is going out. Tell yourselves to stand up and take off your clothes. Don't be ashamed. Use the light of the Exit sign. Leave your clothes where they are. Leave yourselves by the Exit light. Stand up. Do not be afraid.

Home Stay

Hiromi Goto

I'VE GOT SINGLE portions of ground beef all froze up in the freezer. That standing one, not the lying down one," Gloria yelled into the phone, across endless prairie miles, endless winter-dried coulees, sorry stretches of willow shrub and, miraculously, into Jun's ear. "We should be back by 11:00 the latest and you can fry up ground beef even if it's froze through. There's spaghetti sauce in the pantry."

Jun pulled the receiver five centimetres away from his head. Nodded in reply.

"Just keep on stirring is all," Gloria shouted.

"Don't burn down the house, ha, ha," Karl bellowed from the background.

"Oh dear," Jun heard Gloria murmuring to her husband as she set down the receiver, "he might not ..." *Click.*

Jun's hands were chilled aching but he could not drop the frozen palmful. His stomach writhed like a salt-sprinkled slug and he could actually feel beads of sweat curling down the bones of his spine. The stuff he had casually unwrapped, the stuff he had found in the upright deep-freeze with its old-fashioned press lock. The stuff was not ground beef.

Five bulbous goldfish.

They were swollen fatter than bursting, eyes protruding gelatinous, each tattered fin, each glittering scale gleamed in a thin casing of ice. Mouths gaped forever.

Salt pooled tidal in the deep of Jun's mouth and he ran to the washroom, hands held out in front of him. Spine convulsing, his stomach milking bile, Jun didn't drop the fish, just ran, cradling the very thing that was making him ill. But he made it, some strange sensibility made him toss the goldfish into the toilet and he bent his back to heave dryly into the sink.

Janine had called his back poetic. Said she could never imagine loving anyone with chest hair now that she'd been with him. Janine said a lot of things and meant them. At the time. But she had left him for good when he bought her "Bay Watch" beach sandals as a souvenir from San Diego.

"How could you?" she'd uttered coldly.

"What do you mean?"

"Do you know what kind of *show* 'Bay Watch' is?"

"Well, it's about lifeguards, I think. Does it matter?"

"Jun," Janine sank down to the floor.

Jun blinked rapidly. Janine was so, well, strong. Never show a weakness or be damned. He squatted down, peered at her face while he blinked and blinked. She swung away from his gaze.

"I'm sorry?" Jun started.

"Jun," Janine pinched her lips until they disappeared inside her mouth. She caught his hands. Clenched. Let them go. "It's not going to work out. I'm sorry. I thought I might get used to it but I can't."

"What?"

Love is never enough.

They had been married thirteen months.

Jun never did figure out exactly what "it" was. He could only begin at the sandals and trace a vague route backwards. The sandals, the Japanese condoms, the butternut squash, the recliner … Gloria and Karl had been horrified. And guilt-ridden.

"It's because we spoiled her something awful, she came to us when we were almost forty," Karl apologized. Bobbing his bearish head.

"She's not a bad girl," Gloria dripped tears. "She just gets set in her ways and nothing can change her mind."

"You're a good son-in-law, Jun. I wasn't none too pleased when we first met, to be honest," Karl confessed, ignoring Gloria's tiny jerk of chin. "I don't hold much on folks marrying people from different countries, hard enough when you're marrying your own. But you're a decent man. Kind. Generous. Janine could have done a lot worse. She probably will," Karl uttered. Picked at a blackened thumbnail that was starting to come off.

"You move on in with us," Gloria offered. "Until you get your bearings, it's the least we can do."

"We need a young guy to look after our livestock!" Karl winked.

Janine had wanted to keep the pizza shop they ran together. Jun didn't care much for pizza or the business, so Janine bought him out, kept their old apartment and Jun moved on in with her parents.

Jun quite liked the chores, the repetitive nature of caring for animals. There was a certain sensible dailiness about it that he slipped into with pleasure. The dawn walk about to look for early dropped calves. Hauling hay and feed to the wintering pasture. Milking the dreamy-eyed Jersey, old-fashioned style. The frantic flurry of chickens, Guinea hens, the wonder of their blue eggs. Slops and hash for the tragic pigs. Jun wished there were horses so he could write postcards to his college friends, "Married a white girl, got divorced. Now I'm a cowboy." Just as well, Jun thought. He'd started noticing that things he'd thought were matter of fact, concrete, weren't necessarily so. A wife. A home. What was solid could turn liquid. It confused him and made him terribly absent-minded. Probably break his neck if he was on a horse.

Jun dabbed toilet paper to the seam of his lips. He ran the faucet even though there was nothing to wash away, concerned that there might be an invisible film of odour on the surface of the sink and Gloria might wonder.

Goldfish! Dead goldfish! What were they doing in the freezer? Jun shivered and clenched his teeth to bite back the curl of salt that rose once more. He couldn't bear to look at them, now bobbing in the toilet bowl like golden blobs of shit. Four hours till Gloria and Karl got home. He'd decide what to do with them after he'd settled his stomach, might help if he ate something. Tomato sauce was out of the question.

The freezer door was still open, cold misting the kitchen. Jun hurried to press it shut and tried not to imagine what else might be frozen inside. A well-loved cat that Gloria and Karl had euthanized? A treasured parakeet? Stillborn puppies? Jun shuddered, wrapped icy arms around his middle. Who could have done this thing? Practical Gloria? Tell-it-like-it-is Karl? What kind of person saved dead gold-fish in a deep freeze?

Jun boiled spaghetti but didn't bother with a sauce, just fried the noodles with a good dab of home-made butter, fresh garlic, salt and parmesan cheese. He liked Gloria's kitchen. She had the habit of keeping a kettle on low boil on the gas stove. For moisture, she said and Jun had taken to the habit too. The thin wet whine was almost compan-ionable. He ate his simple dinner and drank iron-tasting water that came out of Gloria and Karl's well.

"Don't go," his mother had said, looking at the clock that hung above the doorway. The always-on television blared behind his back.

Jun hadn't answered. Blinked. Blinked. Had stared at the hot water pot, plastic decal of a tiger, peeling and brown-curled. It was so old. He should have got her a new one.

"You're the only one now." His Okasan tapped tea leaves into the red-clay tea pot. She palmed the press on the hot water urn, hiss of liquid boiled, spouting. His mother poured tea with her diamond-shaped hands, nudged a cup into his palms. They drank. Jun, sip, sipping. The always-on television, pots dangling on hooks above the sink tinked through the dull roar of a semi-trailer on the raised free-way, Kubotas, next door, laughing over a late dinner, the noodle soup seller playing his plaintive tune, a beacon for the last hungry businessmen straggling off a late subway. Jun sipped and sipped loudly until his cup was empty, until his mother reached out her hand. She poured more tea for him. They drank, filling the pot from the electric urn, nudging cups back and forth until all of the water was gone.

"Well," his Okasan wrapped up sweet bean manju for him to take back to college. "I guess it's time."

Jun ducked his head and slipped his light jacket over his graceful back. The air was sweet with fall and the metal stairs click clacked with his shoes. When he looked up, his mother was not watching from the kitchen window.

His mother never cooked with butter but that was some-thing he'd taken to as well, since living with Gloria and Karl. Janine wouldn't touch the stuff, called it teat grease. Cooked butter always tasted good, but Jun hated the way the stuff congealed after it cooled down. Traces left on his plate squirming with the pattern of pasta, weals of harden-ing grease like sandworm tracks left on the beach. And how awful, the water. When Janine had first taken Jun to visit her parents, and he had tasted their well water, Jun'd spit it back out into the sink. Gloria and Karl had laughed.

"It's because there's so much iron and the water's so hard," Karl had gasped. Wiping his eyes. "You'll get used to it. And you can't even tell when you make up some coffee.

Later on in the day, Jun had poured out the kettle for some tea and was shocked when chunks of white rock fell out. He had thought they were playing a trick on him, hard water, ha, ha. And when he told them this, they burst laughing until they cried, Janine rolling on the linoleum, ran to the washroom, bladder held by desperate hands.

"Come in," his mother had said, a small dimple in her cheek though she wasn't smiling. His Okasan in the steamy pool of the public bath and the water cupped her neck. Jun had taken small, careful steps on slippery tiles. Had placed one foot in the hot liquid.

"Ohhhh," he mouthed. One step. Then another. The silky water sliding up his thin and childish legs, his still baby-blue bum. The public bath echoed with the voices of other small children, laughing with mothers, grand-mothers, aunties. But the steam softened the sounds cloudy. The other patrons were misty shapes, not solid.

"Lie back," his mother murmured. And Jun had. The soft silk heat of liquid surrounding. His mother held him, floating, with only one diamond-shaped hand gently cupping the back of his neck.

Jun smiled. Stopped smiling with a sudden flurry of blinks.

The goldfish. Still in the toilet. Shit. But he didn't feel squeamish anymore. Funny, he thought. Why had he in the first place? He put the frying pan into the sink, plate, cutlery and poured perpetually boiling water on top of everything. Watched the reams of used butter melt away. Jun cleared off the few dishes and tidied up. Ignored the washroom and went in to watch some television.

He never sat in Karl's recliner, some sort of territorial reflex, he wasn't sure, but Karl had etched his body into the leather, and sitting in it would be like sitting in his lap.

"Let's fuck here," Janine had giggled. Gloria and Karl long gone to bed, still chuckling about hard water.

"What?"

"I want to fuck in Karl's chair!" Janine pushed Jun backward so he thumped heavily into the Karl-shaped leather, Janine tugging her sweater over her head as she giggled. Jun withered in his underpants. Janine stuck her tongue between Jun's slender lips, curved her hands down the graceful lines of his back. When Janine slipped her hand inside Jun's waistband, he felt innocuous. An exposed salamander.

"Isn't that just like a man!" Janine had thrown her exaggerated hands into the air and stomped to the basement. Left Jun in the cradle of Karl's lap.

No, Jun sat now, neatly on the beige Sears sofa, feet placed on the shag carpet.

Gloria and Karl didn't have cable and sitcoms held no humour for Jun. He'd heard that that was the last test of whether or not you've accomplished another language. If you could understand humour. Jun blinked and blinked. He stared at the television, the roars of recorded laughter, until Gloria's ridiculous cuckoo clock ground out a sound. 10:30. Gloria and Karl. Shit. Jun's lips curled toward his right cheekbone, a Janine-imitation he had picked up. He hoped that any deep emotional ties Gloria and Karl may have had with the dead goldfish were well frozen. How bonded could a person get to fish anyway? He knew some people in Japan sat in their koi ponds and fed the glorious creatures out of their hands. Koi, he could understand, but really, who in their right mind would have *feelings* for these mutated excuses of pets?

211

Chopsticks would be just the thing to get them out of the toilet with ease, but Karl "would starve to death if they ever had to eat with sticks" so Gloria had none in the house. Jun would have to ladle the carcasses out.

He found a slotted spoon in the third drawer beside the stove, a zip-loc bag in the pantry. He would put those disgusting creatures back in the freezer and next time someone went looking for single portions of ground beef, they'd damn well see what it wasn't before they'd unwrapped it.

Jun nudged the washroom door with his foot. Flicked the light switch on with his elbow. Swallowed. Blinked.

The deformed fish. Those coffins of ice. Melted.

And alive.

They swam in the iron-stained stink of the toilet bowl, swam sluggish circles with gaping gills, tattered fins, remnants of disease. Their popped-O mouths, open, shutting, thawing from an icy sleep into awakening hunger. The tiny hairs on Jun's arms, nape, the curve of his graceful back, they rose and tingled cold crazy. Shuddered almost into wet. My god. My god. A miracle. A sick sick miracle. A portent. A fucking sign. He made a small noise. Ladle clattering to the floor.

"What—Jun? Are you okay?" Gloria knocked at the partially open bathroom door. She was pushed in by Karl, crowding, concerned. Together, they peered at Jun, caught movement in the toilet bowl, pressed forward to stare into the toilet. Gloria and Karl, their eyes popped, bulged in disbelief, mouths O in wonder and Jun guffawed, couldn't hold it back, gasped hysterical from the pit of his belly. He bellowed, one hand holding his gut and the other pointing to the miracle of fishes, pointing back to Gloria and Karl. He convulsed with laughter, unable to stop, barely able to stand.

Gloria pinched her lips inside her mouth.

Karl flushed the toilet.

Jun's body contorted, gasping, tears streaming down his face, choking laughter like vomit. It's not funny! he thought, there's nothing funny, only to be torn apart with an explosive guffaw. Gloria lowered the lid of the bowl and determinedly sat Jun down. He gulped air, erupting with convulsive gasps, swallowing it into his slender body. Trembling with the effort. Gloria reached out both arms and pulled Jun's face into her soft bosom.

She smelled like baby powder.

Jun blinked. Blinked.

Jun wondered if he ought to move his head side to side between the cushy orbs of Gloria's breast.

Jun wondered if this was a motherly gesture on Gloria's part or if he was supposed to get physically excited. Perhaps both at the same time, in that Occidental way?

Jun wondered what good ol' Karl was thinking.

He pulled, his head slightly back and tipped his eyes upwards. Karl loomed over Gloria's shoulder. A grin on his bearish face, he gave Jun a thumbs-up sign. Jun shook his head slightly.

"There, there," Gloria murmured, Stroking Jun's glossy hair with one hand, keeping his head in her bosom with the other. "There, there."

What should he do? Jun wondered. What did they mean? Something felt terribly off but he couldn't put words to it, it only yawned before him in growing darkness and he scrambled away from the crumbling edge. The goldfish, Jun thought, just think about the goldfish.

"Goldfish," he muttered.

"Shhhh, shhhhhhh," Gloria murmured. "They're gone now, don't worry your head about it." She tipped her head toward Jun, and Karl knelt down in front of him. Karl slipped one arm under the back of Jun's knees, and one cradled his back, Karl lifted Jun up like he was an injured animal, a well-loved pet and Jun's eyes gasped open.

A grown man! Carried like this! Jun could feel the verge, the tip of the chasm and he shuddered, shuddered at the incredible depths, the vertigo plunge and—and—

"He must be freezing!" Karl exclaimed.

"It's the shock," Gloria said, decisively. "Let's put him in our room. We can turn up the heat on the waterbed."

Gloria pulled back the satiny covers and Karl deposited Jun on the unstable surface. It sloshed beneath him like nausea. The sheets smelled of Gloria's baby powder, Karl's hand cream, and Jun's teeth chattered though he hadn't thought he was cold, Karl leaned over him to unbutton his shirt, Gloria tugging the socks off his feet.

Someone started tugging on the fly of his jeans.

"Yamete," Jun whispered, clutching at his pants.

"Leave him be," he heard Gloria advise. Her voice low. "He can sleep with his jeans on for one night, at least. Poor pet. He can sleep between us and we'll keep him warm."

"He's shivering away!" Karl exclaimed. "You've got to fatten him up some, Glory, he's all skin and bones. He's lighter than you are!"

"Oh, you stop!" Gloria giggled. Tucking the satiny comforter firmly around Jun's slender neck.

"Do you think, ah," Karl coughed, "the child's been a bit touched?"

"Oh honey, I just don't know." Gloria smoothed the hair from Jun's brow and he stared upward. Not blinking. "We can't really know what he's thinking, can we?"

"He's like a son to me, a real son," Karl stated.

"He's as pretty as a cat," Gloria murmured. She changed into her flannel nightdress and sloshed into bed. Sat up, absentmindedly stroking Jun's glossy hair, watched Karl put on his pyjamas.

"Leave the hall light on. In case he gets worse during the night," Gloria called out. So Karl just switched off the bedroom light, the weight of the door slowly swinging itself shut. And as Karl sloshed into the bed on the other side of Jun, their middle-aged backs fencing him in between them, the door slowly closed and the wedge of light slivered into darkness.

Totem

Thomas King

BEEBE HILL stood at the reception desk of the Southwest Alberta Art Gallery and Prairie Museum and drummed her fingers on the counter until Walter Hooton came out of the director's office. She was annoyed, she told Walter, and she thought other people were annoyed, too, but were too polite to complain about the noises the totem pole in the far corner of the room was making.

"It sounds like gargling."

Walter assured her that there wasn't a totem pole in the entire place including the basement and the storage room. The current show, he explained, featured contemporary Canadian art from the Atlantic provinces.

"It's called 'Seaviews,'" Walter said, smiling with all his teeth showing. There had been, he admitted, a show on Northwest Coast carving at the gallery some nine years back, and, as he recalled, there might have been a totem pole in that exhibit.

Mrs. Hill, who was fifty-eight and quite used to men who smiled with all their teeth showing, took his hand and walked him to the back of the gallery. "Gargling," said Beebe. "It sounds like gargling."

Mrs. Hill and Mr. Hooton stood and looked at the corner for a very long time. "Well," said the director finally, "it certainly looks like a totem pole. But it doesn't sound at all like gargling. It sounds more like chuckling."

Mrs. Hill snorted and tossed her head over her shoulder. And what, she wanted to know, would a totem pole have to chuckle about. "In any case," said Mrs. Hill, "it is quite annoying and I think the museum should do something about the problem." It would be a fine world, she pointed out, if paintings or photographs or abstract sculptures began carrying on like that.

Walter Hooton spent much of the afternoon going over the museum's records in an attempt to find out who owned the totem pole or where it had come from. At four o'clock, he gave up and called Larue Denny in the storeroom and asked him to grab Jimmy and a hand cart and meet him in the gallery.

"The problem," Walter explained to the two men, "is that this totem pole is not part of the show, and we need to move it someplace else."

"Where do you want us to take it," Larue wanted to know. "Storeroom is full."

"Find some temporary place, I suppose. I'm sure it's all a mistake, and when the secretary comes back on Monday, we'll have the whole thing straightened out."

"What's that sound?" asked Larue.

"We're not sure," said the director.

"Kinda loud," said Jimmy.

"Yes, it was bothering some of the patrons."

"Sort of like laughing," said Larue. "What do you think, Jimmy?"

Jimmy put his ear against the totem pole and listened. "It's sort of like a chant. Maybe it's Druidic."

"Druidic!"

"There was this movie about Druids on a flight from England to New York ... they did a lot of chanting ... the Druids ..."

Larue told Jimmy to tip the totem pole back so they could get the dolly under the base. But the totem pole didn't move. "Hey," he said, "it's stuck."

Larue pushed on the front, and Jimmy pulled on the top, and nothing happened. "It's really stuck."

Walter got on his hands and knees and looked at the bottom. Then he took his glasses out of their case and put them on. "It appears," he said, "that it goes right through the floor."

Both Larue and Jimmy got down with the director. Larue shook his head. "It doesn't make any sense," he said, "because the floor's concrete. I was here when they built this building, and I don't remember them pouring the floor around a totem pole."

"We could get the chainsaw and cut it off close to the floor," Jimmy volunteered.

"Well, we can't have it making noises in the middle of a show on seascapes," said Walter. "Do what you have to do, but do it quietly."

After the gallery closed for the evening, Larue and Jimmy took the chainsaw out of its case and put on their safety goggles. Larue held the totem pole and Jimmy cut through the base, the chain screaming, the wood chips flying all around the gallery, Some of the larger chips bounced off the paintings and left small dents in the swirling waves and the glistening rocks and the seabirds floating on the wind. Then they loaded the totem pole on a dolly and put it in the basement near the boiler.

"Listen to that," said Jimmy, knocking the sawdust off his pants. "It's still making that noise."

When Walter arrived at the gallery on Monday morning, the secretary was waiting for him. "We have a problem, Mr. Hooton," she said. "There is a totem pole in the corner, and it's grunting."

"Damn!" said Hooton, and he called Larue and Jimmy.

"You're right," said Larue after he and Jimmy had looked at the totem pole. "It does sound like grunting. Doesn't sound a thing like the other one. What do you want us to do with this one?"

"Get rid of it," said Walter. "And watch the paintings this time."

Larue and Jimmy got the chainsaw and the safety goggles and the dolly, and moved the totem pole into the basement alongside the first one.

"That wasn't hard," said the director.

"Those grunts were pretty disgusting," said the secretary.

"Yes, they were," agreed Walter.

After lunch, the totem pole in the corner of the gallery started shouting, loud, explosive shouts that echoed through the collection of sea scenes and made the paintings on the wall tremble ever so slightly. When Walter returned, the secretary was sitting at her desk with her hands over her ears.

"My God!" said Walter. "How did this happen?"

That evening, Walter and Larue and Jimmy sat in Walter's office and talked about the problem. "The trick I think," said Larue, "is to cut the pole down and then cover the stump with pruning paste. That way it won't grow back."

"What about the shouting?"

"Well, you can't hear it much from the basement."

"Alright," said Walter. "We'll give that a try. How many poles are in storage?"

"Three with this one, and we haven't got room for any more."

The next day, the totem pole in the corner was singing. It started with a high, wailing, nasal sound and then fell back into a patient, rhythmic drone that gave Walter a huge headache just above his eyes and made him sweat.

"This is getting to be a real problem," he told Larue and Jimmy. "If we can't solve it, we may have to get some government assistance."

"Provincial?"

"It could be more serious than that," said Walter.

"Maybe we should just leave it," said Jimmy.

"We can't just leave it there," said the director. "We need the space for our other shows, and we can't have it singing all the time, either."

"Maybe if we ignore it, it will stop singing," said Jimmy. "It might even go away or disappear or something. Besides, we don't have any place to put it. Maybe, after a while, you wouldn't even notice it ... like living next to the train tracks or by a highway."

"Sure," said Larue, who was tired of cutting down totem poles and trying to find space for them. "Couldn't hurt to give that a try."

The totem pole stayed in the corner, but Jimmy and Larue were right. After the first week, the singing didn't bother Walter nearly as much, and, by the end of the month, he hardly noticed it at all.

Nonetheless, Walter remained mildly annoyed that the totem pole continued to take up space and inexplicably irritated by the low, measured pulse that rose out of the basement and settled like fine dust on the floor.

How Can a Black Writer Find His Way in This Jungle?

Dany Laferière
translated by David Homel

I WAS SITTING in the park thinking about it all. For instance, what can I talk about next?

"Me."

"What?"

"Talk about me."

I turned around. A young black woman was standing there. Insolent mouth, red fingernails, firm breasts. A burning package of rock-hard desire, held in check by an iron will. The kind that won't let go of the piece she's sunk her teeth into. Pearly white teeth, by the way, but that's a cliché.

"Excuse me, but I'm not following."

"How could you not? You're a writer, and you're looking for a subject. Well, I'm the subject."

"Why should I write about you?"

"You give too much press to white women, if you ask me."

"You have no reason to envy the coverage, I assure you."

"Curse me or praise me, as long as you talk about me and spell my name right—that's what they say."

"What's your name?"

"Erzulia."

"You know that's the name of a dreadful voodoo goddess."

"Of course. And I can be just as cruel as she is."

"I suppose you're used to getting what you want."

She smiled briefly. Scarcely moved the corner of her mouth.

"Let's say I agree to write about you … But you understand, this isn't Oxfam or CARE here. There are no holds barred. Would you agree to any kind of portrait?"

"I don't know how to write, but I know what a book is. I can't stand complacency. When a book isn't honest, I throw it away."

"I can tell you understand the problem."

"I'm no fool. I know, I look young …"

"Why do you want to be in a book when you know very well you might get massacred?"

"I want to be famous. That's it. I'm no different from anybody else."

"Everybody isn't famous."

"Those who aren't don't exist."

A pause.

"I see …"

"Especially in my line of work. I have three strikes against me: I'm black, I'm a woman, and I'm not famous."

"But you're sexy."

"They know they can have that for free—if not from me, then from someone else. Guys don't give you anything for that any more. A piece of ass isn't worth a red cent. Besides, they're all fags. Nothing shaking in that neighbourhood."

"Why me?"

"I'm tired of listening to black writers advertising for white women. White writers only talk about white women. So now with black writers onto white women, too, we don't stand a chance."

"We're only trying to protect you."

"Go fuck yourself."

"Maybe you're not a proper subject."

"How can that be?"

"If a white writer starts fantasizing about you on the page, he'll be accused of colonialism."

"That *is* a problem …"

"And if a black writer writes about you, you both end up in the ghetto."

"And when white writers write about white women, which they do one hundred percent of the time, what does that produce? Incest?"

"Now, listen—"

"Don't talk to me like that, you remind me of my father. And that's no compliment, believe you me."

"You don't leave the others much room."

"I'm being honest with you, and I don't give a shit if you like it or not."

"I'm trying to tell you that it's difficult to talk freely about someone who's in an inferior position."

"God, are you complicated! Do you always talk that way?"

"I'm just trying to make myself understood."

"That's right, take me for an idiot."

"I'm saying that a black writer can get away with expressing his most violent fantasies about white women without creating too large a scandal because the white woman is higher than the black man on the Judeo-Christian social scale. As soon as you get the power to realize your fantasies, it becomes harder to express them."

"You really believe that nonsense? You don't think that machos express themselves? They're all we hear about in the papers, on TV, at the movies. I got it all figured out: all men think about is fucking women, whether they're black, red, white or yellow, rich or poor, big or little, healthy or handicapped, Catholic or Protestant. I know from personal experience."

Her eyes challenged the entire world.

"All men don't think just about women," I said.

She burst out laughing. True, physical laughter, the laughter of someone who's essentially honest.

"You're right. One point for you. All men don't think just about women."

"There's more to life than sex."

"There's only sex," she replied definitively.

The two camps had said everything they had to say on the subject.

"I want you to put me in your book."

"Back to square one! I still believe that a black writer portraying a black female character doesn't provide enough contrast. Why don't you consult a white writer?"

"I'm starting with you."

"Why not a woman? There are women writers around, these days."

"They don't interest me."

"A woman would understand you better."

"Women aren't any good unless they're talking about men."

"That's not my opinion."

"It's not the way you think it is, either. Women have a bone to pick with men. Talking about men gets them mad, and that's when they start getting good."

"I think that women know men better than they know themselves," I argued, "since they spend three-quarters of their time with men."

"You're beating around the bush. Is it too much to ask to be in your book?"

"I don't know if you've ever heard of freedom of expression."

"You know what you can do with your freedom of expression! You wrote a book to get famous; I want the same thing you do. I want to be in your next book for the same reason. I don't care what you write about me, and to be perfectly honest, I don't even think I'll read your book. If you weren't famous, I wouldn't waste my time telling you my life story. That's all I'm asking ... Check you later!"

She headed towards a group of musicians playing by the park entrance. I watched her. She was facing the sun. Then she turned and came striding back towards me.

"What do you care whether I'm in your book or not? I've got everything I need to be in a book, and you can't imagine what I might do!"

Nipple Gospel

Suzette Mayr

I AM THE DAUGHTER of the daughter of a Baptist preacher and when I see the reverend, my grandfather, his cardboard face resting comfortably in our album, all I see is God. A face bright, black and noble. Dead years before I was born. But alive in our house, under my baby fingers.

The Bible under his thick, wrinkled two-toned fingers crushes the pulpit. A photograph album that lies forever open. White pencil letters written on black. Gold leaf letters HOLY BIBLE stamped also on black.

1

My face brown and squished against the inside of the car window. Stick my tongue out and taste the cool, bitter glass.

Perfumed slap of mother's church program on the top of my head. Focus on the back of her perfumed head, the naked scalp under her hair.

Comic books colour in the story of Samson and Delilah, read it in the back seat of the navy-blue Fiat, advertised as a family car and much much more. The backs of my bare legs stick to the vinyl seats. Trace the imprint of the vinyl stitching down the reddened skin on the backs of my thighs.

Delilah and her tight, naked belly stretched over Samson, scissors stretched over long, thick, brown hair.

2

Parable of the wise and foolish virgins but really a Sunday school cartoon about twelve fish carrying lamps to their clam shell homes. Look for spilled pearls among the oyster people. If I had a pearl, I would keep it in my month, cup it in the bowl of my tongue. A virgin is a fish.

3

Red and green sprinkled shortbread cookies and milk, paper dolls coloured in of the baby Jesus. Paper angels dangle crayon-scrawled from the lowest branches of the Christmas tree. I wear my favourite shoes with the strap across the top to the Sunday school Christmas party. I look hotter than hot.

4

The daughter of the daughter of a Baptist preacher, children are bought in grocery stores, found in parsley patches, retrieved from hospitals, the back seats of cars.

> Look what Mum and I found for you, a baby brother!

I know where brothers come from, found a baby blanket in the back garden. Bring my friends over for a look.

Mothers shit babies, they tell me, and you were almost flushed down the toilet. That girl from down the street has hair long and soft brown and her mouth twists out words: nooky, vagina, stupid anus, shit. I think of dogs licking their bums and genitals touching. My father in the tub, baby brother and I play tidal pool and rubber ducks in his navel.

He stands up from the bath, hot dripping steamy, his penis curled, a baby banana.

First the baby cube of bread, then the baby cup of purple juice.

Can I take the cup home mummy?

Perfumed slap on the arm, don't talk so loud in church. We stand up and sing. Can see mother's bra through the front of her blouse.

5

Christmas. Mother's see-through shirt tucked under a tailored lady's jacket. Take the candle home from the service, the corners of my mouth tucked cooky crumbles, cookies in the shape of bloated preggers Mary on a donkey.
Climb that night into bed. Think of Mary's premarital sex. Her see-through shirts.

6

Steam erupts tears and I have my period for the very first time. Underwear smeared with rust and ping pong nipple buds. Why not just a paper bag over my head? Who am I she her can't be me. Underwear bloodied and smoky. Wrestle oozy blood clots. The brown varnish of blood-stained pews.

Getting kind of big in the hips there?

Hey you growin' boobs there?

Nibble the bits of skin on the insides of my cheeks, pull at the pimples on my scalp until they bleed, run cool and soggy under my hair.

7

Lilies ache cylindrical. The bell of his trumpet, mouth-piece jammed against his lips. I don't know his name, only know his smell, only know the pressure of those lips on that instrument, his lily blossom. The sight of his Adam's apple pings nipple tips. Forehead and armpits generate glue sweat and bumps.

God punishes me for being a nerd. Spills milk down the front of my blouse right when the trumpet player stands a cooky-plate away. Makes snot bubbles grow from my nose, slime and phlegm surfaces crack in my throat. Does he even know I exist? Do you even know I exist?

Huh, what did you say? (Man, what a nerd)

And he follows another girl, big and blonde and smelling so good. Those lips. Jammed against the mouth piece of his trumpet, jammed against that girl. Wise and foolish virgins. I am a troubled, aching fish.

8

She talks on the telephone and I hear. I hear: Church? no we gave up going a while back. She still goes though. Think it's because she's in love with a boy in the church band. That's right, the pimply-faced one.

Rudiments of math, count on my fingers forward, June July August September October November December January February. But my parents were married August. Click click hum of flesh calculators.

You did that? You had sex before marriage.
Mum?

Grandfather grumbles in his two-dimensions, crushes
the pulpit harder, a good thing he died when he did, otherwise he would have had a heart attack. His daughter,
premaritally sexed and unmarried. My heart and lung
seizures almost only just about a bastard I could have have
have been. Pregnant wedding photos none of the above.
Pregnant wedding photos only a grandfather two-toned
fingers crushing pulpits. Flash of my mother's embarrass-
ment, of a photograph in a certain slant of light. Cardboard
picture frowns. Think of the burning down there. Down
there. Between my legs at night.

Stumble through begats and begones to drown out my
body's clamouring, chant rabid the Lord's Prayer and sing
loudly, too loudly, through choking candle smoke.
Christmas carols, Praise the Lords God help the hymns preserve me. He raises his trumpet to his lips in celebration.

Nipples titter and pop.

Trumpet jammed against his lips. Crush ping-pong ball
breasts with the black leathered HOLY BIBLE, notice the
second trumpet watching me, watching me. The short
bristles on his upper lip.

9

I hear: These days she even goes to evening service. I didn't
even go that often and my father was a preacher.
My body split in half. Chest swaddled in floral prints,
covered shoulders and two layers of underwear. From the
hips up a fish. Legs too smooth under the skirt, too ready,

too smoothly joined to my hips. Warm and flexible. From the hips down down down. Keep my knees in tight oh so tight, grandfatherly and reverently tight.

Help me Lord.

Sucked down by the short warm bristles on his upper lip. Uncross my arms, flex the biceps. Virginity unwrapped and ready.

Forehead squished against the glass, the inside of the car window. His trumpet in the trunk and hands down the pants, up the blouse, asses cupped. His forehead squished against the glass leaves fog smears.

Almost but not quite.

Around my lips and on the chin, the skin breaks out in a rash from his bristles.

What's that rash you been messing with the next door neighbour's dog again when you gonna learn dogs and your skin don't mix?

10

There is no use in praying now. Can't hear myself over the racket my body makes. Nipples clatter and between my legs the roar of the clitoris. Close the cover of the photograph album on the reverend's face. Close it firmly. Close it squarely. Tired of the trumpet, try the oboe on for size. The hair on his face is softer, face doesn't burn with rash.

11

Nothing but the tick tick of the clock in the hall. I am older, fertile. I have forgotten how to pray.

The smell of mother's insomniac cigarettes hovers until late at night; gentle layer of smoke, smooth low-lying clouds under the kitchen lamp. My glass-wrinkled forehead, the hardening moisture inside my pants clammy as I dance on the tips of my feet up the stairs to my bed. Watch out for mother's suspicious eyes. Eyes without whites.

Are you sleeping with that boy?

Nod, too tired to lie, too wet to stand up straight. Rub the love-sexy forehead, then my cheek, raw from male bristles.

You keep on this way, you open your legs to any and every man you meet and you'll have slept with an entire football team by the time you're twenty-four.

You keep opening your legs this way you're gonna be dead from VD by the time you ready to get married. If you get married. No one wants to marry a slut.

Open legs. Open books, open car doors, open cartons of milk, open the mail. I love to get mail, slice open all my envelopes with a long, thin, straight knife, no scissors for this girl. Scissors are for naked-bellied wimps. Mother frowns. Her lips sizzle and crack cigarette curses.

You did that? You had sex before marriage? Mum?

Whisper echoes.

12

I hear: All that religious education. Wasted.

Her wisdom cupped in the bowl of my tongue, slides down my throat. Her curse lodged in the side of my uterus spreads rat gnawing guilt. Back of my scalp tickles and I itch. I itch.

Yeast infected bath water bubbles to the surface. My throat bubbles and moans. I cry so hard, cannot speak, drown from shame in the bathtub, my concave belly a tidal pool. Just enough water to place my nose and mouth in. Breath in bubble bath. Then she'll be sorry. My daughter the slut. Then she'll be sorry. Inhale inhale inhale cough up lungs and bubbles.

The daughter of the daughter of the Baptist preacher, my body burns with yeast and curses. Nipples chatter, wet from the cold of the air outside the warm tub water, the rough dryness of the towel rubbed across my breasts.

Think carefully of sewing my split hymen back together, put back to right what has been wronged. Light brown thread in the sewing basket, and a thin, curved needle. Sew sew sew myself up so tight can't get a needle up there let alone a penis.

The silence of my body, hymen-broken, kills the florals, loosens the underwear and attaches megaphones to my nipples. Sermons loud and clear.

13

I hear: Oh I don't know. Taking a bath and talking to herself.

As usual.

Art

Leon Rooke

I TOLD THE woman I wanted that bunch down near the pine grove by the rippling stream.

Where the cow is? she asked.

I told her yep, that was the spot.

She said I'd have to wait until the milking was done.

The cow mooed a time or two as we waited. It was all very peaceful.

How much if you throw in the maiden? I asked.

Without the cow? she asked, or *with*?

Both would be nice, I said.

But it turned out a Not For Sale sign had already gone up on the girl. Too bad. It was sweet enough with her out of the picture, but not quite the same.

I took my cut bunch of flowers and plodded on behind the cow over to the next field. I wanted a horse too, if I could get one cheap.

Any horses? I asked.

Not today, they said.

Strawberries?

Not the season, I was told.

At home, I threw out the old bunch and put the new crop in a vase by the picture window so the wife might marvel at them when she came in from her hard day's grind.

I staked the cow out front where the grass was still doing pretty well.

It was touch-and-go, whether we'd be able to do the milking ourselves. It would be rough without a shed or stall.

Oh, hand-painted! the wife said when she came in.

I propped her up in the easy chair and put up her feet. She looked a trifle wind-blown.

Hard day? I asked.

So-so, she said.

I mixed up a gin and tonic, nice as I knew how, and lugged that in.

A touch flat, she said, but the lemon wedge has a nice effect.

I pointed out the cow, which was tranquilly grazing.

Sweet, she said. Very sweet. What a lovely idea.

I put on the stereo for her.

That needle needs re-doing, she observed. The tip needs retouching, I mean.

It will have to wait until tomorrow, I told her.

She gave me a sorrowful look, though one without any dire reproach in it. She pecked me a benign one on the cheek. A little wet. I wiped it off before it could do any damage.

The flowers were a good thought, she said. I appreciate the flowers.

Well, you know how it is, I said. What I meant was that one did the best one could—though I didn't really have to tell her that. It was what she was always telling me.

She was snoozing away in the chair as I tiptoed off to bed.

I was beginning to flake a little myself. Needed a good touch-up job from an expert.

We all do, I guess. The dampness, the mildew, the rot—it gets into the system somehow.

Not much to be done about it, however.

I thought about the cow. Wondered if I hadn't made a mistake on that. Without the maiden to milk her, there didn't seem to be much point in having a cow. Go back tomorrow, I thought. Offer a good price for the maiden, the stream, and the whole damned field.

Of course, I could go the other way: find a nice seascape somewhere. Hang that up.

Well, sleep on it, I thought.

The wife slipped into bed about two in the morning. That's approximate. The paint job on the hour hand wasn't holding up very well. The undercoating was beginning to show through on the entire clock face, and a big crack was developing down in the six o'clock area.

Shoddy goods, I thought. Shoddy artisanship.

Still, we'd been around a bit. Undated, unsigned, but somewhere in the nineteenth century was my guess. It was hard to remember. I just wished the painter had been more careful. I wished he'd given me more chest, and made the bed less rumpled.

Sorry, baby, she said. Sorry I waked you.

She whispered something else, which I couldn't hear, and settled down far away on her side of the bed. I waited for her to roll into me and embrace me. I waited for her warmth, but she remained where she was and I thought all this very strange.

What's wrong? I said.

She stayed very quiet and did not move. I could feel her holding herself in place, could hear her shallow, irregular breathing, and I caught the sweep of one arm as she brought it up to cover her face. She started shivering.

I am so sorry, she said. I am so sorry. She said that over and over.

Tell me what's wrong, I said.

No, she said, please don't touch me, please don't, please don't even think about touching me. She went on like this for some seconds, her voice rising, growing in alarm, and I thought to myself: Well, I have done something to upset her, I must have said or done something unforgivable, and I lay there with my eyes open wide, trying to think what it might be.

I am so sorry, she said. So very very sorry.

I reached for her hand, out of that hurting need we have for warmth and reassurance, and it was then that I found her hand had gone all wet and muddy and smeary.

Don't! she said, oh please don't, I don't want you to hurt yourself!

Her voice was wan and low and she had a catch in her voice and a note of forlorn panic. I lifted my hand away quickly from her wetness, though not quickly enough for I knew the damage already had been done. The tips of my fingers were moist and cold, and the pain, bad enough but not yet severe, was slowly seeping up my arm.

My drink spilled, she said. She snapped that out so I would know.

Christ, I thought. Oh Jesus Christ. God help us.

I shifted quickly away to the far side of the bed, my side, away from her, far as I could get, for I was frightened now and all I could think was that I must get away from her, I must not let her wetness touch me any more than it had.

Yes, she said shivering, do that, stay there, you must try and save yourself, oh darling I am so sorry.

We lay in the darkness, on our backs, separated by all that distance, yet I could still feel her warmth and her tremors and I knew there was nothing I could do to save her.

Her wonderful scent was already going and her weight on the bed was already decreasing.

I slithered up high on the sheets, keeping my body away from her, and ran my good hand through her hair and down around her warm neck and brought my face up against hers.

I know it hurts, I said. You're being so brave.

Do you hurt much? she said. I am so terribly, terribly sorry. I was dozing in the chair and opened my eyes and saw the dark shape of the cow out on the lawn and for an instant I didn't know what it was and it scared me. I hope I haven't hurt you. I've always loved you and the life we had in here. My own wounds aren't so bad now. I don't feel much of anything anymore. I know the water has gone all through me and how frightful I must look to you. Oh please forgive me, it hurts and I'm afraid I can't think straight.

I couldn't look at her. I looked down at my own hand and saw that the stain had spread. It had spread up to my elbow and in a small puddle where my arm lay, but it seemed to have stopped there. I couldn't look at her. I knew her agony must be very great and I marveled a little that she was being so brave for I knew that in such circumstances I would be weak and angry and able to think only of myself.

Water damage, I thought, that's the hardest part to come to terms with. The fear that's over you like a curse. Every day you think you've reconciled yourself to it and come to terms with how susceptible you are, and unprotected you are, and then something else happens. But you never think you will do it to yourself.

Oil stands up best, I thought. Oh holy Christ why couldn't we have been done in oil.

You get confident, you get to thinking what a good life you have, so you go out and buy yourself flowers and a goddamn cow.

I wish I could kiss you, she moaned. I wish I could.

My good hand was already behind her neck and I wanted to bring my head down on her breasts and put my hand there too. I wanted to close my eyes and stroke her all over and lose myself in the last sweetness I'd ever know.

I will too, I thought. I'll do it.

Although I tried, I couldn't, not all over, so I stroked my hand through her hair and rolled my head over till my lips gently touched hers.

She sobbed and broke away.

It's too much, she said. I'm going to cry. I am, I know I am.

Don't, I said. Don't. If you do that will be the end of you.

The tears burst and I spun above her, wrenching inside, gripping the sheet and wiping it furiously about her eyes.

I can't stop it! she said. It's no use. It burns so much but I can't stop it, it's so sad but I've got to cry!

She kept on crying.

Soon there was just a smear of muddled color on the pillow where her face had been, and then the pillow was washing away.

The moisture spread, reaching out and touching me, filling the bed until at last it and I collapsed on the floor.

Yet the stain continued widening.

I had the curious feeling that people were already coming in, that someone already was disassembling our frame, pressing us flat, saying, "Well here's one we can throw out. You can see how the house, the cow, etc., have all bled together. You can't recognize the woman anymore, or see that this once was a bed and … well it's all a big puddle except those flowers. Flowers are a dime a dozen but these are pretty good, we could snip out the flowers, I guess, give them their own small frame. Might fetch a dollar or two, what do you say?

Railroading
or:
Twelve Small Stories With The Word "Train" In The Title

Diane Schoemperlen

Love Train

FOR A LONG time after Lesley and Cliff broke up, Cliff was always sending her things.

Flowers.

Red roses by the dramatic dozen.

Delicate frilly carnations dyed turquoise at the edges (which reminded Lesley of a tradition they'd observed at her elementary school on Mother's Day when each child had to wear a carnation, red if your mother was alive, white if she was dead—there were only two kids in the whole school whose mothers were dead—and what then, she wondered, was turquoise meant to signify?)

A single white orchid nestled in tissue paper in a gold box, as if they had a big date for a formal dance.

Cards. Funny cards:

"I thought you'd like to know that I've decided to start dating seals again, and ...oh yes, my umbilical cord has grown back!"

Sentimental cards:

"I love wearing the smile ... you put on my face!"

Funny sentimental cards:

"You You You You You You You You You You You

You … These are a few of my favourite things!"

Apology cards:

"Please forgive me … my mouth is bigger than my brain!"

and:

"I'm sorry, I was wrong … Well, not as wrong as you, but sorrier!"

Pretty picture cards to say:

"Happy Thanksgiving!"
"Happy Hallowe'en!"
"I'm just thinking of you"
"I'm always thinking of you"
"I'm still thinking of you!"

Letters. Mostly letters.

Often Cliff would call during the day and leave a message on Lesley's answering machine, apologizing for having bothered her with another card or letter when she'd already told him, in no uncertain terms, that she needed some space. Then he would call right back and leave another message to apologize for having left the first one when she'd already told him to leave her alone.

He did not send the letters through the mail in the conventional way, but delivered them by hand in the middle of the night. Lesley never did catch him in the act, but she could just picture him parking his car halfway down the block, sneaking up her driveway in the dark or the rain, depositing another white envelope in her black mailbox. Where she would find it first thing in the morning.

At first it gave Lesley the creeps to think of Cliff tippy-toeing around out there while she was inside sleeping, but then she got used to hearing from him in this way. She took to checking the mailbox every morning before she put the coffee on. Waiting in her housecoat and slippers for the toast to pop and the eggs to poach, she would study the envelope first. Sometimes he put her full name on it, first and last; sometimes her first name only; once, just her initials.

Inside, the letters were always neatly typewritten on expensive bond paper. They began with phrases like "Well no ... " or "And yes ... " or "But maybe ..., " as if Cliff were picking up a conversation (one-sided though it might be) right in the middle where they'd left off, or as if he still thought he could still read her mind.

One of the first letters was dense with scholarly historical quotes on the nature of war. Cliff had set these erudite excerpts carefully off from the rest of the text, single-spaced and indented:

> In quarrels between countries, as well as those between individuals, when they have risen to a certain height, the first cause of dissension is no longer remembered, the minds of the parties being wholly engaged in recollecting and resenting the mutual expressions of their dislike. When feuds have reached that fatal point, all considerations of reason and equity vanish; a blind fury governs, or rather, confounds all things. A people no longer regards their interest, but rather the gratification of their wrath. (John Dickson)

And later in the letter he wrote:

The strange thing about this crisis of August 1939

was that the object between Germany and Poland was not clearly defined, and could not therefore be expressed as a concrete demand. It was a part of Hitler's nature to avoid putting things in a concrete form; to him, differences of opinion were questions of power, and tests of one's nerves and strength. (Ernst von Weizäcker)

Lesley could not imagine that Cliff actually had a repertoire of such pedantic passages floating around inside his head, just waiting for an opportunity to be called up. But she couldn't imagine that he had really gone to the library and looked them up in order to quote them at her either.

Still, this letter made her mad enough to call him. When she said on the phone, "I don't take kindly to being compared to Hitler, thank you very much," Cliff said, "Don't be ridiculous. That's not what I meant. You just don't understand."

And she said, "Well no ... I guess not."

He apologized for making her mad, which was exactly the opposite, he said, of what he was intending to do. But the more he apologized, the madder she got. The more he assured her that he loved her even though she was crabby, cantankerous, strangled and worried, hard, cynical and detached, mercenary, unsympathetic, callous, and sarcastic—the more he assured her that he loved her in spite of her self—the madder she got. Until finally she hung up on him and all day she was still mad, also feeling guilty, sorry, sad, simple-minded, and defeated. She promised herself that she would send the next letter back unopened, but of course there was little real chance of that. She tried several times that afternoon to compose a letter in answer to his repeated requests for one. But she got no further than saying:

What it all comes down to is this: in the process of getting to know you, I realized that you were not the right person for me.

It should have been simple.

In the next letter, two mornings later, Cliff turned around and blamed himself for everything, saying:

At least understand that all of this was only the result of my relentless devotion to you.

Lesley took a bath after breakfast and contemplated the incongruous conjunction of these two words.

Relentless.

Devotion.

After she'd dried her hair and cleaned the tub, she looked up "relentless" in the thesaurus. Much as she'd suspected, it was not an adjective that should be allowed to have much to do with love:

relentless, *adj.* unyielding, unrelenting, implacable, unsparing; inexorable, remorseless, unflagging, dogged; undeviating, unswerving, persistent, persevering, undaunted; rigid, stern, strict, harsh, grim, austere; merciless, ruthless, unmerciful, pitiless, unpitying, unforgiving; unmitigable, inflexible, unbending, resisting, grudging; hard, imperious, obdurate, adamant, intransigent; uncompassionate, unfeeling, unsympathetic, intolerant.

The next letter was delivered on a windy Saturday night when Lesley was out on a date with somebody else. It was sitting there in the mailbox when she got home at midnight.

The weather had turned cold and her driveway was filling up suddenly with crispy yellow leaves. When she opened the back door, dozens of them swirled around her ankles and slipped inside. She imagined Cliff crunching through them on his way to the mailbox, worrying about the noise, which was amplified by the hour and the wind, then noticing that her car wasn't in the garage, and then worrying about that too.

In this letter, Cliff said:

I love you like ten thousand freight trains.

Lesley thought she rather liked this one, but then she wasn't sure. She thought she'd better think about it. She hung up her coat, poured herself a glass of white wine, and sat down in the dark kitchen to think. The oval of her face reflected in the window was distorted by the glass, so that her skin was pale, her eyes were holes, and her cheeks were sunken. She did not feel pale, hollow, or sunken. She felt just fine.

I love you like ten thousand freight trains.

This was like saying:

I love you to little bits.

Who wants to be loved to *little bits*?

This was like saying:

I love you to death.

Who wants to be loved to *death*?

I love you like ten thousand freight trains.

Who wants to be loved like or by *a freight train*?

The more she thought about it, the more she realized that she knew a thing or two about trains; railroading; relentlessness.

Dream Train

As a young girl growing up in Winnipeg, Lesley lived in an Insulbrick bungalow three doors down from the train tracks, a spur line leading to Genstar Feeds. Trains travelled the spur line so seldom that when one passed in the night, it would usually wake her up with its switching and shunting, its steel wheels squealing on the frozen rails. She would lie awake listening in her little trundle bed (it wasn't really a trundle bed, it was just an ordinary twin bed, but every night at eight o'clock her mother, Amelia, would say, "Come on, little one, time to tuck you into your little trundle bed").

Lesley liked to imagine that the train outside was not a freight train but a real train, a passenger train: the Super Continental, carrying dignified wealthy people as carefully as if they were eggs clear across the country in its plush coaches, the conductors in their serious uniforms graciously bringing around drinks, pillows, and magazines. She imagined the silver coaches cruising slowly past, all lit up, the people inside riding backwards, eating, sleeping, playing cards with just their heads showing, laughing as if this were the most natural thing in the world. She imagined that the Super Continental could go all the way from Vancouver to St. John's (never mind the Gulf of St. Lawrence—there must be a way around it) without stopping once.

If the train on the spur line did not actually wake Lesley up, then it slid instead into her dreams, disguised as a shaggy behemoth with red eyes and silver hooves, shaking the snow from its curly brown fur as it pawed the rails and snorted steam.

Train Tracks

As a teenager, Lesley walked along the train tracks every morning to Glengarry Heights High School. On the way, she usually met up with a boy named Eric Henderson, who was two grades older and dressed all year round in faded blue jeans, a T-shirt, and a black leather jacket with studs. Occasionally he condescended to the cold weather by wearing a pair of black gloves.

After a couple of weeks, Eric took to waiting for Lesley on the tracks where they crossed her street. He would be leaning against the signal lights smoking when she came out her front door. They never walked home together at four o'clock because, even though Lesley sometimes loitered at her locker hoping, Eric was never around at that time, having, she assumed, other more interesting, more grown-up, things to do after school.

Every morning Lesley and Eric practised balancing on the rails with their arms outstretched, and they complained about the way the tar-coated ties were never spaced quite right for walking on. Lesley kept her ears open, looking over her shoulder every few minutes, just in case. Her mother, Amelia, had often warned her, "Don't get too close to a moving train or you'll get *sucked under.*"

Sometimes Eric would line up bright pennies on the silver rails so the train would come and flatten them. Lesley would watch for the pennies on her way home from school, would gather them up and save them, thin as tinfoil, in a cigar box she kept under the bed. She never put pennies on the tracks herself because she was secretly afraid that they would cause a derailment and the train would come toppling off the tracks, exploding as it rolled down the embankment, demolishing her house and her neighbours' houses and everything in them. It was okay though when

Eric did it, because somehow he could be both dangerous and charmed at the same time.

Every morning Eric told Lesley about what he'd done the night before. Lesley was not expected to reciprocate, which was just as well, since all she ever did in the evening was homework and dishes and talk on the phone.

One Monday morning Eric said he'd gone to the Gardens on Saturday night to see the Ike and Tina Turner Revue. He said Tina Turner was the sexiest woman in the world and the way she sang was like making love to the microphone right there on stage. He said he thought he'd die just watching her, and all the other guys went crazy too.

On the phone every night after supper, Lesley told her new best friend, Audrey, every little thing Eric had said to her that morning, especially the way he'd said, "I like your new haircut a lot," and then the way he'd winked at her in the hall between History and French.

"Do you think he likes me?" she asked Audrey over and over again.

"Of course he likes you, silly! He *adores* you!"

This went on all fall, all winter, all spring, until the raging crush which Lesley had on Eric Henderson could be nothing, it seemed, but true true love.

The week before final exams, Eric asked Audrey to the last school dance.

Lesley spent the night of the dance barricaded in her bedroom, lying on the floor with the record player blasting Tina Turner at top volume. She propped a chair against the door and would not let her parents in. She was mad at them too: at her father, Edward, because he'd laughed and said, "You'll get over it, pumpkin!"; and at her mother, Amelia, because she was old and married, probably happy, probably didn't even remember what love was *really* like, probably hadn't explained things properly in the first place, should have warned her about more than freight trains.

She would, Lesley promised herself savagely, spend the entire summer in her room, learning all the lyrics to Tina Turner's songs, and reading fat Russian novels which were all so satisfyingly melancholy, so clotted with complications and despair, and the characters had so many different, difficult names. Especially she would reread *Anna Karenina* and memorize the signal passage where Anna decides to take her own life:

> ... And all at once she thought of the man crushed by the train the day she had first met Vronsky, and she knew what she had to do ...
>
> " ... And I will punish him and escape from everyone and from myself ... "
>
> ... And exactly at the moment when the space between the wheels came opposite her, she dropped the red bag, and drawing her head back into her shoulders, fell on her hands under the carriage, and lightly, as though she would rise again at once, dropped on to her knees ...
>
> ... She tried to get up, to drop backwards: but something huge and merciless struck her on the head and rolled her on her back ...
>
> ... And the light by which she had read the book filled with troubles, falsehoods, sorrow, and evil, flared up more brightly than ever before, lighted up for her all that had been in darkness, flickered, began to grow dim, and was quenched forever.

And she would probably carve Eric Henderson's initials into her thigh with a ballpoint pen, and she would probably not eat anything either, except maybe unsalted soda crackers, and she would not wash her hair more than once a week, and she would stay in her pyjamas all day long. Yes she would. She would LANGUISH. And for sure she would never ever ever ever fall in love or have a best friend ever again so long as she lived, so help her.

Night Train

When Lesley moved away from home at the age of twenty-one, she took the train because there was an air strike that summer. Her parents put her on the train in Winnipeg with a brown paper bag full of tuna sandwiches and chocolate-chip cookies, with the three-piece luggage set they'd bought her as a going-away present, and a book of cross-word puzzles to do on the way. They were all weeping lightly, the three of them: her parents, Lesley assumed, out of a simple sadness, and herself, out of an intoxicating combination of excitement and anticipation, of new-found freedom, and, with it, fear. She was, she felt, on the brink of everything important. She was moving west to Alberta, which was booming.

Seated across the aisle of Coach Number 3003 (a good omen, Lesley thought, as she had long ago decided that three was her lucky number) was, by sheer coincidence, a young man named Arthur Hoop who'd given a lecture at the university in Winnipeg the night before. His topic was nuclear disarmament and Lesley had attended because peace was one of her most enduring interests.

After an hour or so, Lesley worked up enough courage to cross over to the empty seat beside him and say, "I really loved your lecture." Arthur Hoop seemed genuinely pleased and invited her to join him for lunch in the club car. Lesley stashed the brown-bag lunch under the seat in front of hers and followed Arthur, swaying and bobbing and grinning, down the whole length of the train.

263

Arthur Hoop, up close, was interesting, amiable, and affectionate, and his eyes were two different colours, the left one blue and the right one brown. Arthur was on his way back to Vancouver, where he lived with a woman named Laura who was sleeping with his best friend and he, Arthur, didn't know what he was going to do next. Whenever the train stopped at a station for more than five minutes, Arthur would get off and phone ahead to Vancouver, where Laura, on the other end, would either cry, yell, or hang up on him.

By the time the train pulled into Regina, Lesley and Arthur were holding hands, hugging, and having another beer in the club car, where the waiter said, "You two look so happy, you must be on your honeymoon!"

Lesley and Arthur giggled and giggled, and then, like fools or like children playing house, they shyly agreed. The next thing they knew, there was a red rose in a silver vase on their table and everyone in the car was buying them drinks and calling out, "Congratulations!" over the clicking of the train. Arthur kept hugging Lesley against him and winking, first with the brown eye, then with the blue.

They spent the dark hours back in Arthur's coach seat, snuggling under a scratchy grey blanket, kissing and touching and curling around each other like cats. Lesley was so wrapped up in her fantasy of how Arthur would get off the train with her in Calgary or how she would stay on the train with him all the way to Vancouver, and how, either way, her real life was about to begin, that she hardly noticed how brazen they were being until Arthur actually put it in, shuddered, and clutched her to him.

Lesley wept when she got off the train in Calgary and Arthur Hoop wept too, but he stayed on.

From her hotel room, Lesley wrote Arthur long sad letters and ordered up hamburgers and Chinese food from room service at odd hours of the day and night. On the fourth night, she called her mother collect in Winnipeg and cried into the phone because she felt afraid of everything and she wanted to come home. Her mother, wise Amelia, said, "Give it two weeks before you decide. You know we'll always take you back, pumpkin."

By the end of the two weeks, Lesley had a basement apartment in a small town called Ventura, just outside the city. She also had two job interviews, a kitten named Calypso; and a whole new outlook on life. She never did hear from Arthur Hoop and she wondered for a while what it was about trains, about men, the hypnotic rhythm of them, relentless, unremitting, and irresistible, the way they would go straight to your head, and when would she ever learn?

It wasn't long before she was laughing to herself over what Arthur must have told the other passengers when she left him flat like that, on their honeymoon no less.

Train Ticket

All the way home to Winnipeg to spend Christmas with her parents, Lesley drank lukewarm coffee out of Styrofoam cups, ate expensive dried-out pressed-chicken sandwiches, and tried to get comfortable in her maroon-upholstered seat with her purse as a pillow and her parka as a blanket. She tried to read but could not concentrate for long, could not keep herself from staring out the window at the passing scenery, which was as distracting as a flickering television set at the far end of the room. All the way across Saskatchewan, the train seemed to be miraculously ploughing its way through one endless snowbank, throwing up walls of white on either side of the tracks.

She didn't feel like talking to anyone and closed her eyes whenever the handsome young man across the rocking aisle looked her way hopefully. She had just started dating a man named Bruce back in Ventura and she did not like leaving him for Christmas. But this was her first Christmas since she'd moved away from home and the trip back for the holidays had been planned months ago. Once set in motion, the trip, it seemed, like the train once she had boarded it, could not be deflected. She was travelling now with a sorrowful but self-righteous sense of daughterly obligation that carried her inexorably eastward. For a time she'd believed that moving away from her parents' home would turn her instantly into a free, adult woman. But of course she was wrong.

She kept reaching into her purse, checking for her ticket. She memorized the messages printed on the back of it, as if they were a poem or a prayer:

> RESERVATIONS: The enclosed ticket is of value. If your plans are altered, the ticket must be returned with the receipt coupon intact, for refund or credit. If you do not make the trip, please cancel your reservations.

> ALCOHOLIC BEVERAGES: Alcoholic beverages purchased on board must be consumed in the premises where served. Provincial liquor laws prohibit the consumption of personal liquor on trains except in the confines of a bedroom or roomette.

> BAGGAGE; Personal effects consisting of wearing apparel, toilet articles, and similar effects for the passenger's use, comfort, and convenience (except liquids and breakables) are accepted as baggage. Explosive, combustible, corrosive, and inflammable materials are prohibited by law.

The train trip took sixteen hours. The inside of Lesley's mouth, after 1300 kilometres, tasted like a toxic combination of diesel fuel and indoor-outdoor carpeting.

Her parents were there to meet her at the Winnipeg station, her father, Edward, smiling and smiling, his shy kiss landing somewhere near her left ear; her mother, Amelia, looking small in her big winter coat with a Christmas corsage of plastic mistletoe and tiny silver bells pinned to the lapel. The train pulled away effortlessly in a cloud of steam and snow.

Freight Train

They had a saying in Ventura—when Lesley was still living there with Bruce—a saying that was applied, with much laughter and lip-smacking, to people, usually women, who were less than attractive.

"She looks like she's been kissing freight trains," one of the boys in the bar would say, and the rest of them round the table would howl and nod and slap their knees. Lesley would laugh with them, even though she felt guilty for it, and sometimes, calling up within herself noble notions of sisterhood, sympathy, and such, she would sputter uselessly something in defence of the poor woman they were picking on.

But she would always laugh too in the end, because she knew she was pretty, she knew she was loved, she knew she was exempt from their disgust and the disfiguring, inexorable advent of trains.

Runaway Train

There was a story they told in Ventura—when Lesley was still living there with Bruce—about the time Old Jim Jacobs stole the train. It was back in the winter of 1972. Old Jim was a retired engineer who'd turned to drink in his later years. He sat in the Ventura Hotel day after day, night after night, ordering draft beer by the jug with two glasses, one for himself and one for his invisible friend. He would chat amiably for hours in an unintelligible language with the empty chair across from him, politely topping up the two glasses evenly and then drinking them both.

"At least he's never lonely," Bruce would always say.

On towards closing time, however, Old Jim or his invisible friend, or both, would start to get a little surly, and soon Old Jim would be jumping and cursing (in English), flinging himself around in the smoke-blue air of the bar.

"I hate you! I hate you!" he would cry.

"Let's step outside and settle this like men!" he would roar, hitching up his baggy pants and boxing in the air.

"So what then," Bruce would wonder, "is the point of having invisible friends, if you can't get along with them?"

Lesley knew Old Jim from when she worked in the grocery store and he'd be standing in the line-up in his old railway cap with a loaf of bread, a package of baloney, and some Kraft cheese slices. By the time he got to the cash register, he'd have made himself a sandwich and, wouldn't you know it, he must have left his wallet in his other pants—as if he even owned another pair of pants.

When he wasn't drinking or shopping, Old Jim was sitting in the long grass beside the CPR main line, counting boxcars, and waving at the engineers.

At the time of the great train robbery, he'd been bingeing, so they said, for eight days straight (this number could be adjusted, at the story-teller's discretion, to up to as many as ten days but never down to less than six) in Hawkesville, a nearby town twelve miles west of Ventura. He'd been barred for two weeks from the Ventura Hotel for sleeping on the pool table, which explained why he was drinking in Hawkesville in the first place. So Old Jim was getting to be a little homesick after all that time away from his old stamping grounds, and on the Friday night he decided it was high time to get back, seeing as how his two weeks were up on Saturday. But he was flat broke after his binge, pension cheque long gone, no money for a cab, and it was too damn cold to hitch-hike. So he decided to take the train.

So he hopped right in, so they said, to the first engine he found in the yard, fired her up, and off he went, hauling forty-seven empty boxcars behind him (this number too could be adjusted, interminably up, it seemed, because, after all, who was counting?). He made it back to Ventura without mishap, parked her up on the siding behind the Ventura Hotel so he'd be good and ready when they opened in the morning and he knew they'd give him credit for a day or two. He curled up in the caboose and went to sleep. Which was where the railway police and the RCMP found him when they surrounded the runaway train, guns drawn, sirens screaming, at 5:36 a.m. (the time of his legendary capture was unalterable, a part of the town's history which could not be tampered with).

"But what then," Bruce would wonder whenever he heard the story again, "is the point of stealing a train, when you can never take it off the tracks, when you can only go back and forth, back and forth, back and forth, and you can never really get away?"

Express Train

One summer Lesley and Bruce took the train up to Edmonton where his brother was getting married. Halfway there, they were stopped on a siding in the middle of nowhere, waiting for a freight train to pass. Bruce was getting impatient, sighing huge conspicuous sighs as he fidgeted and fussed in his seat, while Lesley beside him read on peacefully.

Spotting a white horse from the window, he said, "Sometimes simple things glimpsed in the distance can bring great comfort."

Train Trip East

All the way back to Winnipeg for her Uncle Mel's funeral, Lesley drank beer out of cans and wrote postcards to Bruce in Ventura. She bought the cards at various train stations along the way and then she mailed them at the next stop. She suspected that Bruce was on the brink of having an affair with a French-Canadian woman named Analise who was spending the summer in Ventura with her sister. All of this suspicion, sticky and time-consuming as it was, had left Lesley feeling sick and tired, a little bit crazy too. On the back of a green lake, she wrote:

> I tried to take pictures from the train, of a tree and some water, some sky, but they wouldn't hold still long enough.

On the back of a red maple tree:

> I saw a coyote running from the train, also white horses, brown cows, black birds, and a little girl in Maple Creek wearing a pink sunsuit with polka dots, running. All of them running away from the train.

Black city spotted with blue and white lights:

> There was a station wagon stopped at a crossing. It was filled with suitcases, babies, and basket-

balls. For a minute, I wanted to scream: "Stop! Stop! There's a train coming! We'll all be killed!" Then I remembered that I was the train and I didn't have to stop for anything. Trains are so safe from the inside.

Yellow field of wheat:

> What else is there to do on a train any more but remember? I thought of a witchy woman who lived on the corner of Cross Street and Vine, in a wooden shack with pigeons on the roof and chickens in the porch. She watched me through the window when I walked by to Sunday School. The winter I was eight she got hit by a train. For a time I had nightmares ...

Here she ran out of room on the card and finished up her message on the next one. Purple mountain:

> ... about arms and legs broken off like icicles, about a head rolling down a snowbank wearing a turquoise toque just like mine. Then I forgot all about her till now. I remember rocking my cousin, Gary, in his cradle, the way he couldn't hold his head up yet, and now he's the chef at a fancy French restaurant.

Sitting at her Aunt Helen's kitchen table in Winnipeg, surrounded by relatives, neighbours, warm casseroles, and frozen pound cakes, she wrote on the back of a sympathy card:

> I've still got the sound of the train in my head. It makes it hard to think of anything but songs. Tomorrow.

War Train

In Lesley's parents' photo album, there was a picture of her mother and her Aunt Helen seeing her father and her Uncle Mel off at the train station. The women were waving and blowing kisses from the platform, stylish in their broad-shouldered coats and little square hats with veils. The men were grinning and walking away, handsome in their sleek uniforms and jaunty caps. They were all very young then, and splendid. The silver train was waiting behind them, its windows filled with the faces of many other young men. They went away to the war and then some of them came back again.

After her Uncle Mel's funeral, Lesley's father told her about the time he'd ridden the train all across France with Mel's head in his lap, Mel nearly dying of ptomaine poisoning from a Christmas turkey, but he didn't.

Train Trip West

All the way back to Ventura after her Uncle Mel's funeral, Lesley slept fitfully or looked out the train window and thought about how everything looks different when you are passing through it in the opposite direction. On this return journey, she was riding backwards, facing where she'd come from, as if she had eyes in the back of her head.

The train whistled through the backsides of a hundred anonymous towns, past old hotels of pink or beige stucco, past slaughterhouses, gas stations, trailer parks, and warehouses. Children and old men waved. Dogs barked, soundless, powerless, strangling themselves straining at their chains. White sheets tangled on backyard clotheslines and red tractors idled at unmarked crossings.

Lesley never knew where she was exactly: there are no mileage signs beside the train tracks the way there are on the highway. There is no way of knowing how far from, how far to. No way, on train time, of locating yourself accurately inside the continuum. You just have to keep on moving, forward and forward and forward, or back, trusting that wherever you are heading is still out there somewhere.

Horse and Train

One year for her birthday in Ventura (or could it have been Christmas ... could it have been that same year when Lesley bought Bruce the guitar he'd been aching after, the Fender Stratocaster, and when she couldn't take the suspense a minute longer, she gave it to him on Christmas Eve instead of in the morning, just to see the look on his face, and then they stayed up all night playing music and singing, drinking eggnog till dawn ... when Bruce took the guitar to bed with him and Lesley took a picture of him cuddling it under the puffy pink quilt her mother had sent, and then she kept him awake even longer, telling her theory that if men were the ones who had babies, then there would no more war ... the best Christmas ever, it could have been then), Bruce gave Lesley a framed reproduction of the Alex Colville painting *Horse and Train*.

In the painting, a purple-black horse on the right is running headlong down the tracks towards an oncoming train on the left. The landscape around them is gravel and brown prairie grass. The ears of the horse are flattened, its tail is extended, and the white smoke from the black train is drifting across the brown prairie sky at dusk.

Bruce hung the painting over the couch in the tiny living room of their basement apartment and Lesley admired it every time she walked into the room.

After Bruce left Lesley and moved to Montreal with Analise, Lesley took the painting off the wall and smashed it on the cement floor, so that she was vacuuming up glass for an hour afterwards, weeping.

When Lesley moved back to Winnipeg a few months later and rented the little stucco bungalow on Harris Street, she had the painting reframed with new glass and hung it on her bedroom wall. She liked to look at it before she went to sleep at night.

She looked at it when she was lying in bed with Cliff, who had his hands behind his head and the ashtray balanced on his bare chest, who was talking and smoking and talking, so happy to be spending the night. She looked at it as she tried to concentrate and follow Cliff's train of thought, but really she was thinking about how they'd been seeing each other for three months now and it wasn't working out.

But really she was thinking about an article she'd read in a women's magazine years ago, and the writer, a marriage counsellor, said that in every romantic relationship there was one person who loved less and one who loved more. The important question then, which a person must face was: which would you rather be: the one who loves less or the one who loves more?

When Lesley asked Cliff this question, she already knew what his answer would be.

Which would you rather be: the one who loves less or the one who loves more?

This was like saying:

Which would you rather be: the horse or the train?

It should have been simple.

Ottawa

Gail Scott

THE SUMMERY breeze blew the curtains. I lay in bed with my bathing suit on. Too hot. Then too cold. Now too hot. Very still. My knees drawn up in a hump. My mother taking her Sunday afternoon nap. The Sunday roast hardened in the oven.

That poor country boy was racing angrily toward the canal waving the portable radio he gave me hotly in his fist. (I couldn't help laughing. He bought one nobody made batteries for.) The pearl ring was in his pocket. I stretched my toes and cried a while. It was delicious. Then I noticed they'd stuck the plastic Mountie in the plant box.

The door slammed. The young Royal Canadian Mounted Policeman from the prairies came into the oak-panelled foyer. The organdy curtains fluttered. I ran upstairs. "You'll have to excuse her," said my mother to him, sort of embarrassed.

I sneaked out the back. My father was playing the violin. Turkey in the straw. He played it every Sunday. I'd sit on the verandah and listen. "You're tone deaf." I guess he felt kinda silly only knowing the one song. That country boy went by in a cloud of dust, braking sideways.

My mother called me into the parlour. I could feel the Mountie's thin lips. "I want to tell you how to avoid rape," she said. She couldn't see him concealed behind the curtains. "Boys are horrid when they don't feel so hot about themselves. So stoop to conquer. Turn the other cheek. Wear a white sweater."

A solid gold Cadillac drove up outside. I went to the window. My mother pursed her lips. She has the Mountie's mouth. My father's is soft and wrinkled like overripe fruit. The Mountie stepped out from behind the curtains. The Caddy slid off into the sunset. I couldn't see who was driving. My cheeks turned pink. "You're too romantic," whispered my mother.

So when the bus passed I stepped on without a word to anyone. Soon we were driving by the canal. The moon made it blood red. It reminded me of the movie Moon River. We were entering the city of Ottawa.

MOON RIVER

Holly Golightly is the heroine. She is a gentleman's escort who manages never to come across. (No tits.) "Change for the powder room please?" she asks. (She's quite classy.) They give her a fifty. She flees down the fire escape with it in the pocket of her skinny black shift.

The Y had two blue signs, one on each side of the road. YM and YW. Behind them the Peace Tower rose into the sunset. The third-floor room was hot and dusty. Yet if you opened the window a crack in came a strange chill. Down below the boys were stopping at stoplights. They would take their hands off the wheels and put them under the girl's skirts (thinking nobody could see).

Francine in the next bed flicked on the radio. Elvis. I had my knees up. He has a way of saying words. Soft baby lips. Those fat cheeks of southern boys. They laugh quietly when they're in a mood to kill. "You should see Chris," said Francine. "Ottawa's Elvis," She was wearing a gold lamé bathing suit. Waiting for her underwear to dry.

YOU'RE WIDER THAN A MILE

We crept past Ramsay the receptionist. Me, Francine, and the girl with the bandaged wrists. (Just a little razor-blade trick.) The moon was full. Christ slithered into the lights. Francine shoved towards the stage. He didn't give her a glance. I climbed into his gold Caddy.

His hand crept under my sweater. I was wearing a high-wire beauty bra. My nostrils quivered. Between my half-closed eyes I could see the moon bathing the road. A couple was kind of locked together on the front lawn. French-kissing. Chris brought his full lips close to mine, forcing my mouth open. I smiled, sort of embarrassed. He moved away. "What I wanted was a natural woman," he said.

They're tearing down Main Street for a shopping mall. Chasing the rats into the Rideau. I watched from the Y window. His picture's on top of Sally's Yukon Saloon. Between two high-rises. Francine smiled in her gold lamé bathing suit. (It gave her stretch marks.) "There's a trick to French kissing," she said. I could see her purple tongue in her deep throat. The Peace Tower rose palely at the end of the street. On the hill you could see the officers come and go.

Aunt Heloise was presiding over the roast. Her husband the officer smiled as my mother took a bite. Her lip twitched it was so juicy (compared to hers). My cousin Heloise invited me upstairs. Her big breasts bounced thoughtfully. She opened her dresser drawer. Inside, neatly stacked, were used Kotex napkins. Red-Brown. She asked me if I wanted to share an apartment with her.

The moon shone ever brighter on the canal. Rideau Street was full of boys with chains hanging from their belts. And ladies in powder blue suits. My spike heel caught in the grille of the Capitol Cinema. The movie was Moon River. I went in again. Holly Golightly is running up the fire escapes. Chasing her cat. In her simple black shift. She runs smack into the arms of a writer. He keeps her warm. Beside me sat a short fat girl. Connie-the-concert-pianist. She said she had the record.

Connie and I took her stairs two at a time. (Her Moon River record was caught in a scratch.) Then she disappeared through the chintz curtains. I could hear funny sounds coming from the roof. I looked out the window. When she came back in I said: "Do you think Holly was a call-girl?" She laughed in her high sing-song voice. "No she's an artist. And doesn't look back."

I wasn't ready for the black-slip business. Ramsay was climbing the YW stairs. (I'd been watching the sunset.) She handed me my suitcase. Something about an underdressed woman in the window. "Worse than Amsterdam," complained the YM man (calling from across the street). Francine looked smug. I crept by that poor country boy playing his portable in the lobby. A gold Caddy passed. My cheeks were crimson. Connie said to meet her on The Driveway.

We slid down the rock terrasse. Elliott stood there, his thin legs among the drooping daffodils. His neck was surrounded with a Swiss collar. He looked hostile. On the other side of the canal, the Russian ambassador cast a huge shadow on the stone wall. Elliott's father was caught in a Cold War scandal.

On the hill you could see the officers come and go. Speaking of Michelangelo (according to Aunt Heloise). *The Citizen* said the Chinese were going to overrun Canada. The geography teacher drew up a map. They needed the space. I was wearing a black shift, slim at the calves. Sick and tired of Teachers' College. My cigarette holder was concealed in my purse. The bus for the country came up outside.

My mother sat in the orange hall, waiting for the roast. Watching me with her dark eyes. Burnt holes in paper. My cousin Heloise was there too, dressed in smooth blue. "Baked Alaska," whispered my father, his weak mouth against my ear. "Warm on the outside, cool as a cucumber in." The bus braked in the dust.

I climbed off at Connie's (close to the canal). I took off my clothes and crawled under the covers. Elliott came up unexpectedly. I threw off the blankets (the better to show off my Jantzen's slimline bathing suit). He just stood there looking kind of worried. His legs were pretty skinny. Connie saw him the first time she crawled out on top of her roof. His family was moving in across the street. He said he'd brought me a book. He leafed through the pages for a few minutes and then left. He hadn't stayed long. I had the feeling he was saying to himself on the way downstairs: "No class."

I'M CROSSING YOU IN STYLE SOMEDAY

Aunt Heloise smashed a pimple and covered it with powder. "We should strike at the Russians first," said my uncle. Then she hid it in the shade of her organdy chapeau. Her skin smelled like fresh cream. There was going to be a garden party. The whole family set out for Parliament Hill. The pavement was hot and sticky.

"This isn't the swan song it sounds," she murmured to me. "I'm referring to a girl sitting in a beautiful cottage by a shiny river plunging down to a paper mill. She is playing solitaire and singing to herself. A man walks by. Hearing the voice he stops and stares through the glassed-in porch. 'This is the girl I am going to marry,' he says to himself. And he does. So you see, if it happened to me it can happen to you," finished my aunt. "Maybe," I said, "but I don't know how to sing."

We kept walking. Chris's hit song wafted through a car window. Hands on sticky nylon stockings. "Hasn't he called you yet?" said my mother. Taking me from behind. Yes we have no bananas. The new shopping centre smells of plastic. No he hasn't called. Yes the Mountie has moved to Manitoba. No the country boy … as far as I know he's still jerking his radio down the road. Like a drop stitched. I smiled. I don't look back. Another rock star rose out of the shingles over Sally's Yukon Saloon. Squeezed between two high-rises.

On the hill we could see the officers come and go. Drinking PIMM's. "And avoiding husband-hunters," said Aunt Heloise. People were spread in the prickly heat on the Parliament grass. The band broke into the Pirates of Penzance. Someone was washing a frog off the Parliament façade.

Heloise straightened her back. Diefenbaker went by in a buggy. A handsome officer was approaching. Mindful of Aunt Heloise's hint about husband-hunters I decided to be discreet. Only a small smile for my mother. But now the band was in a slow march. He moved on up the hill. Almost in time to the music. I looked at Heloise. Her sky-blue eyes were trained on another pair identical to her own. Buttoned tight in a tunic, to his chin.

I drew my knees close to my chest. My father used to try and force them down. (It was a game.) The ladies were dispersed on the grass in their Easter bonnets. Suddenly I caught sight of Connie lying on a car roof. Outside the grilled gate. I decided to take a stroll. A white potato face stuck out of the car window. "I'm Gerry-the-General's-son," it said, grinning. He handed me a mickey. I took a swig. There was a flutter of organdy beside me. My old Sunday School teacher grasped me in a tight embrace. The bottle was behind my back. She smelled of lavender powder.

Underneath the pink roses on her dress I could feel her steel corset.

We drove slowly down The Driveway. Connie was stretched out nonchalantly on the roof in her black shift. "You have bedroom eyes," he said. Looking straight ahead. (They're brown. Like my mother's.) His mickey was between my feet. We came to the canal. The moon began to shine. Elvis's head came up behind a sand-dune. The neon lights were flickering around the billboard. Elliott stood knee-deep in the drooping daffodils. His father was fired.

YOU DREAM MAKER YOU

The job ad said: *Wanted: Cultivated salesgirl. Thirty yrs. or over. Well-spoken. French and English.* With the right makeup I could pass. I could wear a high-necked sweater and horn-rimmed glasses like Holly Golightly. When she was after the Iranian student prince. She would sit in the public library and study oil prices. He couldn't help but notice.

I walked by St. Griffith's-sur-le-Rideau. They were discussing Michelangelo and the Archangel. Whether theirs was an authentic copy of his. Or something. The saloon door beside the Church suddenly opened. Chris came out. You should see the tawny hairs on his golden chest. He wore a motorcycle belt buckle. His picture was surrounded by star-shaped bulbs. He watched my beehive hair-do passing in profile. "You're too self-conscious," he said.

The choir revved up into resurrection music. It was so hot the flowers on the Easter bonnets seemed to fade. Heloise's engaged! Aunt Heloise screamed with delight. Heloise had hot cheeks (for once). I shivered beside her ice-blue dress. My mother watched me sadly. One thing was for sure. I was leaving Teachers' College.

After the hot came the cold. The fog fell. The Peace Tower stuck up like a Sherlock Holmes mystery. Trying to see was like trying to draw tiny drops back from across your eyes. Veils of tears. A bicycle slipped through the daffodils. Elliott in a Swiss collar. In his hand a note for the Russian ambassador. "Meet me by the match mill," he whispered. "We can climb to the Chateau. The PCs are having a party."

It's the party that gives the best parties. Gerry-the-General's-son was there. He gave me his mickey. I dropped it on the marble. We switched to a bottle of burgundy. Somebody complimented me on my spotless black sheath. "Simplicity itself," he said, grabbing my bottom. I complimented him on the spotless marble of his scalp, where his hair used to be. Elliott gave me some Russian schnapps. The red tunics twirled around. (Or was it me?)

Dief the chief was supposed to show up. They started rolling down the red carpet. In the corner of my eye I thought I saw Connie sitting outside the window. A smile on her lips. Someone said he was coming in a solid-gold Cadillac. An attempted mollifier from the Americans. I stepped gingerly on the plush and started forward. Hoping to get a glimpse. Suddenly a chinless organizer was standing in front of me: "Heh, heh, we'll have none of that here."

I woke up in the fur coat room with a rug over my back. Waiting for the cats. That was my first thought: waiting for cats. Holly Golightly didn't wait for cats. She ran after them. That's how she found the writer. Chasing one up the fire escape. She felt cold. He put his arms around her.

My white hand stuck out the window. It was in the left wing of the Chateau Laurier. Down below the swans were skirting the whirlpool below the matchmill. I crossed the corridor and entered the elevator. "Madame or Mademoiselle?" asked the elevator operator. It was dripping on the daffodils. The soldiers went by. I thought of sketching the Peace Tower. In the morning mist, two lips ... It was a Craven A advertisement. Except it started coming closer. The soft red mouth.

Chris took my arm and we went back to the furry chamber at the Chateau Laurier. "La Chambre Chatouillante," he said. "Madame or Mademoiselle?" said the elevator operator. Chris kissed me all over. The rock scene wasn't so hot. Elvis was turning Hawaiian. He started undressing me, kinda depressed. I could feel his velvet tongue. He took off my high-wire beauty bra. He said it was too bad I had such small breasts. "Get dressed and I'll take you home."

YOU HEART BREAKER

The record was still playing, so scratchy you could hardly hear the words. Connie was nowhere to be seen. I looked out the window. Across the way they were sweeping the floor of the new Bohemian Café. A girl came in with a mandolin under her flowing breasts. I don't know why but it made me want to have books.

That's when Elliott came up again. I was lying in bed thinking I'd build myself a library wall when he entered. He had a book in his hand. He kept leafing through the pages, looking at me like I wasn't listening. I was but I couldn't hear. A terrible racket had started up outside.

Downstairs my father's friends the non-commissioned officers were sitting in the back seat, singing "Oh here we come all full of rum." It was Heloise's husband-to-be's stag. I got in the car. A chill swept in under the door. My father smacked his lips and said something. Baked Alaska? They all laughed, their mouths wide-opened. I got out.

A horn honked behind. Heloise's husband. Almost. I was still at Teacher's College, wasn't I? It would be nice if I could come to the cadet cotillion. Connie sat on the roof outside the chintz curtains. Perfectly silent.

WHEREVER YOU'RE GOING

My mother dreamed I was famous. Gail Groulx saves four out of six from flames, said *The Citizen*. Mme. G. Groulx was struggling through the smoke with three of her children in her arms after her frying pan caught on fire when she suddenly remembered little Liette was left in her cot. Putting the three down she fought her way back for the fourth. Finally she staggered from the house, carrying all four. A huge crowd had gathered. The people cheered loudly.

Ottawa, 1962. The department store had no opening. I couldn't go back to Teacher's College. They said I'd spoiled my chances. I pulled on my tight white sweater and went to Parliament Hill to sketch the Peace Tower. Nobody noticed except a kid from the cleaning staff. He had a girl's name. Jocelyn. French. He wanted to go to law school but his father refused. "Learn English first." I looked at my paper. Maybe there was more to being an artist.

I'M GOING YOUR WAY

I chose wedding white. My mother said I could always come back to the country. A job at the egg-grading station. The breeze lifted the organdy curtains. My chest broke out in a red rash above the cardboard stays. My mother's eyes watched me dress. Connie was practising the piano. The notes were so high they hurt the eardrum.

The rain tinkled down. The silver limousine pulled away from Aunt Heloise's. My fake rabbit shortie was wet enough to smell a little like Campbell's vegetable soup. Heloise's husband kept his aristocratic nose straight ahead. The ballroom was awash with bright lights and tightly buttoned tunics. It was the national flag contest.

A quick shadow passed by the opened French windows, Connie, causing a small smile to tickle the corners of my mouth. At the same moment a pain began creeping unmistakably up the centre of my stomach. The band started. Oh you'll take the high road and I'll take the low road. Two cadets came crashing forward. I took the most sober. Jacques was laced up so tight in his tunic his neck hung over the edges. "Be ladylike," I said to myself. I thought of Heloise's well-kept hands. Was that something moist seeping onto my panties? Connie was in the window, her hand over her mouth.

The band broke into a souped-up version of the Pirates of Penzance. The damp air came in through the curtains. People marched around the floors by twos and by threes. (His friend had my other arm.) The full moon rose. They were stringing up the new flags. Red-tunicked cadets bordered each side of my white brocade. My slip got damper. Heloise chatted animatedly. The red spot spread outward. I could see her working her way behind me trying to see. Connie was heaving with laughter. Only moments before discovery. Chances are I wore a silly grin.

The Man with
Clam Eyes

Audrey Thomas

I CAME TO the sea because my heart was broken. I rented a cabin from an old professor who stammered when he talked. He wanted to go far away and look at something. In the cabin there is a table, a chair, a bed, a woodstove, an aladdin lamp. Outside there is a well, a privy, rocks, trees and the sea.

(The lapping of waves, the scream of gulls.)

I came to this house because my heart was broken. I brought wine in green bottles and meaty soup bones. I set an iron pot on the back of the stove to simmer. I lit the lamp. It was no longer summer and the wind grieved around the door. Spiders and mice disapproved of my arrival. I could hear them clucking their tongues in corners.

(The sound of the waves and the wind.)

This house is spotless, shipshape. Except for the spiders. Except for the mice in corners, behind the walls. There are no clues. I have brought with me wine in green bottles, an eiderdown quilt, my brand-new *Bartlett's Familiar Quotations*. On the inside of the front jacket it says, "Who said: 1. In wildness is the preservation of the world. 2. All hell broke loose. 3. You are the sunshine of my life."

I want to add another. I want to add two more. Who said, "There is no nice way of saying this?" Who said, "Let's not go over it again?"   The wind grieves around the door. I stuff the cracks with rags torn from the bottom of my skirt. I am sad. Shall I leave here then? Shall I go and lie outside his door calling whoo—whoo—whoo like the wind?

(The sound of the waves and the wind.)

I drink all of the wine in one green bottle. I am like a glove. Not so much shapeless as empty, waiting to be filled up. I set my lamp in the window, I sleep to the sound of the wind's grieving.

(Quiet breathing, the wind still there, but soft,
then gradually fading out. The passage of time,
then seagulls, and then waves.)

How can I have slept when my heart is broken? I dreamt of a banquet table under green trees. I was a child and ate ripe figs with my fingers. Now I open the door—

(West-coast birds, the towhee with its strange cry,
and the waves.)

The sea below is rumpled and wrinkled and the sun is shining. I can see islands and then more islands, as though my island had spawned islands in the night. The sun is shining. I have never felt so lonely in my life. I go back in. I want to write a message and throw it out to sea. I rinse my wine bottle from last night and set it above the stove to dry. I sit at the small table thinking. My message must be clear and yet compelling, like a lamp lit in a window on a dark night. There is a blue bowl on the table and a rough spoon carved from some sweet-smelling wood. I eat porridge with raisins while I think. The soup simmers on the back of the stove. The seagulls outside are riding the wind and crying ME ME ME. If this were a fairy tale, there would be someone here to help me, give me a ring, a cloak, a magic word. I bang on the table in my frustration. A small drawer pops open.

(Sound of the wind the waves lapping.)

Portents and signs mean something, point to something, otherwise—too cruel. The only thing in the drawer is part of a manuscript, perhaps some secret hobby of the far-off professor. It is a story about a man on a train from Genoa to Rome. He has a gun in his pocket and is going to Rome to kill his wife. After the conductor comes through, he goes along to the lavatory, locks the door, takes out the gun, then stares at himself in the mirror. He is pleased to note that his eyes are clear and clam. *Clam?* Pleased to note that his eyes are clear and clam? I am not quick this morning. It takes me a while before I see what has happened. And then I laugh. How can I laugh when my heart is cracked like a dropped plate? But I laugh at the man on the train to Rome, staring at himself in the mirror—the man with clam eyes. I push aside the porridge and open my *Bartlett's Familiar Quotations*. I imagine Matthew Arnold— "The sea is clam tonight ..." or Wordsworth—"It is a beauteous evening, clam and free ..." I know what to say in my message.

The bottle is dry. I take the piece of paper and push it in. Then the cork, which I seal with wax from a yellow candle. I will wait just before dark.

(The waves, the lapping sea. The gulls, loud and then gradually fading out. Time passes.)

Men came by in a boat with a pirate flag. They were diving for sea urchins and when they saw me sitting on the rocks they gave me one. They tell me to crack it open and eat the inside, here, they will show me how. I cry No and No, I want to watch it for a while. They shrug and swim away.   All afternoon I watched it in pleasant idleness. I had corrected the typo of course—I am that sort of person—but the image of the man with clam eyes wouldn't leave me and I went down on the rocks to think. That's when I saw the divers with their pirate flag; that's when I was given the gift of the beautiful maroon sea urchin. The rocks were as grey and wrinkled as elephants, but warm, with enormous pores and pools licked out by the wind and the sea. The sea urchin is a dark maroon, like the lips of certain black men I have known. It moves constantly back/forth, back/forth with all its spines turning. I take it up to the cabin. I let it skate slowly back and forth across the table. I keep it wet with water from my bucket. The soup smells good. This morning I add carrots, onions, potatoes, bay leaves and thyme. How can I be hungry when my heart is broken? I cut bread with a long, sharp knife, holding the loaf against my breast. Before supper I put the urchin back into the sea.

(Sound of the wind and the waves.)

My bottle is ready and there is a moon. I have eaten soup and drunk wine and nibbled at my bread. I have read a lot of un-familiar quotations. I have trimmed the wick and lit the lamp and set it in the window. The sea is still tonight and the moon has left a long trail of silver stretching almost to the rocks.

(Night sounds. A screech owl.
No wind, but the waves lapping.)

I go down to the sea as far as I can go. I hold the corked bottle in my right hand and fling it towards the stars. For a moment I think that a hand has reached up and caught it as it fell back towards the sea. I stand there. The moon and the stars light up my loneliness. How will I fall asleep when my heart is broken?

> (Waves, then fading out. The sound
> of the wild birds calling.)

I awoke with the first bird. I lay under my eiderdown and watched my breath in the cold room. I wondered if the birds could understand one another, if a chickadee could talk with a junco, for example. I wondered whether, given the change in seasons and birds, there was always the same first bird. I got up and lit the fire and put a kettle on for washing.

> (The iron stove is opened and wood lit.
> It catches, snaps and crackles.
> Water is poured into a large kettle.)

When I went outside to fling away the water, he was there, down on the rocks below me, half-man, half-fish. His green scales glittered like sequins in the winter sunlight. He raised his arm and beckoned to me.

(Sound of the distant gulls.)

We have been swimming. The water is cold, cold, cold. Now I sit on the rocks, combing out my hair. He tells me stories. My heart darts here and there like a frightened fish. The tracks of his fingers run silver along my leg. He told me that he is a drowned sailor, that he went overboard in a storm at sea. He speaks with a strong Spanish accent.

He has been with the traders who bought for a pittance the sea-otters' pelts which trimmed the robes of Chinese mandarins. A dozen glass beads would be bartered with the Indians for six of the finest skins.

With Cook he observed the transit of Venus in the cloudless skies of Tahiti.

With Drake he had sailed on "The Golden Hind" for the Pacific Coast. They landed in a bay off California. His fingers leave silver tracks on my bare legs. I like to hear him say it—Cal-ee fórn-ya. The Indians there were friendly. The men were naked but the women wore petticoats of bulrushes.

Oh how I like it when he does that.

He was blown around the Cape of Good Hope with Diaz. Only they called it the Cape of Storms. The King did not like the name and altered it.   Oh.

His cool tongue laps me. My breasts bloom in the moon-light. We dive—and rise out of the sea, gleaming. He decorates my hair with clamshells and stars, my body with sea-lettuce. I do not feel the cold. I laugh. He gives me a rope of giant kelp and I skip for him in the moonlight. He breaks open the shells of mussels and pulls out their sweet flesh with his long fingers. We tip the liquid into our throats; it tastes like tears.   He touches me with his explorer's hands.

(Waves, the sea—loud—louder. Fading out.)

I ask him to come with me, up to the professor's cabin. It is impóss-ee-ble," he says. He asks me to go with him. It is impóss-ee-ble," I say. "Not at all."

I cannot breathe in the water. I will drown. I have no helpful sisters. I do not know a witch.

(Sea, waves, grow louder, fade, fading but not gone.)

He lifts me like a wave and carries me towards the water. I can feel the roll of the world. My legs dissolve at his touch and flow together. He shines like a green fish in the moonlight. "Is easy," he says, as my mouth fills up with tears. "Is nothing." The last portions of myself begin to shift and change.

I dive beneath the waves! He clasps me to him. We are going to swim to the edges of the world, he says, and I believe him.

I take one glance backwards and wave to the woman in the window. She has lit the lamp. She is eating soup and drinking wine. Her heart is broken. She is thinking about a man on a train who is going to kill his wife. The lamp lights up her loneliness. I wish her well.

A Day in The Life Of
Thomas Macomber

Guillermo Verdecchia

H<small>E'S TRYING</small> to get it right so he can explain it later. On the screen people wander through a field of trash. They live off the garbage dump. They pick through stuff in the dump and sell it. Or use it. Or something. They live there, on the dump. Or maybe not quite on the dump. It's hard to tell exactly because they're talking Spanish or Mexican or whatever and it's hard to read the words of the translation of what they're saying. Subtitles. That's what they're called. Sometimes the subtitles disappear against the background. Or maybe his eyes are going. Doubtful with all the pot he smokes. That's good for your eyes. Glaucoma. Or something. Terminal eye patients get dope as medicine. Totally. So it can't be his eyes. It's the subtitles. They should invent some kind of system where the subtitles change colour depending on the colour that's in the background. He should invent it. Make a lot of money if you could do something like that. Like if the garbage dump is brown, then the subtitles could be the opposite colour.

"What's the opposite of brown?"

No answer.

It's somewhat of a downer this TV program. Or maybe it's the dope. Lately, whenever he tokes up, Tom gets depressed. Of course, watching documentaries about garbage dump dwellers doesn't help. It's fucking terrible. Like all those panhandlers on the street now. You can hardly turn around without bumping into somebody who's bumming for change. And every other person who isn't panhandling is rooting through the garbage or recycling, looking for beer bottles or whatever. There were like four-teen Indians in the alley the other day, looking for bottles. But they lost out 'cause old Mrs. Chow was already through them all at like five in the morning. With two giant bags on a pole that she carried across her back. That's why he prefers to drive. Avoid the panhandlers.

"Dad, I wanna dig a grave for Rascal."

"Jesus Bobby, you scared the crap out of me." The kid's gotten really quiet lately. Taking to sneaking around. He just shows up in the room, like a ghost. Freaky.

"Can we bury Rascal today?"

"What?"

"Can we bury Rascal today?"

"Hey, what's the opposite of brown?"

"Daaaad."

"What?"

"Can we?"

"What?"

"Bury Rascal."

"Where's your mum?"

No answer. Spooky.

Bobby is training. He is getting better and better at slipping in and out of rooms, houses, yards and conversations unnoticed. The ninja, Bobby knows, is a master of stealth and secrecy, silent as a cat, leaving no trace of his passage. Inside his kangaroo jacket pocket, he feels for his shuriken: deadly throwing stars, often coated with poison, favoured by the ninja. Nine of them. An auspicious number.

The Old Man is getting slower, Bobby thinks. Stupider too. From all the dope he smokes. It will not be long now before The Tong comes. Bobby will not defend The Old Man. He will not be sad when they take him, cut off his head and stick it on a yari for all to see. The ninja is loyal to no one but himself. Stupid Old Man.

Ninja Bobby sits on his front step watching ordinary people walk by. He could kill them with a soundless flick of his wrist. But he doesn't.

It would be something like when they colour in old movies. Colourizing. They could do the same thing with the subtitles. You do the regular subtitling. Then you go back and colourize them. But you could do it way simpler now. With computers. You just program when to change the colour depending on when the background changes and it does it automatically. It's so simple. He's amazed no one's thought of it until now.

That would be so much better than the way they work now. And also better than movies that are dubbed. That's the worst, when their mouths are moving and it's so obviously not what they're saying that you're hearing. That looks retarded. On the TV, a dog is making funny faces. He loves this commercial. He laughs.

"What's so funny?" Lori asks, dragging shopping bags into the house.

"Hey, where have you been?"

"I went to the bank."

"In what city?"

"In this city, goof. I had other stuff to do too. What's so funny?"

"It's that commercial with the mental dog that—"

She comes into the living room.

"Tom. This place is a dump."

"What?" He was supposed to clean up the living room. That's why he was in here in the first place. Now he remembers. Shit.

"The living room is a dump. I asked you when I left to clean it up. Look, you got your shit everywhere."

"It's not everywhere. It's not just my stuff."

"I asked you. Jesus. It's not much to ask."

Flick. The first shuriken goes flying. Deadly accuracy. The man crumples silently to the ground.

"What the hell have you been doing all afternoon then?"

"I've been watching this doc—It's really interesting. People living off—Look, it's the weekend. It's a day off. I'll get around to it."

Flick. Another shuriken. Another dead body. A ninja feels no pity, no remorse, no sorrow.

"When?"

"Jesus, what's the hurry? I'll do it now."

"My sister's coming over. That's all."

"Well, I didn't know that."

"You did so. I told you about eighteen times."

"You did not." She did so.

"I did so."

"No, you didn't. I think I'd remember that."

Outside, the sidewalk is littered with dead bodies. Ninja Bobby turns his back on the carnage, calmly walks past the squabbling Old People to his bed chamber. They do not notice him. To empty his mind, Ninja Bobby draws in his notebook. A city scene: roads, cars.

"Did you get rid of Rascal?"

"What?"

"Did you at least bury the dog?"

"Hey, don't yell at me."

"You didn't, did you? I told you, I'm sick of having that dog in my freezer."

"Hey, stop yelling. People can hear you, you know."

"Is Bobby home?"

"Yeah. I don't know. I guess. Bobby?"

She shushes him. "Don't call him, you idiot. I didn't know he was home. I wouldn't've talked about the dog like that if I knew he was home. D'ya think he heard me?"

"Probably. The whole city probably heard you."

Ninja Bobby adds houses and apartment buildings to his drawing. Stores, people walking, birds in the sky. Construction in one corner.

Inexplicably, Tom finds himself in the kitchen. Did he already clean up the living room? Why doesn't he do things like he says he will? He unpacks the groceries she bought. Cookies. Excellent.

"Would you leave that? Go clean up the living room."

"I'm just trying to help." Crumbs fall from his mouth.

"You can help by cleaning up the living room. And then you can bury Rascal. I told you yesterday I wanted him out of the freezer and I told Bobby we could bury him in the backyard."

"I think he was asking something about that."

"Of course, I told him we could do it."

"In the backyard?"

"Yeah."

"Is that …" He searches for the right word. He searches for a long time. "Safe?"

"Safe? Of course it's safe." She hates the sound of her voice, cannot stand the way she sounds. But she has no energy to change it. Not now. Maybe later. Maybe tonight. Maybe tomorrow.

"Well, what if something digs it up?"

"What, like a voodoo guy?"

"Yeah, make a zombie."

They're smiling at each other now.

"Rascal, you are a zombie. Your soul is mine to command. Go piss on Mrs. Chow's cabbage."

They're laughing now. Bobby cannot hear them. He is finishing his drawing. A Chinese Crested (a rare, hairless breed) rushes out into the busy street and is crushed under the wheels of a car that does not stop. Two blocks away, a little boy is looking for the dog. The little boy goes in the wrong direction and finds the dog much, much later. On the boulevard. He draws the person, a Good Samaritan, who stopped to check the dog and remove him from the road. The Good Samaritan is in her car seeing the accident. She can see it happening because she has long lines of sight coming straight out of her eyes. All seeing, alert.

Tracy, Lori and Tom sit in the back yard, drinking beer. The sun is low enough to be in their eyes. Tracy is talking.

"It's one of the sacred places of the planet."

"Oh yeah?" Tom shields his eyes so he can see her better.

"Uh huh. Paul has this book with all the sacred places and it's in there. I'm totally excited to be going. It has amazing energy, right? I mean spiritual energy?"

"Cool." Tracy has nice tits. He can see her bra. It's shiny, pretty. She's smiling.

"Sacred for whom?" Lori asks, putting an extra hum on the final phoneme.

"For everybody."

"What makes it sacred? I mean why is it in this book?"

"Well, it's a book of all these special places, these sacred spaces, on the planet, and it's one of them."

"Right." Tom is smiling and nodding like one of those dolls with the springy heads. At least he tidied the living room.

"Is this one of the UN places?"

"What?"

"One of the places, you know, World Heritage Places, designated by the UN?"

"The UN?"

"The United Nations?"

"Yeah, I know what the UN is Lori."

"What difference does it make if the UN says it's designated?" Tom asks.

"I'm just asking. I'm trying to understand."

"What's to understand?" Tracy finishes her beer. "It's this gorgeous place with great energy."

"Yeah, what more do you need to know?" Tom agrees.

"Maybe it's a sacred burial ground."

"Oh," Tracy jumps. "Bobby where did you come from?"

"My little ninja," Lori smiles and brushes the hair from his eyes. He pulls away.

"Mom. Don't."

"Hi Bobby. How are you?"

"Hey Aunty Trace. Where's Uncle Paul?"

He's not really your uncle. He hates that: Uncle Paul. What is it? It's 'cause he's not around, so he's special. It's way easier to be an uncle than a father. Fathers have to do all the crap stuff. Uncles just cruise in whenever, birthday, Christmas, take you for a ride on their motorcycle and that's it. Pals forever.

"Oh, he's working tonight."

"Is he coming by to get you later?"

"No, I've got the car."

"You want a burger, Bobby?"

"Not hungry," he growls and walks away slowly.

"Gosh he's cute. Getting so big," Tracy says.

"Yeah, he's growing up." A silence settles with the sunlight.

"Hey, you guys want to smoke a mighty doob?" Tom asks this as much to break the silence as out of desire for more.

"Mmmm. Sure." Tracy smiles. "If I can have another beer."

"You got it."

Inside the house he can hear Tracy and Lori laughing. About what? Sisters. There is a strange thing there. Something he is not privy to, something he does not know or understand. Maybe he left the spliff on the bookshelf.

"Are we gonna bury Rascal?"

"Jeeeezuz, Bobby. You can't do that. You gotta make some noise when you walk. What?"

"When can we bury Rascal?"

"I don't know. Tomorrow?"

"Tonight."

"No, not tonight. We have company."

"Aunty Trace won't mind."

"Tomorrow." He finds the joint and goes into the kitchen to get more beer. "Hey," he calls out the back door, "what's the opposite of brown?"

Tom and Lori walk down to the curb to see Tracy off. Lori leans in the car window, still talking. Tom hangs back, his hands in the pockets of his shorts. They wave goodbye when Tracy drives away and then turn around to return to the house. Bobby is standing there. Holding something in his arms. The dog.

"Bobby."

"I want to bury him."

"Honey," Lori says, "it's late now. We'll do it tomorrow."

"You said we'd do it today."

"I know honey, but."

"I wanna do it now. He needs to be buried properly."

"Okay." Lori says.

Somehow, Tom does the digging even though it was Lori that agreed. He moves two large rocks with his hands. The only light comes from the back porch and Bobby insists on lighting candles. He sings a strange little song and shuttles to and fro around the burial site.

"Shit. This is—I don't know if this is deep enough."

"Six feet under," Bobby says. "It must be six feet."

"I'm not digging six feet."

"Rascal, oh my Rascal, we bestow your body to this ground," Bobby says. Lori wonders where he gets these things. Tom watches Bobby, normally withdrawn, suddenly expressive, his face alive with something: ceremony, mystery? Kids are wild.

"Now raise the candle," Bobby commands. Tom bends over, groans, picks up the candle in its holder. It throws irregular shadows across the boy's face and the plastic wrapped dog's body he holds in his arms. He was a sweet little dog. His nails skittered across the linoleum. He could jump like nobody's business. Poor thing. Bobby climbs into the hole, places the body in the centre of the pit, then climbs back out. He crouches by the side of the hole, says, "Bye-bye Rascal."

Tom throws a clod of earth in. It falls against the plastic. Tom shivers. He throws another shovelful in. He feels sad. Why did the dog have to die? He feels stupid. Maybe it's the doob. Another mouthful of dirt. He's crying. It's been a sad day. The whole day, though he can't remember why. Hot tears run down his nose. Stupid Lori has gone inside so she doesn't know and the ninja crouched at his feet only stares fixedly at the dirt piling up in the hole. He pushes the dirt in quickly now, awkwardly. He's doing a lousy job of it. Well, there's no light. How're you supposed to fill in a hole when it's dark?

He pushes the dirt with his foot. It sinks. He stands a moment thinking that he doesn't want to see it in the morning, a newly dug grave in the backyard. After Bobby goes to bed, he'll put the kids' swimming pool over top of it. Bobby is still crouched, his head against his knees, one hand on the mound of dirt. He's humming quietly. Then Bobby gets up abruptly, walks away, apparently no longer interested.

"Good night Bobby," mumbles Tom. He wipes his face with his t-shirt sleeve, tosses the shovel aside. He tries to pick up the swimming pool but it is round, plastic, filled with water, and, therefore, slippery, unmanageable, and immovable. Tom grunts, curses, and flicks his hands at the pool as if dismissing it. A voice calls quietly, "Dad?"

He turns. Bobby is standing on the steps of the back porch, his little boy's chest exposed to the cool air. "Bobby."

"Thanks. For doing that."

"Oh, no problem." Tom turns back to regard the grave. "We can fix it tomorrow, pack down the earth, when there's more light. I tried to put the swimming pool on it, but maybe some grass seed would be better, eh? Or flowers?" He turns back to Bobby, hoping the boy will see his smile through the darkness. Bobby is gone, vanished silently into the house.

Tom picks up the shovel. Leans it carefully against the rickety toolshed. He goes in. He adjusts the kitchen light just so that it casts a low, warm glow and sits at the kitchen table. From upstairs he can hear Lori and Bobby talking as Bobby gets ready for bed. He can't make out what they're saying but the sound of their voices creates an agreeable murmur. He listens to them and looks at his dirty hands, rubs his index finger. For a moment he has the impression that his life is very rich and that all is as it should be.

And the Four Animals

Sheila Watson

THE FOOTHILLS slept. Over their yellow limbs the blue sky crouched. Only a fugitive green suggested life which claimed kinship with both and acknowledged kinship with neither.

Around the curve of the hill, or out of the hill itself, came three black dogs. The watching eye could not record with precision anything but the fact of their presence. Against the faded contour of the earth the things were. The watcher could not have said whether they had come or whether the eye had focused them into being. In the place of the hills before and after have no more meaning than the land gives. Now there were the dogs where before were only the hills and the transparent stir of the dragonfly.

Had the dogs worn the colour of the hills, had they swung tail round leg, ears oblique and muzzles quivering to scent carrion, or mischief, or the astringency of grouse mingled with the acrid smell of low-clinging sage, the eye might have recognized a congruence between them and the land. Here Coyote, the primitive one, the god-baiter and troublemaker, the thirster after power, the vain-glorious, might have walked since the dawn of creation—for Coyote had walked early on the first day.

The dogs, however, were elegant and lithe. They paced with rhythmic dignity. In the downshafts of light their coats shone ebony. The eye observed the fineness of bone, the accuracy of adjustment. As the dogs advanced they gained altitude, circling, until they stood as if freed from the land against the flat blue of the sky.

The eye closed and the dogs sank back into their proper darkness. The eye opened and the dogs stood black against the blue of the iris for the sky was in the eye yet severed from it.

In the light of the eye the dogs could be observed clearly—three Labrador retrievers, gentle, courteous, and playful with the sedate bearing of dogs well schooled to know their worth, to know their place, and to bend willingly to their master's will. One stretched out, face flattened. Its eyes, darker than the grass on which it lay, looked over the rolling hills to the distant saw-tooth pattern of volcanic stone. Behind it the other two sat, tongues dripping red over the saw-tooth pattern of volcanic lip.

The dogs were against the eye and in the eye. They were in the land but not of it. They were of Coyote's house, but became aristocrats in time which had now yielded them up to the timeless hills. They, too, were gods, but civil gods made tractable by use and useless by custom. Here in the hills they would starve or lose themselves in wandering. They were aliens in this spot or exiles returned as if they had never been.

The eye closed. It opened and closed again. Each time the eye opened the dogs circled the hill to the top and trained their gaze on the distant rock. Each time they reached the height of land with more difficulty. At last all three lay pressing thin bellies and jaws against the unyielding earth.

Now when the eye opened there were four dogs and a man and the eye belonged to the man and stared from the hill of his head along the slope of his arm on which the four dogs lay. And the fourth which he had whistled up from his own depths was glossy and fat as the others had been. But this, too, he knew in the end would climb lackluster as the rest.

So he opened the volcanic ridge of his jaws and bit the tail from each dog and stood with the four tails in his hand and the dogs fawned graciously before him begging decorously for food. And he fed the tail of the first dog to the fourth and the tail of the fourth to the first. In the same way he disposed of the tails of the second and the third. And the dogs sat with their eyes on his mouth.

Then he bit the off-hind leg from each and offered it to the other; then the near-hind leg, and the dogs grew plump and shone in the downlight of his glance. Then the jaw opened and closed on the two forelegs and on the left haunch and the right and each dog bowed and slavered and ate what was offered.

Soon four fanged jaws lay on the hill and before them the man stood rolling the amber eyes in his hands and these he tossed impartially to the waiting jaws. Then he fed the bone of the first jaw to the fourth and that of the second to the third. And taking the two jaws that lay before him he fed tooth to tooth until one tooth remained and this he hid in his own belly.

Notes On Contributors

André Alexis was born in Trinidad and came to Canada at age three. He is a playwright and novelist. His first book of fiction was *Despair and other stories of Ottawa*, first published by Coach House Press in 1994 and republished a few years later by McClelland & Stewart.

David Arnason was born in Gimli, Manitoba. He is a founding editor of Winnipeg's Turnstone Press, an important purveyor of short stories and other fiction. He has published several novels and volumes of poetry. His short story collections include *The Happiest Man in the World*, from Talonbooks, 1989.

Margaret Atwood was born in Ottawa and now lives all over the place, but often in Toronto. She writes two kinds of short fiction–realist stories, often in the first person, and more innovative texts. *Wilderness Tips* (M&S, 1991) and *Good Bones* (Coach House, 1992) are recent examples.

Clark Blaise was born in Fargo, and has lived all over North America. Many of his stories work the acres of autobiography, and grow hybrid texts. He directs the famous writing program at Iowa, and continues to investigate the nature of short fiction. Recent books include *If I were Me*, from Porcupine's Quill, 1997.

George Bowering was born in Summerland, and currently lives in Vancouver. He has edited numerous books of short fiction, and written several novels and volumes of stories. His most recent collection is *The Rain Barrel* from Talonbooks, 1994.

Clint Burnham was born in Comox because he was an air force brat. He is a polymath, having published a theoretical volume on Fredric Jameson as well as scurrilous chapbooks of poetry. He is a non-traditional editor and teacher. His controversial stories, *Airborne Photo*, were published by Anvil Press in 1999.

Matt Cohen was born in Kingston. His first books were marked by their experimental nature. He then wrote many novels and stories in a realist mode, before turning to further experiments late in his life. His last book of stories was *Getting Lucky*, Knopf, 2000.

Candas Jane Dorsey was born in Edmonton and lives in Edmonton. She is a veteran of the Canadian science fiction scene, acting often as an editor. Her recent collection of stories, *Vanilla*, won a Howard O'Hagan award. "Sleeping in a Box" won an Aurora prize.

George Elliott was born in London, Ont. He worked in journalism and advertising and stayed away from the CanLit scene. His book of connected stories, *The Kissing Man*, Macmillan 1962, is perhaps our most famous neglected classic.

M.A.C. Farrant was born in Sydney and now lives in Sidney. She is a pure short story writer who has published a succession of short collections. Her stories are usually anti-realist constructions about very peculiar yet recognizable contemporary people. Recent books include *Word of Mouth*, Thistledown, 1996.

Brian Fawcett was born in Prince George. He began his writing career as a poet, turned to short stories, and then to novels. He now writes non-fiction. He takes the political and the social as his topics, but always looks for non-conventional forms. Talonbooks published four collections, including *Cambodia: A Book for People who find Television too Slow* (1986).

Timothy Findley was born in Toronto and lives in Stratford. He was for some years an actor, and is a successful playwright. His novels are always on the bestseller list, but he regularly offers short stories as well. His most recent collection is *Dust to Dust*, HarperCollins, 1997.

Keath Fraser was born in Vancouver. He is a slow and careful writer of novels and short fiction. He has been called "the best unknown writer in Canada," which has to be a bum rap. His largest and most ambitious book of stories is *Foreign Affairs*, published by Stoddart in 1985.

Hiromi Goto was born in Chiba-ken and brought up in southern Alberta. Her novel *Chorus of Mushrooms* (NeWest, 1994) won a Canada-Japan book award, and her second novel, *The Kappa Child*, was published by Red Deer Press in 2001. She is part of the Calgary renaissance.

Thomas King was born in Roseville, California. He has taught Native Studies in the US and Canada, most recently at the University of Guelph. He has edited Native writing, and written fiction for adults and young folks. A recent collection is *One Good Story, that One*, HarperCollins, 1993.

Dany Laferrière was born in Haiti, where he became a journalist. He went into exile to Montreal in 1978, and caused a stir with his first novel *How to make Love to a Negro Without getting Tired* in 1985. The story in this anthology is from *Cette grenade dans la main du jeune Nègre est-elle une arme ou un fruit?*

Suzette Mayr was born in Calgary, where she currently teaches English and writing. Part of the Calgary renaissance, she has published two innovative and comic novels, *Moon Honey* and *The Widows*, both from NeWest Press. She is currently trying to write a novel about Trudeau and race.

Leon Rooke was born in North Carolina and currently lives in Winnipeg. He has published more short stories of a literary quality than anyone in Canada. His fiction explores the range of vocality, and combines hilarity with great seriousness. His most recent work is *Painting the Dog*, Thomas Allen, 2001.

Diane Schoemperlen was born in Thunder Bay. She writes stories as books rather than collecting scattered stories from time to time. She likes to set up frames constructed of fairy tales or books of instruction, and explore human lives in the light of those restraints. See *Forms of Devotion*, Viking, 1998.

Gail Scott was born in Ottawa, brought up in two languages, and moved to Montreal, where she has been a journalist, translator and novelist. Her novels are truly experimental and dense; the latest, *My Paris*, features a diarist who frames her writing on a French edition of Walter Benjamin's Paris project.

Audrey Thomas was born in Binghamton, and moved to Vancouver part way through her university life. She is a novelist, but has always retained high interest in the short story. Her first books were published by Talonbooks. The latest is the selected *The Path of Totality,* Viking, 2001.

Guillermo Verdecchia was born in Buenas Aires and brought up in southern Ontario. He is best known as a successful playwright and director, based in Toronto. *Fronteras Americanas* is probably his most famous play. Talonbooks published his first book of stories, *Citizen Suárez,* in 1998.

Sheila Watson was born in New Westminster. She would become the principal figure in Canadian literary modernism with the publication of her classic *The Double Hook.* An extremely spare writer, she published one other novel, a collection of essays, and a thin book of stories, *Five Stories,* Coach House, 1984.